MICHELA'S MUSINGS

Michela's Musings

Michela Volante

Michela's Musings
Michela Volante

Published by Greyhound Self-Publishing 2021
Malvern, Worcestershire, United Kingdom.

Printed and bound by Aspect Design
89 Newtown Road, Malvern, Worcs. WR14 1PD
United Kingdom
Tel: 01684 561567
E-mail: allan@aspect-design.net
Website: www.aspect-design.net

Cover Design Copyright © 2021 Aspect Design
ISBN 978-1-909219-81-6

For Dee and Marion

CONTENTS

A NUN'S TALE

From the time of their meeting seven years previously Joan and Marie had formed a lasting friendship, half of which they had shared together in the convent. The Sisters of Mercy lay concealed beneath the Mendips, within easy reach of the diocese cathedral. The convent lay in such obscurity that it was quite a surprise when Marie confessed to her friend that she feared she was pregnant. At first she had been extremely evasive, but Joan had known her for too long to be fooled by such prevarication, and through floods of tears she discovered the truth.

An Open Order, nuns were free to walk the hills and moorland and Marie had taken to wandering among the numerous footpaths and byways of the dale. One bright afternoon she happened upon a tiny hamlet with a few scattered cottages, general store, post office and pub. The village was small yet she was tempted by the promise of forbidden fruit, feeling drawn to satisfy her hunger for social intercourse, the company of others – basic human contact. Man, she felt, was a gregarious beast; if this wasn't the case why had the Almighty given us siblings and communities in which to congregate? From a large family, where her elder sister had pushed her swing, passed on hand-me-downs, and taught her the mechanisms of femininity; and where she had in turn carried her younger brother on her shoulders so that upstairs on buses he could run his hands along the ceiling, she had felt a part of something – a belonging. At the convent she had problems with the Great Silence, when speech was forbidden throughout the evening until the following morning's Lauds or morning prayer.

On one expedition to the village clothed in her solitary outfit of mufti she had met Jamie, a shy lad who after a couple of encounters persuaded her to escort him to the pub. Following a subsequent visit and a gin too many and whilst seeing her to the Convent gates he made a pass at her, and to her surprise she enjoyed the attention. From that time onwards the couple sought any ruse to engage in a series of clandestine liaisons on the moors. The pub was an altogether different environment to her daily constraints. Banter around the bar became more diverse when the clientele learned she was from the convent, although nun-jokes were generally kept within certain parameters: in her hearing these were restricted to puns such as "nun for the road" or "all for nun and nun for all". She chuckled to herself that she felt rather nun-plussed by their effrontery: there were as many nun puns as gnome ones! One thing led to another and suddenly the duo's harmless petting had morphed into a burst of passion Marie had been unable to control.

Joan headed towards the cathedral to pray for her friend. She was in pensive mood as her brisk steps brushed aside the twisted and scorched beech leaves on the avenue floor, portent of another autumn she mused. Across the cathedral forecourt, she passed beneath the large monkey tree immersed in a bed of bright yellow rudbeckia (black-eyed susan) and the vibrant silky multi-coloured blooms of Californian poppies. From the half-open cathedral door drifted a cacophony of so many misplaced notes it took an effort for her to recognise the tune to *Jesu, joy of man's desiring*. Slipping into the cavernous depths of the lofty sanctuary, she proceeded to the high alter where she fell to her knees in devout supplication. 'Please God, let it be a mistake; please don't allow Marie to be with child, I beg you,' she fervently pleaded running devotive beads through trembling fingers. 'Sister Marie is a good person, a devout nun. She always kneels by her bedside each morning to repeat the Lord's Prayer and catechism and 50 Hail Marys before Lauds, adores her *lectio divina*s – and is never late for Compline.'

Her prayers went unanswered. A week later Marie's doctor confirmed the tidings she was dreading: Tidings with which she was forced to confront the Mother Superior. Here she was calmly informed that she was not suited to the contemplative life and asked to pack her bags without delay. The brutal words still rang in her ears as she moved silently along the cloistered confines leading from the Mother's office. Through much sobbing and recrimination Joan learnt of the encounter, before she too was summoned to that daunting chamber. 'Sister Joan, I have called you here today to warn you that Sister Marie has committed the cardinal sin of conceiving outside of wedlock. As the two of you were close, I felt it my duty to inform you of her lapse. In the wake of this unholy act she has been summarily dismissed from these premises –'

'But she is a good person –'

'Don't interrupt child. God's work will continue in this place. We are a beacon that shines resolutely through this vale of tears. Each of us is placed on this earth to suffer temptation, and to strengthen our souls by the rejection of such temptation. I suggest you visit the cathedral to pray for the salvation of Sister Marie's soul: you may go.'

Never having had men show interest in her, Joan couldn't understand why Marie had fallen so heavily from grace. What was the mystical power they were able to wield over the female psyche? Perhaps it was true, perhaps it was the Devil's work! *She* looked forward to the quiet intercessions, the latin Vespers before supper, the study time following afternoon tea and making a fuss of *Winston* the convent dog; she didn't mind rising at 5 and the ensuing early Vigil (psalm or scripture reading and meditation) or even wearing the shapeless Benedictine habit. Undoubtedly she would miss having her friend around yet she would pray for strength, secure in the knowledge that she herself was a true bride of Christ.

ADRIAN *(THE ALIEN)*

If asked, Maisie was never sure when she'd first met Adrian. In a way he just appeared on the scene and she'd simply accepted him. It was as though he'd always been there. Compliant and agreeable with an implacable smile, he was intent. Often she caught him gazing as if he was studying her. She felt he could get inside her head. She would use his name in coaxing tones; in much the same way that she talked to a succession of furry friends; and this spilled over to include her Barbie dolls. She was sure she'd known him since she was 5 years old. Next month she would be 7.

They had met at the bottom of the garden, where her father had said the fairies dwelt. Adrian was cowering inside an ornamental tub in the potting-shed. He measured a mere 6 inches head to toe, and was formed similar to human-kind with a few subtle embellishments. He possessed a pale green pallor and his eyes, sunken deeply into his head, were further apart than normal and nestled below an over-large forehead. Originally dressed in a peplum resembling a Roman toga, Maisie had altered his appearance by clothing him in 'action-man outfits', and Adrian didn't seem to object. She fed him the scraps she saved from drawn out vacant meal-times, and he slept contentedly upon her pillow.

He accompanied her everywhere; although she had worried that he might be discovered when at school he had stowed away in her backpack in the locker room. When forced to leave him on his own she gave him strict instructions regarding security. She saw him as somewhere between one of her animals and an

Action man. She wasn't sure why she's chosen his name, but it seemed appropriate. Adrian had told her he was not from far away, but that he would one day have to return.

Her mother was oblivious to her occupation with toys, and anyhow it kept her out of the way; with the bonus that any benefits gained from her playthings would reap dividends in later life. She never addressed Maisie in endearing tones and treated her as another adult. The woman was often out, and Maisie suspected her of having secret amours. Her father was simply absent, away on business or so he said. A rep for an oil company, he spent long months abroad. Maisie had grown to be independent and became used to being alone. For her birthday she was expecting a smart-phone, although she wasn't too sure who she would call.

The moment she first realised Adrian could speak would stay with her forever. She'd been sitting on the floor, engaged in 'moving in' a couple of newly-weds to her doll's house; when by accident the loaded removal van had run over his foot. She had noticed him wince and peering closer she observed his normally serene countenance bore an anguished expression. Lying flat on the floor, and leaning towards him she plainly heard him utter as a reproach the word: 'Maisie!'.

One half-term, mother suggested a trip to Baker Street and Madame Tussauds, after carefully checking the Guide and noting there was nothing on the tele unless you liked snooker. So they left father staring vacantly at a melange of coloured balls that progressed with varying velocity to and fro across the green baize, and headed for the station. Following a tour of the museum, including the Chamber of Horrors where Masie was sure she had caught a glimpse of her father, and a brief lunch; mother suggested a visit to the Planetarium situated next door.

Inside, her mother stayed at the elevated rear of the auditorium, while Maisie insisted on sitting in the front. As the lights gradually dimmed and the calm evocative voice-over began: 'There are 100 billion galaxies in the observable universe…' the indigo domed ceiling filled with stars. Maisie became aware of a frantic scuffling from within the confines of her rucksack. This frenetic scrambling was followed by the emergence of Adrian who seemed agitated with behaviour far removed from his usual placid demeanour.

Within the obscurity of the dim lighting she held him gently on her lap but he wouldn't settle and his tiny head was turning frantically from side to side as he craned to gaze in wonder at the spectacle of the night sky. Passing the orbits of Jupiter and Saturn distant stars grew brighter, to just as suddenly dissolve into darkness. The ever changing vista gradually shifted as light years of travel passed in seconds through space. Blazing comets soared in orbit across the ether to disappear amid nebulous clouds of milky celestial clusters.

Adrian was becoming more and more animated as he marvelled at the multiple images. She felt him thrashing uncontrollably, and raised him to her ear as he gesticulated towards a certain spot over their heads. Pointing directly at an approaching star formation, she heard him yell: 'There! There! There!…' Andromeda. With a desperate cry he was gone. She searched all over for him, in her rucksack, under the seat, in adjoining rows to the annoyance of fellow star-gazers, to no avail. She thought that at the time she had detected a dull thud above the sonorous sounds of the narration; this she had put down to sound effects within the commentary.

Eventually the lights went up in measured stages, as the voice returned the enraptured audience gently back to earth. Even her mother noticed her distraught features as Maisie returned with tear-stained cheeks. 'I've lost him! Adrian's gone!' she wailed dragging her mother to inspect where she had been seated. 'Pull yourself together child. It's only a doll. We'll buy you another if it's <u>that</u> important' was her mother's disinterested response.

A message came over the tannoy that caused some amusement in the stalls. Apparently someone had thrown a projectile with such velocity that it had made an indent in the domed ceiling: An occurrence to which the management took a very dim view. The chatter subsided and the audience began to disperse. Her mother snatched Maisie's hand and the pair headed for the exit.

There, lying ahead in the centre aisle, Maisie spotted Adrian's rigid lifeless body. She ran over and tearfully cradled him in her arms. She had never realised how much he had missed home. That was the moment Maisie came of age; realising that time moves on, and in Tinsel Town toys will be toys! Poignantly she thought to herself, Adrian once told me he came from not far away; in the myriad stars in the heavens, the cosmos, the universe, we were virtual neighbours!

ANIMAL RESCUE

When it comes to the lesser animals, traditionally the dog takes pride of place as a valuable asset to mankind. We are all familiar with the exploits of our canine friends and of course there are many who enjoy an intimate relationship with them. From hunting to guarding and guiding to chasing criminals and sniffing out drugs or illegal immigrants, and even distinguishing themselves under fire, dogs have proved their worth. The lives of the two species canine and homo-sapiens remain indelibly intertwined and on a one-to-one basis there is much evidence of close bonds and partnerships becoming established. Yet, is the dog man's best friend? There are certainly other contenders for the prestigious title. Mankind's history abounds with numerous documented accounts of altruistic acts performed by diverse members of the animal kingdom especially where human lives have been at risk.

The humble pigeon is often cited for carrying vital messages during wartime, notably for their assistance in the trenches of WW1 and across front lines in WW11; but the dog in warfare has assumed a more dangerous role i.e. that of the bomb sniffer and searcher. Treo, an eight year-old cross-breed, was in the news in 2010 when he received the Dickin Medal, the animal equivalent of the VC, for services beyond normal animal pursuits. This award was introduced by Maria Dickin the PDSA founder in 1943. Treo won his accolade for sniffing out two hidden bombs in Helmand Province in Afghanistan. Having earned retirement from active duty, today he is the family pet of Sgt. Heyhoe his handler who has worked with him for five years.

It is not only in warfare that dogs have shown acts of extreme courage. In 2008, a woman and her young son were returning to their car after having been at a playground when they were confronted by a man wielding a knife. He directed the pair not to move, when suddenly from nowhere appeared a large pit-bull terrier which raced at the man, who speedily turned and fled.

Back in 1982 a 2 year-old Texan child had been walking in the garden with his grandmother and family dog Arf, when the dog became agitated. Gran took the youngster inside and told Mrs Sparks, her daughter. Mrs Sparks came outside to find Arf fighting with a 2 foot North American coral snake. She promptly shot the snake, but not before Arf sustained multiple bites and scratches which kept him in the veterinary hospital for 24 days before making a sturdy recovery.

In Britain, Brenda Owen was walking her dog along a river bank when they came across an abandoned wheelchair. Within the flow, Brenda saw a woman struggling against the current. Her calls to the hapless female achieved no response, so she shouted to her dog Penny to 'Fetch! Fetch!' Immediately the fit 10 year-old dived into the water and pulled the fortunate woman ashore.

Dogs' arch-enemy the cat won't allow the canines to steal the limelight, having been responsible for much valour on their own account. A case in point occurred at the home of Dianne Busscher woken at 4.45am by the family cat Oreo who was crying out from the garage. Upon entering the garage she was greeted by smoke and flames mixed with toxic fumes. She quickly alerted her husband and five children who ran to safety. The fire demolished the garage as well as a bedroom. Previously the family had not been fond of the cat; now Oreo had become a favourite member of the family. Another cat Baby also saved her family from fire. A further feline, Simon, served on HMS

Amethyst during the Yangste incident and also won the Dickin Medal for bravery under fire. Although wounded by shrapnel, he continued to dispose of a multitude of rats that had stowed away onboard. He carried out this feat in the midst of shell-fire that was capable of making a hole one foot in diameter in steel plate.

Larger mammals have also contributed to mankind's well-being. Binti Jua a female lowland gorilla received an unusual visitor when a 3 year old boy fell into her enclosure at Brookfield Zoo in 1996. The lad was knocked unconscious by the fall, but the gorilla cradled him in her arms and kept other inmates at bay. She carried the boy for about sixty feet to the entrance where a keeper rescued the child. Ten years earlier at Jersey Zoo in a similar incident a five year old boy also fell to unconsciousness in a gorilla pen. This time a large male gorilla Jambo protected the youngster against others of his species. As the boy awoke and began to cry, the other occupants of the enclosure backed away sufficiently for a keeper to fetch him to safety.

Back in the States, attempting to cross the back pasture of the animal refuge she owns in Arkansas, Janice Wolf was astonished when an 11 month-old Watusu calf stepped out in front of her and blocked her path. She grasped the beast by the horns and tried to manoeuvre it aside, but the calf was having none of it and proceeded to toss its head so that she almost lost her balance. Then she spied a copper-head snake on the path in her direct line. Although copper-head venom is not normally fatal to adults, in her case she was particularly sensitive to insect bites and had just returned home from a lung operation.

Dolphins have performed many daring manoeuvres. There are approx 50 species of this mammal in existence. The toothed whale of the family *Delphinidae*, are streamlined and agile and up to 4.5 metres in length. They move in large groups or schools, feed mainly on fish and often accompany ships for many nautical miles. Intelligent and possessing well-developed abilities for social communication, they are also able to echolocate (a method by which certain animals can sense and locate surrounding objects by emitting sounds and detecting the echo). The common dolphin which is blue-black with a white belly and striped body grows to approximately 2.1 metres. The Bottlenose, with its small beak, is grey-blue and reaches a length of 4m. This is a shallow water species popular in dolphinariums and has been the subject of much research into the social habits, behaviour and language of whales. The porpoise belongs to a different family (*Phocoenidae*).

One hot August day Todd Endris, a 24 year-old owner of a Monterey Aquarium, decided to go surfing along with a few friends. Out of the blue a 15 foot shark attempted to engulf both the surfer and his board in its massive jaws —in fact the board saved him as it came between the shark and his vital organs, however skin was stripped from his back. Todd was able to fend off the predator by clinging to the board and kicking out at the shark's snout. Yet he was gradually becoming drained of energy. From nowhere appeared a pod of dolphins which formed a protective ring around the swimmer until he was able to ride his board to shore and gain emergency assistance from his friends.

Another occasion of a similar rescue saved a British-born lifeguard Rob Howes out for a swim with his daughter and friends off the North Island of New Zealand, close to Whangarei. They were enjoying a relaxing swim when they were herded together by a group of dolphins. Howes attempted to drift out of the circle but was guided back by the dolphins; then he spotted a 10 foot great white shark approaching at speed. He admits turning pale as the beast approached to within a couple of metres distance. It became clear that the dolphins had corralled the swimmers in order to protect them. After around 40 minutes the sharks lost interest and drifted away to allow the group to swim the 100 metres to shore. Another lifeguard spotted this episode from a patrolling life-boat and corroborated this unusual behaviour. Ingrid Visser of Orca Research verified that this was natural dolphin behaviour against sharks, using measures they would adopt with their young, circling in a protective ring and slapping the water with their fins.

Again, in southern Italy off the coast of Manfredonia in Puglia, 14 year-old Davide Cecci a non-swimmer fell off his father's boat and was within minutes of death by drowning. The dolphin Fillippo, a local tourist attraction, pushed the lad up from beneath and out of the water and then approached the boat where his father who had been unaware of his son's plight was able to return him onboard. Davide's mother called the dolphin a 'hero' with an 'instinct to save human life'. It is often the case that dolphins seem to have no fear of humans.

The above has shown the importance of efficient stewardship concerning vulnerable creatures and their habitat. Is it common sense to neuter dogs and cats as well as providing water and avoiding sealing them in airtight cars in the heat of the sun; also to avoid carelessly discarding plastic waste which can choke our streams and rivers and cause hazards to wildlife in our oceans; to maintain our hedgerows and meadows to encourage a natural habitat for birds, wildlife and insects; to drive responsibly, especially on rural roads and report any cruelty we may encounter? As mere custodians, a respectful and caring approach to our environment would surely reap dividends wherein mankind ends up the richer.

AQUADUCK

I felt pleased with myself – I prided myself on my organising ability, my thoroughness and my attention to detail. Geoff seemed to share such faith in me. We had known each other for around twelve months and became firm friends. It had been a while until he introduced me to the other love of his life, but since that misty morning in North Devon where *Aquaduck* and I first made acquaintance Geoff and I had sailed in her across the Solent to Cowes, around the mouth of the Severn calling in at Portishead, past the Charleston Rocks and over to Avonmouth. He even hinted at taking me on a jaunt to the Med someday.

The *Aquaduck* was an Ericson 27 and Geoff's pride and joy. His ex-wife had run a successful clothes company and with the settlement he was able to pursue his passion. The Ericson's engine was inboard and she was not speedy but capable of 6.5 knots cruising speed under full sail, running on diesel with a reinforced fibreglass hull and teak cockpit, tiller steering, and she measured 9' at the beam. She was a competent craft, with the owner's cabin forward of the engine room, and aft an extra double cabin for a pair of guests which served as extra storage. She was not the fastest on the pond but she was steady and reliable and that suited me.

Geoff had rowed to port leaving me in control of the yacht (I should have donned the skipper's cap!). He had gone in our tiny rigid fibreglass tender boat for the mainland to pay a call on the harbour-master and add to our supply of diesel. He was also topping up our meagre stock of provisions: we were careful with how much we stored on board, space was paramount.

Despite certain trepidation as to our competence to control the craft if we got into difficulties Geoff had been on sailing courses and obtained all necessary qualifications; and he insisted on my taking maritime classes to ensure I was seaworthy. He assured me that due to modern innovation two able-bodied seamen were perfectly capable of handling the vessel. Such innovations as warping winches made it easier to muscle in a spring line, even against wind and current; and joy-sticks and Trac thrusters allowed for less dangerous docking. We of course had none of these luxuries but I had confidence in Geoff, he was very meticulous and thought things out carefully before acting.

He must have charmed the private owners of the Clovelly harbour, for somehow he had procured us a berth for three nights. Clovelly is a tiny unspoilt village on the N Devon coast – enjoying private ownership since 1738, the 19th century was its heyday and now it remained delightfully entrapped in that era. Cars were banned, where inhabitants used sleds over the steep cobbled streets to shop for goods in the local stores; 16th cent cottages abounded, and well-stocked flower tubs of scented blossoms were everywhere – with no tourist tat allowed. Geoff had booked us into the exclusive Red Lion Hotel right by the harbour-side and where the locals bar was awash with Poldark lookalikes. At £100 pp per night I was glad it was a short stay. The restaurant was excellent and as well as local lobster the menu boasted Red Ruby Devon beef.

**

I had never taken to Peterssen, a Dutchman of dubious disposition who made a pass at me at the Club. He was continually putting

Geoff down, using snide remarks about amateur matlows or weekenders as he called them. He had taken a swing at Geoff when on a particularly stiff bender, Geoff had admitted to me. He liked his liquor and Brandy was his nemesis. Of course he had a 60-footer with 4 extra cabin beds and a deck lounge, as he never tired of informing the Club-house. Here he was drawing alongside *Aquaduck*, he must have been watching for Geoff to leave the vessel.

'Mind if I come aboard?' he queried. What could I say? Geoff was a bit of a softie who was only too keen to learn any nautical tips from a competent seaman. It was the man's arrogance I found overbearing: 'I prefer to add a comfortable motion at sea and high bulwarks, while preferable to walk the deck to windward, high bulwarks give footing to leeward if needed...' was typical of the man. 'Yes, but Geoff will be back in a tick...' I answered rather too defensively. 'Drink', I offered to make certain his hands would be occupied. 'Thank you, a stiff gin and tonic would be great.' I made my way to the galley believing him behind me – but realised he had vanished. On a 27-footer he couldn't have gone far. I hastily searched him out accompanied with his G and T and my Campari. It wasn't an easy passage with the slight slap and swell of the tide. He'd gone aft along the side deck, and I discovered him sitting upon a locker where we stored ropes and scuba gear by the winch next to the ensign staff.

I attempted small talk although Peterssen seemed uneasy. I slipped anxious glances towards the shore where other yachts swayed at anchor in the breeze, searching the bay for Geoff's return: no sign. I briefly took in the sun sparkling on the slight swell that rocked us at anchor and spread to the rocky shoreline – the water was clear around *Aquaduck* and I spied molluscs and other sea-creatures beneath the surface and clumps of low rock formations embedded in the sand: above, echelons of seaweed floated lazily on the tide. If only Geoff would hurry back.

Peterssen had seemed rather flushed and rudely drank down his liquid in a single draught, and lifting the grapnel from his dinghy he stepped over the side: 'Thanks for the drink, regards to Geoff…must be away,' he shouted as he assumed a brisk stroke for shore.

Well I thought, that was short and none too sweet, but I was suspicious as to why he had beaten such a hasty retreat – had he been up to mischief? Diligently I did a check round the vessel, the scuba gear was still intact, he hadn't been near the wheel house, the anchor chain appeared secure, the cabin ports were untouched, trailing the deck were the canvas deck awnings with all ropes neatly coiled – no nothing appeared out of place.

Then it hit me, I had failed to inspect perhaps the most important item of all – the seacocks! With trepidation, I felt under the muffler and risers for moisture (we were taught this procedure early in the course). Sure enough they oozed dampness…an unmistakable sign they'd been tampered with. Perhaps I had arrived just in time. Urgently, I searched the tool locker for the special wrench, but it wasn't there. Geoff where are you?

BELIEF

Under cover of darkness, a small army detachment had reached the intimidating outskirts of a deep forest, and the terrain was foreign to them. They were a troop of five, a small platoon that had been sent on a secret mission into enemy territory. The five had been friends since birth, not that unusual given their upbringing. With Sergeant Bull their leader the group included Hoppy, Skippy, Deadpan and Jumpy. Their mission was to seek out a fresh base, while noting but avoiding any enemy activity along the way. Essentially they were required to move speedily, with minimum disruption to the environment, achieve their objective and return to base.

At that moment the sergeant was delivering a last minute briefing: 'Now guys, don't let anyone wander off. Stay close. We are closing in on the hardest part of the mission. Keep in orderly file and don't leap around too much.' They each appeared attentive except for Deadpan who kept his eyes averted.

Stealthily the column entered the dingy woodland and fell to the ground crawling on their bellies in close order.

Jumpy whispered: 'Pitch-black: What are we doing in this poxy wood anyway?'

After a pause Skippy answered: 'Dunno, but it gives a new meaning to "mission creep" don't it!? Oi! You're showering me with mud, you slimy Kermit!'

'I'd rather be home,' said Jumpy.

'You've gotta be joking mate, 'e'll 'ave us out 'ere till our feet go numb and we crave for water. <u>You</u> see!' answered Hoppy.

'Talking of water, there's none in sight. It's all woody, isn't it?' responded Jumpy.

'What do you fink, Deadpan?' enquired Hoppy of his partner.

''E never finks nuffin, dunno why you bovver,' said Skippy.

'Stop whining you lot, we're 'ere on a mission 'aint we', hissed Bull: 'We agreed it 'ad to be done. A little less croaking and more listenin', eh?'

The sudden snap of a twig nearby broke the silence, from eleven o'clock at about ten metres to the left. The troop froze in their tracks, all except Skippy who uttered, 'I'll skirt round and investigate…' 'Stay where you are!' ordered Bull through clenched teeth, but he was too late. A further rustling was followed immediately by a desperate cry and a scuffling that gradually diminished leaving in its wake a deathly hush. After a brief pause Sergeant Bull said: 'Righto, all follow me, and keep behind in column formation,' as he searched his backpack for a torch.

They moved quietly, keeping the sergeant in contact until he gave the signal to halt. ' Now, careful – careful,' he instructed as each came slowly around; to where Bull shone his torch into a large hole in the ground and then around the troop; two of their number were missing – Deadpan and Skippy had disappeared, swallowed by the gaping void. 'We're gonna have to call down to them and risk blowing our cover', Bull spoke with an authority he didn't feel. He called down softly at first but gradually increased the volume to a yell before a feeble response came from below. 'Now what do we do,' said Jumpy,' they're many metres down and our ropes won't reach.'

'Nil desperandum,' croaked Bull (using his only Latin phrase); 'We'll simply tie all the ropes together and Bob's your aunt, Fanny's your uncle –.'

Jumpy jumped in with 'I didn't bring mine…' A ponderous

silence ensued for a few seconds, then for half a minute the forest shook with the obscenities and oaths of Sergeant Bull.

After he'd calmed somewhat, they lowered the remaining attached ropes. 'Ahoy', called Bull, 'we're lowering a rope down, let us know if you see it…' 'Yes, I see it', came the feeble response. There followed some frantic scrambling from below, then a dismal cry of 'No, I can't reach it.' 'Right, we'll think of something,' Bull shouted back. Who was he kidding, if there was anything he'd have thought of it by now. 'What'll we do Sarge? We're gonna 'ave to get 'elp,' muttered Hoppy; while Jumpy complained that he hadn't volunteered for the mission in the first place. 'Keep your 'eads lads,' offered Bull; and 'Are you bofe alright?' he bellowed into the dim shaft. A few seconds later came a soft reply in the affirmative.

Bull attempted to calm the remnants of his troop while racking his brain for a solution, and projected torchlight into the chasm which was narrow and slippery. To his dismay he was unable to detect anything but darkness below. There seemed no alternative but to go for help, yet help was impossible in hostile territory; at least he knew he could communicate with the desperate pair underground. He called down and explained the predicament and received muffled assent. 'There is simply nothing for it, 'shouted Bull, 'I'm sorry, but you'll both have to take your cyanide capsules '

'No,' asserted Skippy and with conviction, tremendous effort and multiple attempts that left him exhausted he succeeded in reaching halfway to the surface, viewing daylight. ' It's pointless, you'll never make it,' yelled Bull and the other two joined in with 'just give up', 'go back down!' and 'take the pill'. It dawned on Skippy that he was losing the battle. His buddies were right, he just couldn't make it; what was the point of hanging on, clinging desperately to a few tufts of tired grass? He had to give up the futile struggle. With a desperate yell of anguish he relaxed his grip on the dank turf, and fell below down the slippery precipice to his death.

Deadpan however launched himself at the slope as if possessed and continued leaping tirelessly. Stoically, with enormous dexterity and exertion he scrambled his way to the point where he was able to see his comrades who were still frantically yelling that escape from the hole was futile, that he should simply give up and save remaining energy. Seeing them and their animation he jumped even harder.

Then with a gigantic leap Deadpan made it to where a weedy sapling struggled for existence close to the pit entrance; as he clung precariously to the fragile shrub his pals moved swiftly to his aid and lowered the rope; finally they were able to extricate him from the muddy tomb. After a while they regained some vitality, and were able to exercise weary limbs. Deadpan communicated that he was deaf, which solved their unanswered question as to why he had ignored their cries of "no hope" and "suicide as the only option". Deadpan was also able to explain that being deaf he was convinced the others were cheering him on, urging and encouraging him to try even harder, empowering him to succeed. 'Mission aborted,' announced Bull. The four shook slimy legs at one another and hopped off croaking among themselves towards the forsaken lily-pond where they had been spawned; not since young tadpoles had they encountered such a daring exploit.

Words can hold enormous consequences for others, we need to think carefully about what we are saying to someone, it could be a matter of life and death. The secret is for one to hold true to their belief even when all the cards are stacked against them.

CAUGHT OUT IN THE RAIN

'Throw that ball as if you mean it!' Fiona Frobisher's brisk alto rang out across the dank meadow; although she was wasting breath on Samantha Braithwaite. At St Wurstan College the girls held their Games Mistress in high esteem, they emulated her. In her mid-30s, Miss Frobisher was confident, vivacious and forthright, the role-model to whom all aspired and Miss Frobisher was apt to bask in this admiration. She had certain principles to uphold as niece to Olly Leftwing, the over ambitious and rather stretched Tory politician. She took the girls for hockey, lacrosse, netball, tennis, swimming, gymnastics, games theory and Movement; she also opened the batting for the school cricket team. Smartly turned out, following an hour on the tennis court she was daisy-fresh. Normally encountered in flat shoes with little makeup, and extremely proud of her posture, her long hair was neatly presented, plaited, braided or tied back. Confident, punctual, and resourceful, she commanded respect and kept a clear head, held lofty standards and expected no less of others. Her cockney boyfriend amused the girls. At one time, attending a school concert where the *Carnival of the Animals* was played, he caused a fit of giggling when he referred to the piece as 'summat by saen-saun! …don' tell me… Catchy as can be, the melody, they call it Saint Saens!'

Hope Babbington had been at St Wurstans for two years, since her parents parted, and was a rather dysfunctional student. She was fairly introverted until engaged in sport when she came alive, it was as though this was the outlet she craved. On pitch, court or field she assumed her true colours. Not keen on gymnastics she went through the motions: there didn't seem much point in heaving a medicine ball across the shiny chestnut gym floor, nor leaping over the 'horse' or scrambling aloft on wall-bars or thick ropes. She did however excel on cross-country runs and obstacle courses. Her competitive spirit brought her certain hidden accolades and often top grades in sporting activities. The school was in a league wherein prowess on the field formed a 'rite de passage'. Despite being shamed academically she experienced popularity via her sporting acumen, and sought every opportunity to excel. Good at netball, she was useful at lacrosse, but cricket remained her great love: whatever the sport Hope thrived on a challenge.

One day following a workout that involved catching a lacrosse ball, an exercise Miss Frobisher optimistically referred to as 'wake-up time for sleepy heads' she called her to one side. She thought the teacher wanted an errand and enjoyed being singled out, it showed Miss Frobisher had noticed her. 'O, Hope, I see such a bright future for you; if only you would be more attentive in class you would be such a good all rounder. If you were only half as good at lessons as you are at sport... I have a proposition for you. We've the major match with Birlington High coming soon. Now, if you were to make a 50 I might, just might, have a word with Mrs Fisc-Keynes (Economics). There may be a possibility we can get you into Six-form college.' 'Would you Miss? My mum would be so proud if I went on to college.' 'Well, as I said, I can't promise a thing, but I shall have a word with Amasa and we'll see. But first of all there is that small matter of 50 runs!'

The day of the big match dawned clear and bright. Birlington won the toss and decided to bat. They were cruising along, making steady progress at 100 for 5, however this steady progress changed dramatically at the fall of the fifth wicket. This heralded the arrival of Sally Hargreaves, known to some as Slasher Sally.

Within 10 minutes she had knocked up 28 runs, and the 150 was on the board. At this rate, the score would rapidly become invisible to apprehensive St Wurstan supporters. Sally was treating Miss Frobisher's medium-pace bowling with contempt, dismissing her to the boundary twice in successive overs. Yet the Slasher finally ran out of luck, when she mis-timed an ambitious hook shot and spooned the ball to short leg (had she really connected, it would have sailed over the weathered cream pavilion with yards to spare). She had scored 38 and their total stood at 190. Following this spirited performance the tail capitulated somewhat, yet Birlington High finished on a reasonable 218 runs.

St Wurstans began sprightly enough with Miss Frobisher slipping silkily into her stride. She had contributed a worthy 63 when disaster struck. As dark clouds loomed above, she holed out in the deep. Still 83 for the first wicket was respectable. Yet, after three quick wickets fell, 105 for 4 was far less healthy. Maybe the girls were affected by Miss Frobisher's departure. It was make or break time for Hope, and she felt the butterflies flutter as she strode to the crease. Following Miss Frobisher she had to succeed.

Nervousness soon vanished, and after a couple of boundaries she felt the bit between her teeth. Her partner at the other end, Jayne Hamilton, was solid and provided a perfect foil for Hope's stroke-play. Jayne was advancing in resolute fashion, acquiring runs in calculated singles or sneaky twos – essentially keeping her end intact. There were hiccups when Hope was dropped at second slip after chasing an attempted yorker and getting a thin edge; and Jayne was almost run-out only saving her wicket by a desperate full-length dive to the turf. Cheers greeted the 150, then Hope opened her shoulders to a slow bowler; on one occasion advancing to the pitch of the ball and lofting it high over her head for 6. She was enjoying herself. The weather on the contrary failed to share her enthusiasm, and changed from bright blue to acidic grey. Yet there was hope of a positive outcome as a steady breeze sprung up, perhaps this would shepherd away the threatening nimbi.

29 and her eye in, Hope dabbed a fast ball down to the third man boundary, whilst wondering why they had removed the fielder. As the batsmen crossed midfield, Jayne gave her a sly wink. Yes, she thought, we can make it! No – she was sure she felt the faintest of rain-spots on her cheek. She countered her frustration with a resounding cover-drive for 4. The umpires were peering tentatively skywards, and a couple of overs later a fine drizzle began to descend. Please, please, not just yet, she silently prayed. 41 was good, but she wasn't there yet: Nine runs needed to carry her over the line, then she could relax and really let loose.

Jayne drove a ball to the boundary just out of reach of mid-on to bring up the 200. As she became more expansive, Hope was growing more circumspect as she closed in on the magical number. Light rain persisted and the umpires exchanged surreptitious glances over the green sward. With a couple to the mid-wicket boundary Hope reached 49. It hadn't been the nervous nineties but the feverish forties she recalled thinking. This was it, yes the next delivery had pitched in the same spot where she'd previously nicked one to long-off. There it was; NO, it had turned at the last moment, probably slicker with the wet, she attempted to withdraw the bat – too late, the ball caught the inside edge and the faint sound was followed a second later by a tiresome thwack as it embedded itself into a pair of secure leather gloves; a further second and the triumphant cry of 'Howzat!' from behind the stumps was echoed by the close fielders. Looking down the pitch she was saluted by the umpire's doom-laden raised finger.

Katie Elms, the Birlington wicket-keeper, was jubilant as she held the ball aloft. Merde, merde, merde! Dumbness, dismay, dejection rolled into one: Fallen at the final hurdle. Hope put on a brave face as she returned to the pavilion. It wasn't to be. She had experienced some peculiar dismissals – the time the stray had run on the pitch, collected the ball and run with it onto her stumps leaving her a bemused bystander; or when she had been caught on the boundary rope although she was certain she had struck a 6; and that time she had been clean-bowled by Beth Hopkin's devious underarm ploy. She'd had some bizarre dismissals she pondered, yet this was the first time she'd been caught out in the rain.

CHRISTIE'S FOLLY

Miss Christie in her novels subtly combines the best and the worst of the English character. At the same time as cosseting us with a detective thriller in time honoured tradition with the skilful maintenance of tension and mystery, she captures the blatant prudishness and bigotry which epitomises essentially the middle classes of mid 20th century Britain. Despite a confident expose of xenophobia bordering on the ethnocentric, her work is popular with students exploring English as a second language. The archetypal stiff upper lip dramas, played out to a backdrop of fluttering chintz in stuffy English drawing rooms, remain a much prized source of education to foreign students of all nationalities. Miss Christie's appeal worldwide may be fundamentally reduced to a wistful nostalgic escapism.

Although by no means extinct, Miss Christie's characters predominated in the 1930s, 1940s and early 1950s. This hybrid variety of Anglo-Saxon has its roots firmly embedded in the compost of empire. During this time most world maps portrayed Britain's possessions, amounting to two-thirds of global land mass, in a vast pink array.

Christie's writings of this period are rife with the importance of maintaining political correctness. Her novels are handbooks in English etiquette of the mid 20th century; recording a comprehensive and faithful dossier of the behaviour appropriate to a particular social status. Her catalogue of what ought or ought not to be done in a particular social setting is more extensive than the books of Mrs Beaton half a century earlier.

This was a time when, especially for the middle classes, it

was grand to be British. The heritage of the Victorian empire builders par excellence gained greater legitimacy and cohesion as Britain and her commonwealth shared the spoils as victors of two world wars. If domestic politics were not going as planned it was a minor hiccup; after all the jolly chaps in South Africa, New Zealand and the Indian jewel would be there to bail us out. Yet to be British meant more than this. It was ordained from above, the blessing of a benevolent deity – the British were what James Morris called 'God's elite'.

In the 1950s communism posed the new threat to stability and world order. In abeyance to Uncle Sam and Macarthyism, Reds were being discovered in the most unlikely places. Agatha Christie, ever with her finger on the pulse, was quick to use this misguided fervour to add spice and intrigue to her novels. In *They Came to Baghdad* written in the early 1950s characters have names like Victoria or Theodore Darly and of course live in Fitzjames Square, Kensington or Knightsbridge with a country estate in Norfolk. Much of their dialogue embodies the obsessive phobia: 'All this damned communism. War may break out at any moment…the whole country's riddled with it…' Communists, secret agents and Atom Scientists also feature prominently in *Dead Man's Folly.*

In this book is one of the best examples of Christie's caricatures, wherein the stalwarts of Empire appear resolute and imperturbable in the face of political and economic change. (And perhaps this is one of the attractions of Christie's work). The reader skips blithely over words like 'grandiloquently' and phrases such as 'When you're frightfully busy…' It is perfectly natural for one character to comment on the deterioration of the country when Youth Hostel Associations cater for 'both sexes and mostly foreigners'.

The characters present at the garden party (the focal point

of the story) are all upper class caricatures and of course all suspects to the subsequent murder. According to one of the players a Folly is 'one of those little sort of temple things, white, with columns'. And where would we find one? Of course, we have 'probably seen them at Kew'. It is here assumed that Miss Christie's readers are regular visitors to London's Kew Gardens. Yet it's 'nice to be rich' for there are always servants and gardeners to 'make the preparations'...'what's the good of being rich if one has to do everything one's self'. And when one throws a garden party it will probably be 'like Ascot, with big hats and everyone very chic.'

Colloquialisms abound and we expect them, for instance people who are 'absolutely stinking' with money never know what to do with it (with reference to the nouveau riche) and of course they waste it on 'something utterly goddamned awful!' Speech stereotyping is liberally resorted to, and all the familiar participants are represented from the military to the cockney and west country dialects. *Dead Man's Folly* takes place in a Devon country house where naturally if one is not 'frightfully respectable' there has to be 'something awfully fishy somewhere' along the line.

Moral judgements are liberally dispensed eg. the young 'craggy' architect Mr Weyman professes that when the foundation is rotten everything else is in a similar state of decomposure (a possible yearning for the return of the dwindling halcyon era). It would appear there is nothing new in the contemporary plea for a return to basics. Manners are unimpeachable – Inspector Poirot 'bowed over her hand'. And politeness must be seen and heard, no matter how supercilious and superfluous. The English are of course past masters of the false aside which when analysed is meaningless; such as the greeting 'Good Day' (it's teeming with rain and hail). 'How are you?' is not a sympathetic enquiry over a fellow being's condition (if it were so, it would probably embarrass the respondent profusely) – it is simply an extended form of 'Hello'. Christie makes ample use of such worthy small-talk (or time-fillers normally used while people are sizing each other up), as in 'The trains are sometimes too terrible this time of year' (this roughly translates as 'So, you've arrived at last!')

At times Miss Christie waxes poetical. For instance she allows one character to refer to Lady Stubbs (one assumes no relation to the famous artist) as 'A creature of the tropical sun, caught, as it were, by chance in an English drawing room'. However, there existed a question mark over her husband Sir George. The socially mobile tycoon fails to quite measure up, he is in fact 'a complete vulgarian' whose only saving grace is that he frequents the right side of town: 'Chelsea…and all that.'

Patronising references are made to the mentally ill and the working classes. We learn that the asylums are 'always letting 'em out half-cured nowadays', and police are accused of being more concerned with petty offences such as illegal parking while murderers go about their nefarious trade uninterrupted (further topical issues). A snob-ridden condescending attitude is adopted towards youth and the local youth hostel, so that perhaps 'young people should enjoy themselves'. Stereotypical behaviour is evident when the working-class Tucker is castigated by his wife for walking over the 'nice linoleum' in his working boots: 'Twouldn't have took ee tu minutes to be off with them boots', and 'That be someone at the door, that be. Du ee go and see who 'tis.'

Further examples of idiomatic dialogue may be found as the West Country old timer tells us of his former employer: 'Her be a Folliat…' and that 'She've had a hard life, she have…' but, of George Stubbs: 'Us understands that he be powerful rich.'

Perhaps the Stubbs made ideal marriage partners; 'but if her fair hated the sight of him' it would be another matter. Many of these underlings were employed on the estate. Although the household is no longer able to maintain a house keeper the butler is an imperative fixture. (In this instance the butler is innocent of the murder).

Higher up the social scale, polite dinner talk follows after one 'makes a terrific toilet'. We may catch the cut and thrust of indulgent conversation traversing the dining table, such as 'Absolutely asinine of me' and 'Darling, you look divine'. Poirot himself describes an event as a 'scream' (today perhaps the term would be 'riot') and makes reference to a 'music hall parody'. We learn that IQs are one of a collection of 'new fangled terms'; apparently old fangled ones include 'fakum policy'. Mrs Legge didn't leave the table immediately, she 'accepted the dismissal with promptitude'. And the following day Sir George wished Poirot good day 'perfunctorily'. Convoluted dialogue is to be found in 'He forbore to add that those had also been her questions', or the description of a bracelet 'from which depended a multiplicity of small gold objects', and the good gentleman who spoke 'parenthetically'.

Social class barriers are perpetuated. The Englishness of the extensive dinner ritual remains a permanent anachronism of the upper middle classes. Lavish trappings are the drawing room (originally withdrawing room), where luxurious glossy copies of *Vogue* and *Homes and Gardens* lie side by side with the *Tatler*, dinner jackets, evening gowns and the mandatory sherry, port and silverware. On the morning after, the Englishman's breakfast is a meagre offering of scrambled eggs, bacon and kidneys, or alternatively one could make do with a plate full of cold ham and turkey.

Inevitably middle class personages who failed to strictly

adhere to the social norms of the day were merely eccentric, whereas the lower classes were more often than not insane. Those wayward souls of the upper crust who failed to fit the social mould were perhaps 'a bit wanting in the top storey'. The fey Lady Stubbs fitted this category, her position made respectable by her current marriage of convenience to one of the 'financial johnnies' – a solid if crumbling column among the bulwarks of capitalism. Everyone knew his or her place in the pecking order, to the degree that it became 'dangerous' to sacrifice the mundane for greater glory (this was contrary to the war time slogan 'It all depends on you').

The system remained reliable and efficient just as long as one was of the correct stock. One of Christie's characters argues the case for eugenics, ie. Every 'feeble minded person' ought to be excluded from breeding, this natural function ought to remain the preserve of the intelligentsia. Doubtless, and Englishman's home was his castle, all that was required was a stiff upper lip, trust in God, and an ability to keep one's powder dry. The clues of the Murder-Hunt Game (a by product of which is the discovery of the murder proper) appear as Cluedo props, the characters themselves are life-size Cluedo personae (as Christie intended).

There are two major attractions to the work of Agatha Christie and they form a paradox. On the one hand there exists within each one of us longing for a golden past which was somehow stable and dependable (for example an inflexible social class structure). This is noticeably more prevalent at times of economic crisis as people yearn for a return of the 'good old days' when Britain enjoyed a privileged global stature. This is linked with the desolate feeling that all this is unattainable. That perhaps there never was a glorious country where things were done differently. As Miss Christie was writing, the other country was inevitably undergoing a process of cultural change. This social upheaval is ably documented in Miss Christie's work.

Nostalgia is evident despite the inevitable march of progress. For instance 'young women must have irons (electric), modern cookers and television…' But for all that some things could be relied upon, Merle the head gardener had remained at his post for 30 years. So although in some ways it might have been 'a very wicked world' as Mrs Folliat professes, there was still a stability and permanence to daily life. 'Proper stuff the ladies wore in those days. No gaudy colours and all this nylon and rayon: real good silk…' and with reference to today's development of real estate: 'nowadays, one drives through the country and passes place after place with the board up 'Guest House', or 'Private Hotel' or 'Hotel AA Fully Licensed'. All the houses one stayed in as a girl – or where one went to dance. Very sad.'

One of the main props to this drama is the bundle of comics. A further reference to past indulgence – we have comics today, yet there is a tendency to think of the comics of bygone days as more vibrant, lively and entertaining. But of course times are changing: 'people let one down in the most extraordinary way these days' (especially the hired labour it appears). 'Nowadays one has to do nearly everything oneself' pouts Mrs Folliat, so 'what's the good of being rich?' And of course there are more visible novelties like the 'youth hostel tomfoolery' with incumbents who wear incredibly designed shirts and 'just jibber at you'.

A strong theme in Christie's books is one of xenophobia and *Dead Man's Folly* is no exception. This is maintained to a degree which today would be impermissible given the current obsession with political correctness. This of course stems from the heritage of Empire and military successes which inevitably encompassed innumerable excesses in the name of Britannia. For example: 'there were many English people who considered what one said to foreigners didn't count!' The English are naturally incurably romantic, the French and Italians on the other hand are merely lustful or 'hot blooded'.

The latter were the cads and bounders who frequented the hostel. They were 'practically all foreigners,' and the problem was 'you never know where you are with foreigners.' They are evidently up to no good as witnessed by their proclivity to sun themselves – and without their shirts! Apart from having the impertinence not to understand a word you spoke to them, they had the audacity to 'jabber back at you in Dutch or something.' The root of this is obviously a refusal to speak Queen's English, 'which is really too inconsiderate of them.'

This phobia is shared equally with the lower classes. Mrs Tucker is adamant: 'You never know where you are with foreigners.' And the local beat bobby PC Hoskins is also willing to place the blame outside of the cosy local community. Obviously the foreigners are the culprits he declares. The main thrust of his evidence being their tendency to indulge in 'goings-on' and anyway there are 'some queer ones among them' he adds with conviction. The trouble seems to be that 'you never know with foreigners', who are promiscuous, lacking in moral fibre and good British phlegm. Added to this they are unpredictable and likely to 'turn nasty all in a moment.' Christie retreats from the brink by excusing the excesses of this local verdict, blaming it on a 'comfortable' and 'age-long one of attributing every tragic occurrence to unspecified foreigners.' (We can only surmise that Miss Christie's works are read and digested by current British politicians).

Casinos do not abound in England apparently as they do not 'accord with the English character.' Miss Christie would be dismayed to note these characteristically foreign gaming houses springing up in all our major towns, not to mention the forthcoming sale of another exclusively foreign incidental, the lottery ticket. With bitter irony Poirot is told he is 'one of us.' The basis for such a display of magnanimity being that the Belgian detective is 'a friend of the Eliots,' thus the misfortune of his ancestry may be overlooked.

To summarise, Christie remains in the vanguard of English literature. Her credit has been assured by the success of *The Mousetrap* which entered the record books for being the longest running show of all time. It ran continuously in London for more than 30 years. She was writing at a time of great social change: when Britain's class structure was becoming less rigid along with a loss of empire. Her appeal owes much to her ability to remain topical yet true to the times she portrayed. Examples have been cited above. One 'profound truth' may be seen in Britain's social and political problems stemming from the 'incredible apathy of people in this country.' Equally, the location of the discovered body, found buried beneath the concrete base of the ornamental Folly, bears a chilling similarity to the hapless victims of the contemporary murderer Frederick West.

Her prodigious international success seems due to her matchless ingenuity in the contrivance of plots, the sustenance of suspense and an uncanny knack of misdirecting her reader. She also had an ear for dialogue and brisk, unsentimental common sense and humour. Miss Christie was a product of her time and her marked ability one of skilfully interweaving social documentary with mystery and suspense. The closest such an accomplishment may be encountered today may be possibly found in the works of Dorothy L. Sayers and Marjorie Allingham, who both wrote detective novels on the same historical periods and settings; whereas P.D.James could be seen to provide a more topical variation. Theorise we may, the bottom line must remain with the fact that Miss Christie has enthralled many thousands with a ripping good yarn.

References:
Dead Man's Folly – Agatha Christie
They Came to Baghdad – Agatha Christie
Pax Britannica – James Morris
The Precise Oxford Companion to English Literature

DALLIANCE

'Why am I here? – A geographical, rather than philosophical question. Well you may ask! Shivering in this obscure craggy meadow, sporting my finest taffeta and surrounded by sheep, why indeed? Why mar this idyllic pastoral landscape? Here I am, hanging around like an extravagant Edwardian scarecrow peering expectantly into the future; striking the pose of an abandoned figurehead from the prow of some sailing vessel.

Well, we have darling Charles to thank for that, don't we! It could have been worse, I could have caught him inflagrante delecti with Molly the maid, but of course he's too clever for that. To escape the tears (Molly's, not mine) after confronting the strumpet I ran out of the house and across the fields. I had only a moment to snatch this apron as I dashed through the kitchen; I found the stick leaning by the wall. The embarrassment of it all! Lady Faversham hinted all was not well below stairs just last month.

What a fool I've been! Couldn't he choose an assignation with the nobility – O the ignomy! Servants these days are simply getting above their station. Except of course Frobisher: dear sweet Frobisher, always there to intercept trouble. What a blessing that man is, what more could one look for in a butler. As he once remarked to me in his frosty tones: "we also serve, those who stand and wait."

I'll wager they're having a good stare at me from the workers' cottages; I'm sure I saw a curtain twitch. At least the sun's shining, yet the wind's chilly and I fear I'll lose my hat in this strong westerly; and I wish I'd stopped for my coat.

I shan't return. Well, I must think it over carefully… Maybe I shall go back, simply to humiliate Charles. Darn the insects, <u>go</u> away! Oh, – now I've trodden in something!

Why I'm addressing you useless ewes I don't know, you're taking no notice at all; that's right, carry on munching and looking sheepish. I see nothing in the distance and no carts have travelled along the lane, which may be a blessing.

You've no idea what I have to put up with! The letter I intercepted, was from Frobisher's silver salver, as he was carrying the mail along the hall to his master. I seem to have mislaid it, no doubt I dropped it by the chaise-longue as I made my speedy departure. Really, the wording would have made a sergeant-major blush. Perhaps I'll sneak back and collect it; oh, I don't know. Wonder if the royals have such problems, no, George's beard would put most women off; Queen Mary's quite safe. Oh dear, my hem's becoming damp with dew, glad you lot keep the grass down.

But, I mustn't continue in this vein, it's now midday and I only have ten minutes! Get away, curse these insects. Well, well, a magpie on a ewe's flank – there's one for Thomas Hardy to ponder.

The other evening we held a small soiree (dinner a la Russe), Montague was there accompanying the soprano on piano, what's her name, oh yes Sally Winstanley that was it; while Edith brought her cello. Don't know why she brought it but they did sound fine; although, if it wasn't for her corsets she'd never be able to play the thing. Sally sang something by Vaughan Williams; the song of the shepherdess or some such ditty. The fare was well received, game, fish, sweetmeats and roast – you know the sort of thing. No, don't worry, mutton wasn't on the menu.

The Fitzroys were there and that wretched Italian banker Segantini. And the Kimboltons with that horrid little man

Parmeston (I think he's in trade!) – too ghastly! The Martins turned up (Charles calls them the house Martins – he says they're always fouling their nest). And Major Delaware, he's really quite dashing you know, and too much for a gal to handle. His smile was scintillating as, after dinner, I directed him to the smoking lounge.

The charming Frogmortons, the Dolomites and the Somervilles came too; they've a place in London of course, in with the Bloomsbury set. Young Hettie was there, I do like Hettie, in spite of her telling everyone every few minutes she looked like Lillie Langtry. What a time we had, we ran out of Borscht and had to send Cook to the Coddingtons.

The man was so beastly to me, even Nancy Sherbourne could see that. Of course, I've had my suspicions. I once confided my fears to Nancy – she said she was not surprised; although she did add that she herself was too old for such dalliance: "my dear, the days for that sort of business are far behind me."

Such a barren landscape, not a tree in sight: My heart yearns for the Oberammergau pine forests of my youth. As a small girl I would pass long summers with my aunt and the dogs, trekking for truffles beneath the trees: later we'd return to bowls of thick warming soup. I do so love firs, their subtle scent and soft silent carpet of needles. Uncle would cut logs for the cabin fire that spoke to me in sharp crackles in the soft glow of evening. Oh yes, hmm…aah! you startled me …Sebastian not here, the workers' cottages…I thought you'd never come!'

DESTINY

The nagging fear was there as she stirred and turned over although she was unsure from where it came. Muted squeaking came from somewhere among the bed covers, then a low purring drummed in her ears: a soothing sound that was enticing her back to sleep. Suddenly her eyes opened wide and she sprang upright in bed. Reaching for the clock she saw it was ten past eight, she leapt from her bed and slipped into a dressing gown. At last the day had arrived – time to confront her demons. Clasping the tiny bundle of fur to her bosom she tore downstairs. After feeding little Destiny, Miriam washed down a bowl of cereal and banana with a half mug of tea and raced back up for a speedy shower. She thought it prudent to apply minimum make-up. Outside was dull and wet.

Stomach churning, she wished she could use the car and her thoughts flew to the small yellow Suzuki asleep in the garage. Not today, today Su could have a day off – Miriam would be taking the train. This was one visit she was dreading to the depths of her being: perhaps she should go on an extended holiday and not return; something unexpected might crop up and in a magical way she'd avoid the trip – but Destiny? She needed her – Miriam was her lifeline. Escape would merely postpone the inevitable she pondered reaching for her collapsible brolly. It was just after 9.30 that she closed the door and entered a breezy world where there was a rising mist and rain enough to dampen the features and cover the pavements in a glossy sheen.

As she turned the corner she had the good fortune to spot

an approaching bus to transfer her to the station. Arriving, she purchased her ticket and ascended the stairs to cross the line to her platform and sat on the brown-painted bench to await her train; next to an elderly woman in a blue raincoat who stared straight ahead as though divining the meaning of life and all that. 'What am I doing?' she repeatedly asked herself, I suppose out of flight or fight I've opted for the latter. As it was later in the day, there was a marked absence of the faceless grey suits she had jostled with during her commuting days. Her gaze wandered along the platform, where at its furthest extent she saw a few huddled transport staff enjoying tobacco. 'Some people still *smoke*!?' she surmised absent-mindedly, of course she was referring to cigarettes.

Her thoughts turned to little Destiny. In a way the animal had been dumped on her, having had cats when married she hadn't envisaged embarking on the commitment so soon. It had been Elsie's fault: she ran a Sewing shop and the mother cat had given birth to three cute kittens out the back. Well, she couldn't claim she'd been talked into having him – the tiny mite had sold himself. Should I fail to return, she mused, Pat Jarvis along the street would feed him. She'd left ample water and invested in one of those food-dispensers that deliver sufficient biscuit to stall imminent starvation.

Waiting on that grimy platform in the murky drizzle of early Autumn and peering beyond the station into the pervading gloom, she felt her stomach tremble. Her father always advised her to think happy thoughts whenever unpleasant ones were imminent. As a child this had proved simple, she merely conjured up swaying Christmas trees or sparkling colourful crackers set upon tables laden with less common fare such as jittery jellies and pink blancmange, spicy plum pudding and roast turkey; or sunny-beach days, where with bucket and spade she and her brother would construct intricate sandcastles then watch them slowly succumb to the incoming tide.

Throughout the train journey she forced herself to picture the Amalfi coast she'd visited on holiday a year before. She'd gone on a Singles coach tour to southern Italy, where they'd made brief pauses at Rome and Naples before heading further south. She recalled the small coastal town of Amalfi where she'd first sampled Limoncello; Ravello, where tribute operas to Wagner were held in an open-air amphitheatre overlooking the dazzling Bay of Naples; and Positano, in the season home to celebrities and artists who had villas overlooking a sparkling azure sea. In fact it had been difficult to spot the join between sea and sky. She had taken a trip on a coastal boat and visited the isles of Capri and Ischia, and could still smell the fresh salty spray when peering into the blue depths the sun bathed all in warmth and wonder. Graceful white villas and palm trees clung to the hillside above the rapt sightseers skimming the lapping waves. On that trip she had swapped her brolly for a parasol.

These pleasing reminiscences were rudely interrupted by a grating voice that warned of her approaching destination. With apprehension, she gently moulded her stomach to spread the anxiety. Leaving the station precinct, she negotiated a couple of rain-sodden streets to arrive at the hospital gates. With tension mounting she turned from the busy thoroughfare and passed through a high black wrought-iron portico, with at its centre a fleur-de-lys motif, and headed towards the tall building beyond. Approaching, she was vaguely aware of beds of beleaguered wallflowers, their bright orange and yellow heads drooping beneath the constant rain. Pushing through double swing doors she entered and followed the signs to reception.

Her appointment was with Mr Goodson. She fantasized, would she prefer him tall dark and handsome or off the wall with a wacky sense of humour? Would he have a stocky figure and pleasing appearance, or ginger hair freckles and a stutter? Did it matter? She told herself he need only be kind and thoughtful. Would he put her at ease, the meeting would be their first, or would she remain on tenterhooks? Why was she putting herself through all this, could she stay calm? This had never happened to her before; yet it had to others she knew and they had survived to tell the tale. Such events were unavoidable later in life if she thought about it. It would be nice if he smiled, she did appreciate pleasantry. If he wasn't honest and trustworthy, then maybe she would get lucky and not have to see him again. All these thoughts and more crossed her mind as in the waiting area she skimmed the pages of *Woman's Weekly* and *Country Life*.

'Mrs Winborne...?' he was tall and rangy with dark hair greying at the sides; maybe in his fifties, he was dressed in a mink shirt and coordinated tie over black trousers, in fact quite trendy she mused. 'Please come in.' This was it, she was in the presence of the man she had dreaded meeting for over two months. Finally her Waterloo, would she emerge as Wellington or Napoleon she wondered as he ushered her into a small office. The room was sparse, containing filing cabinets, a large desk topped with assorted folders, a couple of chairs and a potted aspidistra by the window. With hands shaking she sat in the proffered seat.

'Now, Mrs Winbourne,' he began, 'your doctor has referred you to me – Dr Redding, I believe – he thought it wise if you came for a visit. I believe you've been having some trouble with...'

Miriam had medical problems that proved beyond her doctor's diagnostic capabilities and eventually he had referred her to Mr Goodson, a consultant at Kensal Green General. With a phobia about hospitals she had convinced herself she would never come out again. Nevertheless, Mr Goodson was charm itself, the nurses sympathetic, and her agonising fears proved groundless. Following a couple of hours of tests and some inevitable waiting, she was released with a clean bill of health and told to report to her GP for medication.

Her grateful thoughts shifted to Destiny and it felt good to be needed, good to be alive. 'What a fool!' she scolded herself. Heading for the station, she knew she couldn't wait to make a big fuss of her Destiny.

DUTY

The monotonous ticking of the clock was driving her to insanity. At 39, she felt it was ticking off the precious moments of her life; draining away her very essence with the insistence of each tock. Listlessly, she allowed her gaze to take in her sordid surroundings: the grim dark kitchen, with its heavy black forbidding stove, the gritty bread-oven, the shiny fading oil-cloth covering the old oak table, and the greasy Belfast sink. Was this the sum of her achievement, her destiny, to spend her waking hours tied to that stove and sink – to never experience laughter among friends, picnics in airy fields on summer days? In lighter moments her mind would wander to the possibility of meeting a dashing young blade, with an open sports car like the one in bright red she'd seen in a magazine; he would be handsome and charming and whisk her far away from her life's drudgery. If only she could escape to Leeds, perhaps there she would realise her dream.

From above her head came the other knocking that ruled her life and measured out her hours. This was more persistent and irregular. Tap-tap, tap-tap, tarrap-tap! Doesn't she ever give up? This sound too she had sought to ignore on many occasions, but it only grew louder and more insistent to be finally accompanied by raucous screeching, as though someone was strangling a tormented parrot. In the end, she always gave in, lit the oil-lamp, opened the latch-door, and climbed the narrow creaking staircase to the next floor. The stairs began immediately the door was opened, ascended steeply without light at the top, and were covered in unforgiving dyed hessian.

Her ailing mother had hung on for years, and she was forced

to take care of her. Wearied by the constant ferrying of food, wash basins, chamber-pots and village gossip, at times she rebelled against the tyranny. Continually at her beck and call throughout the day when she wasn't helping out Ma Collins at the corner-shop; and at times during the hours of darkness when her mother wasn't keeping her awake with her drawn-out snoring that seemed to rattle the floor-boards. All in addition to normal household chores. An endless cycle of degradation from the pans on the stove to the sink, she never took off her apron. As she filled and emptied pans, collected water from the pump, emptied chamber-pots, scoured dishes, fetched coal, made beds, and drained clothes from the copper to the mangle in the back yard, her constant companion was the eternal noise of the clock: always encouraging her to work faster – tick, tock.

She fantasized that somehow she would stop that clock, stop its continual transformation of the present into the past. She would nudge the large ugly wooden frame to place it off kilter, spitefully it would continue its regular rhythm. She would hold the long brass pendulum to arrest its movement, but she knew the moment it was released it would resume relentless motion. At other times she imagined taking a hammer to it, and smashing the glass casing and the haughty black and white face to smithereens. It was only a man-made object after all, an invention ever directing her to her demise. If it ever stopped her mother always knew; she seemed to sense when the wretched mechanism should chime and as it remained silent she soon began her unholy cacophony. This happened when she had to detain the pendulum for its half-yearly polish.

Often she envisaged her escape, she even kept a small suitcase packed with essentials. She would dress in her best blouse, skirt and boots, a little lipstick and she would slip the catch to freedom. It would be so easy, she would wait until her mother's snores were rocking the foundations: and set out as the clock struck ten under-cover of the resonant chimes. Time enough to catch the last train to Leeds at 10.28. She would have to find somewhere for the night, that should be possible around the station; she'd sleep in a doorway if she had to, then look for work in the morning. Once beyond the door, it was a simple matter of ten paving stones to the gate and liberty. She had rehearsed it many times.

Her father had been a kind soul; a shadowy figure dying when she was young, nevertheless she could recall pleasing memories. Possessing a weak chest through working in the pits, he was probably drawn to the shades as a cause of his wife's excesses. She would have tolerated her intransigence had her mother been civil. Instead she was a mean spiteful cantankerous old woman who resented her daughter's nimble dexterity, constantly bemoaned her bed-ridden condition and the state of the world; and took to directing her daughter's world with her husband's cane.

Should she, could she, run off? Repeatedly she returned to the conundrum, as the clock ticked on. She had adopted the habit of reading the day-old newspaper Mrs Collins had given her to keep abreast of events. Yet what good had she gained from the schooling? Tick, tock – a mere implement, yet it came alive to her. At times the sound seemed to grow in intensity, and resound around in her mind until she felt her head would burst, tolling of doom. Surely she deserved better?

She had grown to detest her mother's sallow skin, her beady sunken eyes, her bruised arms, her drawn features, and the surly mouth that sagged at the corners and constantly emitted drools of saliva. She tried to think of a time she had ever loved her mother. For as long as she could recall, the daughter had been resented; although she had tried, really hard.

There was the time she'd spent over an hour collecting wild flowers for her fit and well mother, from along the lanes home after school. This offering was greeted with a scolding for being late, then she was castigated for bringing a handful of weeds into the house. And, when she had mistaken her mother's bitterness for sadness and surprised her with a birthday cake she'd had made at the shop. A fine cake that had been baked and iced on top. 'You'd think that shop could make a better job of a cake!' was her only response. She was everlastingly belittling her father. His wagoner's wages weren't enough, he should have got more schooling and secured the post of a smart clerk in a shipping office in Leeds or Harrogate. She viewed his many acts of kindness as weakness: 'What do you want to do that for 'er for, she does nowt for us?'

Then came the day she made her decision. In the scullery, it had been a normal day of pots, pans, and more pots. In the evening she had laid down her paper at the tapping on the door, when a neighbour called round with flowers for her mother. 'Shall I put them in water, mother?' 'Do what you like with them. She only came around to nose, I know her type!' That was it, something inside of her snapped. She'd had enough, more than she could take of her mother's ungrateful and contrary ways. She decided to execute her plan that very evening.

As her mother's snores spread through the house, she gave herself a thorough wash at the sink using the bar of carbollic, and stepped into her smart clothes. Carefully pinning her hat in place and slipping a cape around her shoulders she surveyed the kitchen; as the chimes began to reverberate, with a last glance in the hanging mirror, she took her suitcase and gloves and pressed the latch. At that moment, from above, came a snort, a cough, then tap, tap, taptap – mother had awoken. 'Sod er!' she muttered. The screams that followed must have been heard through the open door, and the tapping became a frantic thrashing as she hurried over the paving towards the gate.

She deliberated before silently pressing the latch – not to the gate but to the door, as she yelled up the dark stairs: 'Coming, mother!' Perhaps it would be prudent to bear her mother's insults a while longer, at least until she had inherited the house. As she calmly struck the match to light the lamp, she felt something was different. She realised the clock had stopped. The clock had finally stopped, and there was precious little her bed-ridden mother could do about it!

ENCHANTED BAY

The only sounds were the constant lapping of waves against the ebony rocks, the shingle-sucking tide, and the occasional shriek of a herring gull gliding to the shelter of a lofty ledge. A fiery sun slid away in splashes of orange and yellow mosaics leaving a jostling breeze to marvel the splendour of its parting. The solar lustres blended with the sparkling essence of a becalmed ocean, casting a myriad colours across the vacant canvas of the horizon. A haunting tableau re-enacted on countless moments and recaptured in a myriad memories. The scene was as it always had been, always would be on other dusk-laden evenings.

It was the same a short year ago: Alan had shared it with me then and I had felt secure in his warm embrace. My heart skipped a beat when he playfully kissed my nose, or when his pale blue eyes twinkled as he chuckled over some amusing banter. Oblivious to time, we had wandered barefoot along the shore and splashed among the shallows. Laughingly we chased each-other across the warm sand to pause for breath upon an upturned dinghy beached above the water-line. Alan had skimmed flat stones across the placid surface, and we had searched in green rock-pools for marine-life or collected shells and coloured pebbles more precious to me than gem-stones. The fortnight had lasted forever.

It was on that bewitching beach that we'd met. He'd been a little shy at first and I did most of the talking. I'd failed to secure my wind-break; seated on a towel across the beach Alan had come to my assistance. We talked about books we'd read, films we'd seen and places we'd visited, We discussed my teaching and his legal practice. We had seen each other every day, explored all the way over that extensive beach and others too, shared local museums and dined by candlelight. Towards the end of his stay, he was returning before me, he became nervous and withdrawn. At first I thought he was upset at having to leave. I'd made a special fuss of him: soon things were back to normal and his dry sense of humour came to the rescue; later we'd played hide and seek among the rocks like a couple of ten-year-olds.

No, it hadn't lasted…Alan, my Alan –tall fair and handsome, who made me laugh – also made me cry; we had shared so much – yet I realised so little. There were times he would go into his own world – times when he was not with me at all…I was left abandoned and confused – did he really love me? Then we'd had that long chat in the small bistro in a local town. I had quizzed him over these silences and, bless him, he tried to respond. Pulling me close, he said: 'Sophie, listen to me, it isn't you, it's me –' During those dark moments he just needed to be alone – to think things through. He told me he'd been badly hurt before and thought we were moving too fast. He didn't think he was able to commit at that moment: I argued with him, I pleaded with him whilst desperately fighting to hold back the tears.

He mentioned the job: as a lawyer he had the chance of a position in the North. I wondered if this was an excuse: that secretly he felt trapped and wanted to get away…but when the blackness had gone, then we were just two people seeking happiness again. I loved him so… He hadn't written for six months after we'd parted, and then it was only small talk concerning his work and the new neighbourhood. This had been testimony to what I already knew in my heart. Eventually, I had imagined I was over him…

I hadn't intended to return to Lisa so soon. If it wasn't for a mix-up over travel arrangements I would have been basking by the hotel pool in Malaga sipping a long cool cubalibra. It was a couple of months ago that the tour company had contacted me, apologising that the hotel hadn't been refurbished for the season and another couldn't be found so late in the day – they would however refund my money in full and offered me priority booking as well as a hefty discount for the following year. Lisa had been a poppet as ever. As soon as she heard of my plight she offered to put me up. She had lost her husband some time before and, with her two children at home for the holidays was grateful of willing assistance.

'They'll be going to bed soon,' I chastened myself, as I climbed the steep hill that wound from the beach to Lisa's bungalow. It was a pleasant little village nestling a sheltered valley in West Wales not far from St Davids Head. As I climbed, the stiff breeze tugged at my cotton frock and blew my hair into reckless disarray. From the top of the hill the view was stunning across the bay below, where sun sparkled upon the rippling surface against the backdrop of a crimson sky.

'Enjoy your walk, Sophie?'

'Yes thanks Lisa. It's a gorgeous view from the hill – you are so lucky,' I responded.

'Yes, it is rather beautiful…so glad you could come again this year…though I would have understood if you had decided against it – I was worried it might be too painful for you-' 'Oh-it's alright, Alan's in my past,' I answered, I hoped convincingly. 'Anyhow it's good for me to confront the situation, no-one can run for ever. Oh, we shared some wonderful times but I guess I'm not sure of him – and realistically never have been.' It was partly to restore my confidence that I had returned to our favourite beach on the following evening, to dispel my private ghosts.

Once more the beach was mine but for an ageing Labrador who lagged behind its owner, plodding resolutely in pursuit as he rounded a collection of rocks and disappeared from view. I had sat upon a flattish rock covered in barnacles, my eyes lazily following the lateral course of a pink hermit crab as it scuttled for the safety of a shiny clump of kelp. But before long my eyes were drawn towards the distant horizon and the panoramic shoreline we had shared together. I glanced out across the bay as dusk began to settle – revelling in the timeless beauty of the scene. To my left, a forsaken dinghy covered in peeling grey paint loomed phantom-like through a rising sea-mist. Then I saw him. His golden hair shone in the half-light as he passed across my field of vision along the shore. Was he in my past?

'A-Alan', my lips formed the word yet no sound escaped. I wanted to run to him, to collapse into his arms and shower him with kisses – but unable to move I waited spellbound in the gathering twilight. Transfixed, I had remained clamped as firmly to that rock as the hundreds of limpets that clung to its craggy surface. I blinked, of course it hadn't been him: he was the busy solicitor somewhere in the North. His last letter six months ago had been plain enough – he wanted friendship, that was all. The last time we'd gazed upon this scene together had been around, I glanced at my watch, the same time – nine in the evening…my pulse beat faster. Frantically my eyes scanned the empty horizon, to be met by a solitary seagull keeping lookout from a rocky overhang. 'Careful girl, you're starting to see things – keep a grip on yourself!' I cautioned as I turned my back on the beach and the splendour of our favourite vista.

Lisa's children were no trouble at all: they were healthy, well balanced and bright. Lisa was doing a fine job of bringing them up alone. Jamie was eight and into all the scrapes that attend boys of that age: little Meg was five, she'd just started school and looked like a miniature angel with her golden halo of curls.

'Cleaned your teeth yet, Jamie? –Say goodnight to Mummy

then, and don't forget Auntie Sophie…' I thought I wouldn't bother Lisa with my hallucination about Alan, but my mind was on him and not the television as we sat in the back parlour. That night I hadn't slept well. It had been warm and sultry and I'd lain awake tossing and turning, then kicked off the duvet and felt more relaxed covered merely in a gossamer of cool nylon. My thoughts turned to Alan. If only; what if it had been him on the shore? Finally I had fallen asleep to spend the remaining dark hours in fitful slumber.

Of course, I had returned on the following evening. Expectantly I had waited at the same spot on the beach overlooking the tranquil bay – but he hadn't appeared… it had to have been a mirage I told myself, attempting to be as rational as a primary teacher can be, anyhow it had been dusk and the mind is known to play tricks at such an hour. Desolately, I had gazed seaward until the sea appeared as a sullen grey haze and the hands of my watch pointed to half past nine, then I headed for home.

The next evening found me on the shore again: it had been an overcast day, with intermittent sheets of rain drifting across the bay to drum the surface of the sea and draw the dusk in early. I had sheltered from a stiff breeze in the porch of a locked and abandoned beach-hut at the far end of the shore-line. Out to sea I spotted gulls and oystercatchers bobbing on the choppy grey surface, when my eyes were drawn to a large black shape which ducked with the swell in the near distance…at first I thought it was a sea mammal but, no, it had kept roughly to the same area of water without totally submerging…a drifting buoy or some floating debris after all…laughing like a little boy, Alan would have thrown pebbles at it for target practice.

Soon the clouds lifted and I returned across the beach to my situation upon that familiar boulder; inevitably my eyes were drawn towards the opaque grey mass that obscured the horizon.

In the dim twilight he passed again, just beyond clear vision. It had to be him…it just had to be…even his walk seemed the same. Again I sat in silence, still as the stone I was seated on, as he passed out of sight beyond a rocky promontory that stretched towards the sea from the tall cliffs behind me. Then suddenly I was able to break the spell that gripped me and became galvanised into action. I leapt up from that rock and raced across the barren sand, shouting his name into the gathering gloom.

I rounded the cluster of jutting boulders expecting to spy his retreating figure; to be confronted with a vast empty expanse of sand. I appeared utterly alone in the rapidly descending dusk – nothing stirred on that silent shore, but the steady drumming of cascading drops from the encroaching shadowy rocks into a hollowed out pool below. Exhausted and bewildered I remember sinking to the moist sand in a dejected heap, oblivious to the dampness soaking my skin through the thin cotton.

How long I had lain there I cannot tell, but lights glowed from the bungalows as I eventually reached the cliff-top. 'What's happening to me?' I pondered, 'I know I've been working hard recently, staying up late with all that extra paper-work, but really…' Not the sort of person to believe in the supernatural, I had always treated visitations from other worlds with a healthy scepticism. There had to be an other explanation…but what? I couldn't find a logical one – I admit I was baffled – I feared I must be losing control of my senses. Such a condition was not unknown in the profession.

I returned to find the bungalow in a state of chaos: Trish Greene, Lisa's neighbour was settling the children to sleep. Lisa had had an accident whilst out shopping. Apparently she had dashed to stop young Meg from wandering into the busy road, and in the process her scant flip-flops lost purchase on the damp pavement and she tumbled down a small flight of steps. She had been unable to place any weight on her foot and suspected a twisted ankle. But at the Casualty department of the local hospital it was discovered she'd broken a small bone in her foot: the injured limb was encased in plaster and she had been kept in overnight. I busied myself making tea for Trish, in an effort to ease my guilt at not having returned earlier.

'Pieces of eight, Pieces of eight – here comes Peg-Leg!' cheeked Jamie, as we heard the now familiar tapping of Lisa's old cherry stick in the hallway.

'I'm sorry to lay all this on you': Lisa commented as she entered the kitchen, and surveyed me attempting to conjure up the sparkle to the floor-tiles boasted by the manufacturers of the cleaning fluid.

'Now, don't you worry about me – you just get that foot better', I shouted above the whirring washing machine. 'Care for a coffee, the kettle's just boiled-?' Secretly I was glad that for the past four days I'd had to do the chores – it had diverted my mind from dwelling on my private mystery. Although I'd been able to visit the beach at around midday, I was spared my later cryptic visitation: dusk proved to be the busy time when everyone in the bungalow required attention. Yet my thoughts were there, especially around nine o'clock, overlooking the enchanted seascape I knew so well.

Poor Lisa spent most of her time flat on her back – she even watched TV from a sun-lounger I'd found in the garden shed and somehow fitted into the parlour. The doctor had suggested the plaster could be removed in about six weeks: until then the smooth white surface was slowly becoming sullied with obscure graffiti. On one occasion, Jamie's school chums had called round to inspect the invalid, at the same time adding their individual designs and autographs to Lisa's plaster cast. 'Careful what you write boys!' Lisa advised them. There was enough space for them to practice their artwork for, despite the breakage of such a tiny bone, the poor thing had plaster not only encasing her foot but up her leg to just below the knee. Trish was very attentive, many times I had to assure her that everything was OK and I was coping just fine. She said I wasn't to worry about Lisa after I returned home next week: she would look in on a regular basis and ferry the children to and from school alongside her own. 'It's good to have friendly neighbours', I thought to myself, recalling the surly inhabitants of my suburban street.

I guessed it must be Trish when, having tucked the kids up for the night, I was startled from my reverie by a sharp ring on the door-bell. I had been sitting on my bed, my mind's eye conjuring the magical cove below and wondering if... He was tall and fair and neatly dressed in a casual sort of way with a rust coloured parka over an ochre roll-neck and beige chinos: his deep blue eyes shone when he smiled which was almost permanently, actually it was more of a boyish grin. Realising I must look a sight, instinctively my hands flew to my hair, I hadn't bothered with make-up, and I had on a sad baggy T over tired leotards that displayed evidence of the recent confrontation between the little ones and the bath-tub.

'Er- yes, can I help you?' I queried, still patting my hair into place.

'Sorry to bother you, but does Lisa Gooding live here?' he asked, '-only I took her to the hospital after her unfortunate accident the other day and, – well, I really only called to see how she was...?'

'O-oh, well...you'd better come in,' I suggested, leading through to the parlour. 'Excuse the mess,' I added noticing his eyes sweep around the room as I removed a pile of dog-eared magazines from a chair, 'Would you like a coffee?' He said that would be welcome. The interlude served to cover my distracted behaviour and I had hastily applied lipstick whilst slyly glancing in his direction from the kitchen. He was about thirty-five with blonde hair and a deep tan, quite dishy in fact.

'I hope it's not too hot?' I placed the coffee on the table in front of him and sat in the vacant chair opposite. 'No, just fine! – 'Silence hung over the tiny parlour: the air was charged with an expectancy normally reserved for opening night at the theatre. Biting my lip, I garbled: 'Has the rain stopped?'

'I believe so,' he answered in a deep soothing accent, replacing his mug on the table. 'Look, is Mrs Gooding alright–?'

'Oh, yes of course…it was only a tiny fracture to an ankle bone –', I flustered, realising I had totally forgotten the reason for his visit. 'She's sleeping at the moment – she's on pain-killers you see…' I added lamely.

'Ye-s, I understand. They can make a mess of the normal sleep pattern…Are you her sister?'

'Me? No…I'm just visiting – on holiday –'.

'Ah, I see – it's a lovely spot, isn't it?' he put his empty mug on the table and stood up. 'Well, I must be getting along. It's been nice meeting you – Mrs –?'

'Sophie Townsend, a-and it's Miss –', I stammered.

'Right then –'.

'You're sure you won't have another coffee?'

'Thanks, I'd love to, but I have to get back to the nursery,' he explained. 'But perhaps we'll see each other again before your holiday is over. I've enjoyed talking to you …I'm Scott Peters by the way. I have a small business selling cut-flowers from the Appleyard smallholding on the Trensham road.' The smile had started from within those deep blue eyes again, slowly spreading across his sunburnt features in a way no girl could ignore. 'Kindly give my regards to Mrs Gooding for me…' he offered from the doorway as he turned to leave.

'Er, yes of course,' I managed. 'And thank you for your concern', I called in the direction of the retreating rust parka.

In desperation I ran to the nearest mirror where my worst fears were confirmed. Hastily I drew my hair into a bun and applied light make-up; with a dab of Anais Anais behind the ears I felt somewhat better, albeit too late. I found a music station on the radio then sat on the bed and tried to read but the print appeared as a jumbled blur, I couldn't concentrate. I even attempted a puzzle from one of Lisa's magazines but it was no use, my mind continued its erratic dance. I lay back and closed my eyes in a forlorn effort to gather my thoughts, but all I could see was that dashing smile swimming out of the depths of those penetrating blue eyes.

At around seven the following evening of a brilliantly sunny day, I had just made Lisa comfortable and was busy with the evening meal when the sound of Meg sobbing in the garden drew me to the open window. This was unusual as the kids normally got on fine, and Jamie was always attentive and protective towards his little sister; yet some sort of tiff was the only explanation.

'What's the matter then, Meg…Why are you crying like that?…There now sweetheart, dry your eyes like a big girl and tell Auntie Sophie what's wrong –?'

'It's Bungie – I can't feed him–' she wailed. Bungie was the childrens' pet rabbit who spent the summer months out of doors. His cage was kept on top of a high decrepit chest of drawers beyond the reach of furry predators, and also beyond that of tiny Meg. The poor child sat on the grass amid an impressive array of greenery, including lettuce leaves and stalks of dandelion and groundswell; her rosy cheeks, usually creased in smiles, were grubby and glistening with fresh tears.

'Well-Why not ask Jamie to feed him, as he's done before –?'

'Jamie's gone –'

'Gone?...gone where?' I knelt down to her level, as alarm bells began to ring: I hadn't seen him since early afternoon – and he hadn't come for his usual piano lesson. I searched the house and garden and then along the street: no sign of Jamie. With growing concern I checked the immediate neighbours. Trish said she would help me: leaving her husband Roy in charge, she suggested I search the village while she took her car along the back lanes of the perimeter.

I looked in on Lisa before I set out: she was sleeping soundly probably having taken a pain-killer. I thought it best not to disturb her in case it was all a false alarm, and arming myself with a lightweight rain-proof jacket and stout walking shoes headed for the village. I made the Post Office my first stop, then on to the Police House: nobody had seen the young boy, but Gareth Jones the local sergeant offered his services. After walking and running the extremity of the hamlet, and checking each of the three lanes leading from the village I had returned distraught and exhausted.

In my anxiety I had forgotten to look seaward: in a final desperate endeavour I passed by Lisa's bungalow and descended the hill towards the bay. Long shadows were changing the landscape as I stepped onto the cooling sand. A middle-aged couple were strolling along the water-line oblivious to the rapidly approaching athletic jogger in scarlet shorts, who was forced to make a sudden detour to avoid a collision. Apart from these, the shoreline was deserted. My watch showed eight-thirty, and if I wasn't able to find the lad soon I would have to admit my failure to Lisa. After trudging the length of the beach, I had arrived at some water-filled troughs of hollowed sand that heralded the beginning of the rocks.

Beyond a rocky outcrop, as far as I could see, I was again confronted with a vast stretch of beach devoid of humanity. To gain access to this further extent of vacant sand avoiding the encroaching tide, I was forced to clamber over a few low rocks with their scattering of pools throbbing with aquatic life-forms. My desperation caused me to be careless and I lost my footing, splashing into one of those teeming water-worlds as I strove to maintain my balance. It was while I was occupied wringing out the Indian cotton of my damp skirt that I saw him...coming towards me through the failing light.

My heart missed a beat: I straightened my skirt and tugged at a stray strand of hair, trying to appear as nonchalant as I could as I gazed upon the confident masculine stride bringing him ever closer. He had come back to me – that's why he haunted the beach every evening, he was searching for me – his one true love. His golden hair reflected the dying rays of a drowning sun, his strong arms rippled as he strolled along the shoreline looking out to sea.

'Oh, Alan –', the words died on my lips, for as he approached he turned his head slowly in my direction and I could see his face clearly despite the impending dusk. It wasn't Alan – it was Scott Peters, and he was heading straight for me. Ashamed as I am to admit it I forgot everything at that moment, even the vital mission that had brought me there...

Scott told me to go no further, he had walked as far as possible and the beach was empty: He suggested returning to Lisa, and then seeking the help of emergency services. Walking over the sand, we chatted like long-lost cousins, Scott was so easy to talk to: he told me he'd been married briefly but it hadn't worked out: but having met me he couldn't get me out of his mind and wanted to get to know me better. He usually crossed the beach at this time following his evening meal in order to turn on the sprinkler at the nursery. I said I thought I may have seen him once or twice before, in fact he had given me quite a start on one occasion.

'Does that bother you?' he queried, his eyes looking deep into mine.

'Not any more,' I countered as I led him along Lisa's front path.

The door was opened wide and I was greeted by a beaming Trish: Jamie had been found safe and well and playing cricket with four or five school mates in a field close to the village. Lisa had been upset that he hadn't warned anyone and the hapless child had been sent to his room without supper.

'We were just starting to worry about *you* now –', Lisa admitted.

'There's no need to do that any more,' I laughed contentedly. 'Scott, oh Scott' my mind kept repeating as I gazed into the depths of those sea-blue eyes, secure in the knowledge that at last I had laid my ghosts to rest...

ENCOUNTER

Despite having been tempted by the images videos and endless promotions, and the souvenirs brought to her throughout the holiday season, Lisa had never felt the urge to vacate these shores. Enthusiastic friends and colleagues recounting their escapades, bronzed with exuberance, would produce beguiling snapshots on their phones depicting miles of white sun-drenched beaches, breath-taking falls, snow-capped mountain ranges, exploration of the Amazon rain forest, or the verdant rivers of Cambodia and Vietnam; while proffering such exotic gifts as Belgian chocolate, Russian dolls, Egyptian multi-coloured stuffed leather camels, miniature sphinxes or geisha girls in satin kimonos. All failed to stir her wander lust.

Of course on offer from the little screen, avoiding the endless cookery programs – as if the nation was in a state of constant famine (and when not in World Cup year); before she had ordered the Christmas turkey were the continual programs aimed at the enticement of the vulnerable, extolling the virtues of travel to beautiful far-flung shores, where time was spent in deck-chairs on stretches of pristine empty sand beyond a shoreline of gentle lapping waves, fanned by balmy breezes beneath a deep blue sky. And there was every possibility she could survive without building an igloo in Alaska; bungi-jumping over the Niagra Falls; fishing for sharks off the Great Barrier Reef; searching for the Bengal tiger; or ballooning over Alice Springs.

Financially secure, her and husband Jason could afford foreign travel. As Marketing Manager to a local heating firm such trips were accessible to her; if she chose, she could have cruised to the

Northern Lights or cashed in her chips at Las Vegas. She was simply not interested. There were plenty of suitable venues closer to home. She enjoyed trekking the Cairngorms or exploring the Pembrokeshire coastline where her sister lived, or the Malvern Hills, visiting the Cornish Riviera or the Lakes, shopping in Princes Street in Edinburgh or trips to York Minster. The closest she'd come to 'abroad' was the day-trip she made to the Isle of Wight with her son Mark when he was little.

Jason was her saving grace, she wasn't sure how she could have coped without him at her side, issuing words of encouragement or cheering her with his laconic grin. A quiet guy, always thoughtful, a rock to deflect life's stormier tides, and a good indulgent dad. Handsome greying streaks that served as a mark of esteem, and those eyes, orbs of steely grey reassurance. In her book, Jason had a single downside – his obsession with cricket. He travelled miles to watch a match. An avid supporter of Middlesex, he knew the players' names, where all county grounds were situated, and almost drove Lisa up the wall when he began reciting batting averages. When a Test Match was televised the living room became a cathedral: a silent reverence prevailed, when even Churchill the staffie was excluded from the room.

It was during an interval in a series with South Africa that the commentator displayed a competition across the screen, the question was: during the famous 2005 Test Match – England vs Australia, who was the main fielder at square leg to Shane Warne's bowling? She remembered that year vividly, Jason had nursed a malt whiskey as he nervously watched the closing overs. Of course Jason knew the answer, for a laugh he entered by sending the player's name via text on his phone, along with thousands of others he had reflected. Nobody thought any more about it, until a letter arrived in the New Year. Along with congratulations, were included Jason's return flight ticket from Heath Row and his ticket for inclusion to the five days of the last match play in Dubhai. Jason naturally expected Lisa to accompany him.

The couple very rarely argued, this was an exception: 'For the last time, Jason, I am not going!…No! No! No! N – O! Which of those two letters are you having trouble with? Are they in the wrong order for you? - You want me to say it's ON, but it isn't Jason, it's OFF!' 'But you'll be all alone dear.' 'Don't worry about me, you know you want to go, go and enjoy yourself; as I said, I shall visit my sister in Wales, it's time we got together.' She'd thought it over long and hard, to the point it was causing her loss of sleep. She didn't wish to upset Jason, but she felt unable to join him. 'I've never been abroad, and I'm not going to start now!' Set in her ways – the prospect was too daunting. All that packing (worry over what she'd forgotten), passports and visas, insurance, airport schedules (not to mention the flight itself), the language and currency, AND the expense! No, much safer in this country she comforted herself, all too much hassle.

Arriving by taxi in the evening at her sister's cottage, she noted there were no lights on. Alerted, she kept the taxi waiting while she investigated – no one at home. She certainly should have warned her sister a visit was imminent. The taxi took her to a hotel in Haverfordwest (the town her sister referred to as 'Have-a-good-rest', in little England beyond Wales). Her room was adequate with all the customary additions. After showering and dressing she went down to the restaurant, where there were plenty of empty tables at the latter hour, and selected a single by the window.

Few were about, but a pair of cobalt blue eyes directed her way gained her attention. He was also at a single table although in the process of departure. Rising from the table he smiled warmly and, passing, bent towards her conspiratorially, 'Hello', he offered, 'word of warning – don't have the soup, it's revolting!' 'Thank you, but I'm not ordering soup.' With a sharp wink he was gone.

At nine in the morning she returned to her previous table to find he had moved location and now occupied an adjacent one. 'Good morrow, fine lady. I trust you slept well? My name is Alex.' And a while later: ' Do you have transport?' 'Er – no, she replied, 'I took a taxi from the station.' 'Oh, dear,' he said, buses are infrequent around here. Tell you what, I'm taking a trip to the beach at Little Haven – I'd be only too pleased to take you along?' She thought it over, he seemed respectable and she had her phone; 'Alright, if it's no trouble…' After the beach they stopped at the Crown & Anchor for lunch, where over crab sandwiches they discovered much in common. Later they agreed to meet up the following day.

Thus began a charming dalliance. Throughout the week they met at breakfast and spent their days enjoying each-other's company. They explored St Davids and Pembroke Dock and the castles of Pembroke and Manobier, walked around St Brides Bay and the length of Newgale Beach (where she rescued a wounded glossy-black razor-bill); they visited Tenby and Saundersfoot, and a wildlife park close to Carmarthen (where Lisa became besotted with a wild boar piglet, wanting to take her home - loving the way she twitched her tiny pink nose constantly sniffing the air); and Fishguard harbour, in the suburbs of which Alex lived. They had strolled beaches and cliff paths for hours, making light conversation or simply in silence, perfectly at ease with one another; visited museums and monuments, and on one occasion attended a revue at a Tenby theatre. She found him engaging and a true gentleman, in tune with her love of nature, easy-going and undemanding (often following her suggestions or willingly fitting in with her itinerary). Despite having lost his wife a year previously he hardly mentioned her. He had an enquiring mind, treating each new day as an opportunity with the buoyancy of a small boy discovering his first train-set.

As all pleasing interludes must, the week drew to its close. Lisa had found his company heady and intoxicating; it was reassuring to learn that she could feel valued as a person in her own right (unlike the way Doug, the Projects Chief, had treated her at the office party when he had tried to take advantage of her!). He had been charm itself – not once had she felt threatened or awkward in his presence. Yet, she was adult not a giggling schoolgirl; she knew it for what it was, an enjoyable diversion. She loved Jason, always would.

Returning, she found her husband full of his adventure. When he paused for breath during his elaborate and doubtless embellished account, he was reminded to enquire as to how she had coped. She replied that she'd had a peaceful break, one he would have found totally boring. However she had been perfectly content discovering the hidden treasures of Pembrokeshire.

FROM RECCO TO ROCCO

Strolling leisurely through Italian towns has always been a pleasure and in this regard Recco was no exception. A minor town on the Ligurian coast and close neighbour to Genoa, dotted with palm trees interspersed with occasional shrubs of camellia and bougainvillea or the pink flashes of oleander fall gently on the eye. Beneath the welcome shade of this exotic flora the hustle and bustle of Italian life expounds; where brief snatches of jaunty Latin cries and conversation are embellished with esoteric hand signals.

One stop along the rail-line from Camogli, the small town of Recco is celebrating the Madonna; here she is known as Our Lady of Suffrage, their patron and protectress. Each year on the 7/8 September a festival is held whereby bunting flows across streets, tourist events and concerts are held and a general carnival atmosphere pervades. From the station and over a viaduct between a narrow avenue of gleaming parked cars I descend a gentle slope to main street Via Roma; a long straight road with at one end the coast and the other projecting inland, today totally closed to traffic. Turning right into the town I become immediately aware of an electric buzz of expectation; excited chatter, bubbly laughter and exuberance abound as the warm sun smiles from above.

Bunting flaps lazily across the Via and billows from colourful shop-fronts. Gaily decorated market stalls groan beneath a cornucopia of meat, salami, cheeses, fabrics, lace, utilities, fashion, toys, trinkets, nuts, la dolce, cream-cakes, fortune tellers and electrical goods, nail colouring, household linen and appliances; all positioned along one side of the Via Roma in an orderly row and continue beyond the traffic island and out of sight. Across the street everyone is moving in one direction and numbers are growing. I become embroiled in the gently drifting current.

The distant snap of a firework is heard; and always the sun at its zenith within an azure sky. We reach the Manuelina Ristorante patisserie and I enter, lured by the savoury aroma of pastries mingled with Italian coffee wafting onto the street. A speciality of the region is the Focaccia col Formaggio, and those from Recco are claimed to be the region's *migliore*. Sweet smells from deep ovens suggest a huge wafer-thin pastry emitting the light aroma of olive oil. The focaccia is a flat oven-baked Italian bread similar to pizza but with a flakier texture, seasoned with olive oil and salt (not unlike the Greek Lagana). The sweetmeat is often seasoned with rosemary (focaccia col rosmarino) and served either as a side or as sandwich bread, and may be flavoured with vegetables or cheese. Mine has a mild cheesy tang and an addition of lard to give a more flaky texture, and I divide it into bite-size portions using the napkins provided and take time to savour each succulent layer before rejoining the swirl of humanity.

The crowd surge is continuous in the direction of the church of Santa Maria. A brief pause as my eye is attracted to a rack of multi-hued cashmere jumpers displayed beneath a stall awning. Opting for a deep eye-blue, and prompted with thoughts of the imminent English winter chill, I complete my transaction and re-enter the general throng: the while, the warm sun is my constant companion. Ever onwards, then a further pause when tempted by a couple of bangles (two black and silver bracelets). On flows the multitude along the major thoroughfare as if drawn by some invisible thread towards the church. All the while the sights and sounds of an Italian market: shouts, jeers, jokes, barracking and banter: a couple locked in a fond embrace, an olive-skinned woman in a bright green dress barters over a sparkling ring; a pair keep one eye on their boisterous charges the other on a bargain. Yet again I pause momentarily, this time to collect a lacy stamp on third finger-nails, a stencil upon the deep fuschia: such indulgence must be the heady influence of this ancient Roman republic. For a spell I break from the pack and enter a hotel garden off the street, where I request the bar. There follows a welcome repast for reflection and admiration of purchases in the pleasantly cool hotel garden over an ice-cold Peroni; then on again.

The small church is packed, and the throng fill the pavement where organ music serenades, flooding through the open doors to immerse the expectant crowd. The long street stretches beyond the church and into the residential region. Shortly, at the parted doors the jostling ceases and a reverent hush descends as prayers are read. Gradually, with bowed heads and cosseted rosaries, diligently and respectfully people divide to create a path for the procession to pass. In pairs the column emerges, centred by a golden effigy of the crowned Madonna. The entourage of clergy, choir and church officials with a small group of musicians taking up the rear spills across the pavement and into Via Roma; where it makes steady progress towards the coast the jubilant horde flowing in its wake. Faces of awe and wonder are captivated by the parade as it wends through cheers, waves and camera flashes.

Tiring of the herd, I linger behind and wander beyond the church where there is relative calm; as the steady dull thud of the drum slowly fades. Here the paving has been skilfully adorned with a large chalk mural. An optimistic crowned Mary and crowned Child gaze meditatively heavenwards, accompanied by the current year and artist's signature, a certain Collodari. Retracing my steps along the street, now more empty and ensuring more easy a passage, I arrive at an intersection. Here a few token fireworks are detonated watched over by a master pyrotechnic and unobtrusive polizia, the major display is reserved for the evening; so I slowly turn left and head towards the station and Camogli.

Satisfied by my trip to Recco, I decide to attempt a visit to San Rocco during the late afternoon along the Punta Chiappa Trail to complete the day's activities: a visit that had been suggested earlier. Reaching the tiny hilltop hamlet of San Rocco with its covert byways and fatiguing ascent is not for the weary; although completing the testing pathway reaps dividends, affording the traveller the most glorious of spectacular views (3 kilometres, a doddle for someone from the Malvern hills!).

The journey from Camogli begins at Via San Bartolomeo from where one takes a narrow pathway between some municipal buildings and the Caribinari station. At the start one walks alongside a softly descending stream (the Gentile torrent), where the comforting gurgle and babble is music to the ears and birdsong supplies the descant as the Camogli suburbs are left behind. Suddenly the path broadens into wide concrete steps that continue ever upwards. Climbing in the burning sun, in a temperature of 29 degrees C saps the energy if not the spirit and water is essential. One passes houses carved into the incline and terraced gardens running with chickens or geese; protected by stone walls or iron gates that enclose orchards and olive groves burgeoning with produce. The way is thankfully amply blessed with trees that at intervals provide welcome shade. Sometimes the path narrows and is buttressed by stone walls of varying heights, to broaden again into concrete slopes or paved steps, but ever upwards.

At approximately halfway to the summit a thoughtful soul has placed a welcome bench. Upon this bench I encounter a signore from Camogli, and gratefully chat a while and retrieve some breath. Continuing upwards, I am convinced the air is thinning. The incline is sometimes bounded by fencing of wire or wood or by protective stone walling (at times head-high or taller). This can narrow disconcertingly forming roof-less 'tunnels' between garden greenery and gated approaches. Ever rising, towards the church bell-tower and cupola that have only appeared to me as a distant silhouette on the skyline from my breakfast terrace at Camogli. Higher and higher I climb, passing from patches of refreshing umbra into vibrant sunlight with glimpses of a pure azure sky. A further dimension is added to the narrowing and broadening, in the form of twists and turns to the narrower paths. Ascending still, passing mail-boxes at garden boundaries and the chalk-board requesting the senora requires bread or milk today.

Finally, sweaty and red-faced, around a snake-like twist in the path I spot a diminutive sign on the wall that declares the intrepid trekker is entering San Rocco. Passing between closely packed gaily painted houses and a *fruttivendolo* (greengrocer) and ascending a dozen final wide brick-faced stairs I am confronted with the little church of San Rocco painted in white and sand. It is perched on the top of the hill with a steep precipice on three aspects – the fourth leading behind into the village. A tarmac esplanade, Via Franco Molfino, surrounds the church and proceeds to the little town perched on the hilltop; this is hemmed by a low wall painted in keeping with the church's exterior. High above, the small duck-egg blue cupola topped with a golden crucifix twins with the square bell-tower as both gracefully scan the wide blue Mediterranean far below. Entering the church, it is cool to sit in the nave among the pews within the refreshing and reassuring stone walls. It had taken a good hour and a quarter to ascend to the church.

The overall effect of the interior is of bathing in an aura of burnished gold: behind the altar is a cameo of Christ set within the golden rays of the sun beneath an ornate ceiling depicting familiar biblical scenes; all perceived through a saffron haze. Descending a column of steps onto the Via, where people gather to chat and admire the views, I ask a passing signore how many steps there are in the ascent. His reply is markedly ambiguous: "*Ci sono circa tre kilometre a San Rocco*". Yes, I respond, I know it is 3 kilometres, but how many steps? "*Non lo so*," he shrugs, "*Forse, un mille.*" He is correct, there are well over 900 steps and this does not include the multiple pathways and byways in between equally leading aloft. Below, boats appear as tiny models, not more than dots, and the azure sky provides a surreal backdrop to the blazing orb. Across the bay, the coastline of Genoa forms a fortress along the waterline that must have proved formidable in days gone by. Through the trees the constant sparkle of the sun-kissed Med is visible across the deep sapphire Gulf of Genoa far below, the Riviera di Levante.

Passing to the left of the church Via Franco Molfino continues beyond an enticing ice-cream vendor, bus-stop and village hall towards the private residences. Continuing, I come across Bar Pippi that affords a splendid vista over a low stone wall and across the sun-drenched hillside and valley below. We are 220 metres above sea level, and the air is sweet; embracing traces of jasmine and eucalyptus. Seated on the terrace I am treated to the magnificent panorama where, in variegated colours, houses, villas and churches cling to the hillside and decorate the scene like a myriad segments of dolly-mixture scattered at random across the landscape. The patron is friendly as is his wife, and the daughter greets me with a shy "Ciao". Sipping a cool beer and sampling from the bowl of nuts and nibbles my contemplation includes praise for the privilege. Refreshed and revitalised I bid farewell to the family and begin my descent to Camogli. Downhill from here!

Carefully descending, passing now familiar sights and sounds of the hillside I rest for a spell upon the bench where earlier I engaged in friendly conversation. With reducing altitude, I am startled by a vicious canine whose deep explosion of sound is received at ear-level and succeeds in momentarily disrupting the afternoon's tranquillity. Down and down I go, thankful for the declining slope despite the raging heat. Ever descending, until all of a sudden the lane narrows alongside the whispering Gentile torrent, the terrain evens out and I enter Camogli once more.

The sky is so so blue, blue as the sea; at times it is difficult to define the precise meeting of the two. Another memorable day spent sampling the enthralling environment around the Gulf of Genoa and the inscrutable Latin temperament. As the sun goes down over the Camogli coastline I am encouraged to recall the many generous, fun-loving and enigmatic characters I have encountered during many visits to the Italian peninsula and its exotic isles. Like the sun, the focaccia and the olive oil, these people are in the main genuinely warm-hearted and amiable towards a fellow human and only too willing to go the 'extra mile': This, without mention of *la bella figura* and a committed passion for life. *Ci sono simpatici. Viva Italia!*

HERE WE GO AGAIN!

As the train drew into the station he thought: 'Here we go again!'

The three-monthly visit to his cantankerous mother always filled him with despair. It wasn't as if she was ailing or incapable – she was as fit as a fiddle yet for the last three years, since she lost her husband, she had become unbearable. She had let herself go and become uncharacteristically morose and withdrawn. Her house needed a make-over and she could well afford it, his father had seen to that. Her demeanour was as lack-lustre as her decor. Suggestions that she seek help met with sarcasm and derision.

He had grown to resent these demanding visits, the hassle of changing trains and futile hours spent on dirty grey platforms. If he dodged the gauntlet of the school exodus he could not escape the cutting draughts that sought refuge in his trouser-legs, nor the grimy oppressive atmosphere. He had summoned the courage to sample the cafeteria tea – never again. Once he had gone by road, but that entailed an unavoidable erratic crawl through the city centre, followed by desolate miles of suburbs strewn with skulking speed restrictions and predatory cameras. He wouldn't have minded if at the end he received a warm welcome.

Alighting, he was aware of the sun shifting from behind the clouds, the rain had stopped. Then he saw her, edging towards him through desultory groups of hopeful travellers – his mother as he always thought of her: dressed in gay colours and beaming. She embraced him with a loving hug and suggested lunch, no need to hurry home. She had regained her sparkle and over lunch suggested a visit to a new art exhibition. The day passed blissfully.

What a homecoming, he really could not believe it. All doubts evaporated in the soft beams of sunlight that filtered through the gallery windows. His mother was made of sterner stuff; all she needed was time. Avoiding the prescient pitfalls of commenting on her effusive gaiety he kept to the wide and secure paths of small-talk, smiling indulgently immersed in his good fortune.

His mother's house was a revelation. The tired brown paintwork had been replaced with a subtle French ivory. Walls proudly displayed light embossed papers and adventurous emulsions. His mother played Johnny Mathis on her CD player, and proudly showed him her collection of irises in a quiet corner of the sun-dappled garden. That night he fell asleep in his new old room feeling content: thank God – she had weathered the storm.

Rudely awoken and drowsy, the harsh tones of the tannoy warned him of the approach of his destination. As the train-driver applied the brakes the protesting machine juddered to a slower pace. Stumbling into the corridor, he cursed the repetitive chuntering, chuntering, soporific effect of train travel; designed to soothe, to induce that fleeting feeling of comfort until eyelids droop and one finally succumbs. As the train drew into the station he thought: 'Here we go again!'

HOME

She sat alone staring from the window across to where the houses had been built, upon the old field where she would play for hours with her brothers Eric and Harold as well as the Mitchams, the Waters and the Craddocks. Now they had all grown and moved away, or died. As she peered from the window she was aware of the smell of dusty cretonne curtains. Few passed by, her neighbour from the end probably on his way to the betting shop. Change is inevitable she thought as she looked around her room at all the familiar objects. 'Where does all the dust come from?' she pondered. She couldn't envisage being parted from this miscellany. She never did find out the name of the priest, a friend of her father who left her the small picture that hung on her wall: St Margaret Mary Alacoque a 17 cent. nun who had visions and was devoted to the Sacred Heart of Jesus. She had been beatified in 1864 and canonised in 1920.

She had consented to go away, to leave her home with its shelter and food. She wouldn't be sorry to finish her job at the Store. They'd say she'd run off with a fella! The manager was a particular menace, with his: 'Look lively, Miss Cromby!' or 'customers waiting!' he certainly wanted putting in his place. No, she wouldn't miss it that much. They'd be married in a new country, fresh start; yet she felt, fancy being swept off her feet...She remembered her father's violence and her mother's indifference. She feared his dark moods and often got palpitations as a result. Being a girl he would never have gone for her like he did with the boys. Yet, there was such a thing as mental cruelty. Now she had nobody to protect her. Eric was dead and Harold lived abroad. Money was always tight, and after Ma died she brought home her wages to her Da. She'd kept the house together and cared for the younger boys. Anyhow she felt grown up these days, she'd just had her thirty-fifth birthday. Life here had been hard, but now she was about to leave, was it really that undesirable?

She was going to explore another life with Alec – he was a kind easygoing and manly type. They were booked on a night-sleeper to Edinburgh. She cast her mind back to when they met. He was busy painting his gate with his fair locks tumbling over his bronzed face and paint on his chin. Gradually they'd got to know each-other, he would meet her outside the Store in the evenings and see her home. He took her to the cinema or to a smart restaurant: once she'd accompanied him to the theatre. Her father found out and forbade her to see him for no particular reason. One day he and Alec quarrelled and it almost came to fisticuffs, after that the young lovers were forced to meet in secret.

She was leaving the drudgery behind her. The evening deepened beyond her window. The street lamps highlighted the two white envelopes on her lap: one to her father, the other to Harold. Her father was becoming old lately – he would miss her. Sometimes he could be quite thoughtful. Recently he had read to her from his newspaper when she'd been poorly. She remembered too, when Ma was alive, how they'd taken the old banger into the countryside or by the sea and they'd shared a picnic Ma had prepared.

Night was encroaching but she still sat at the window inhaling the odour of dusty cretonne. Her mother's illness had been too much for her father – he hadn't known how to cope. She stood up in sudden desperation. She must escape: Alec would save her, give her life – love too perhaps.

She rushed in confusion to the barrier, the station was full of soldiers with brown baggages. She felt pale and lost – how could she draw back after all he'd done for her? She stood frozen to the cold platform filled with over-whelming nausea; passive as a hapless rabbit caught in headlamps. Her lips in silent prayer, her mind in torment. No, it was not possible, it wasn't her doing this. Alec approached the barrier calling her name. She remained rooted, eyes to the floor without a hint of love, recognition or even farewell. Briskly she turned and in tears ran from the station.

HOME-TRUTH

Comfort found scant refuge in the stone cottage, the few spent embers that brightened the fireplace did little to pierce the chill of Farrs' parlour. Grotesquely magnified flickering shadows cast by the old oil lamp bathed the dull cream walls in a sepia glow. She knew this would be difficult: at best her father was a tetchy customer with an irascible temperament. He'd achieved this brusque manner through gruelling years of dealing with the mill-hands, and bargaining at his weekly market-stall. After a couple of pints people always afforded him a wide berth. She felt thankful on this occasion he'd only had half a glass, perhaps she'd caught him in a relaxed state. But before she could present him with what was on her mind, he gave a rasping cough and began to admonish her:

'You've been spending too much time wi' that floor-walker – what's-'is-name – that Sternby fella.'

'How do you mean spending time with him, I work alongside o' him that's all.'

'Thees snow what I mean lass. Kemple were telling me in't pub, he spotted the pair o' you strolling through Jubilee park, canoodlin' arm in arm…thee should know thy place.' Farr was gaining momentum. 'Right little madam, with all your airs and graces. You be gettin' above yourself my love since you started working at that high-street milliners. The farm were good enough for your ma.'

'It were, till it sent her to an early grave. Got your spies out now, have you?'

Mary drew a few stray strands of wayward hair across her

brow; this was going to be tougher than she'd anticipated: 'Da, now don't go on so. Let me get you another bottle. Listen – there's something I want to say.' But it was too late, Farr was into his stride, maybe he'd had more than a pint on his way home thought Mary ruefully.

'… An' I've kep thee lass – theese don't want for nowt. Up to me elbows in chaff-dust and grain to keep thee and thy mother at 'ome wi' food in't bellies.'

'Huh, you know the mill switched to new machinery after great fire and it all went mechanical!' She felt she had nothing to lose as she thrust the knife home: 'You were allus agen me 'cos I wasn't a boy!'

Farr clenched and unclenched his fists, rose, spat into the dying embers that hissed back at him and lit a cigar: 'That's as maybe – but many a lass takes on a fella's work these days. We allus discussed it, your mam and I, that you'd be learning trade and taking over when I'm gone. You know I'm not getting any younger, and I got the Merchants to run.'

'I stood by you…when Mam passed away, I've cared for the home for 18 months without her – but I'll not be taken for granted.'

'– So you never stop reminding me!'

'Aye, but you're a mean ol' bugger, Bertie Farr. It were different when our mam were alive – she could tame yer!'

'Aye and happen these got her stubborn streak about yer, our lass.'

She felt salty tears well behind her eyes as she recalled her mother's cheerful countenance and winning ways; <u>she </u>knew how to calm the raging bull. 'I've put up with your tempers, your drinking and smoking but thees never grateful. Take that there picture', she changed tack, 'thik one thee got at auction with the money you won at races, when you didn't even think to buy me flowers, I hate it! Ma would've too; you'd not have taken liberties with her, she wouldn't allow half-naked women in '<u>er</u> parlour.'

Farr staggered to his feet, bringing back his arm to take a swing at his daughter, but was checked by his wife's disapproving frown from the frame on the mantelpiece. Thinking better of it he slumped back in his chair.

'Don't you dare lift a finger to me Father. I'm a grown woman of 19 now and entitled to a life of my own.'

With effort Farr controlled his emotions, a calmer approach was called for. He drew deeply on his cigar, tilted his head and blew a smoke ring that spread as it trailed lazily aloft, to dissipate into the grubby obscurity of the ceiling. 'Now lass, it were established years ago that thee should work in't Merchants. See sense girl. What'll happen to business after I'm gone – ?'

'It were established by thee, I were too young to have owt to say.' Despite the sudden flush to her cheeks she was gaining confidence: 'Happen I've got me sights on getting a place of my own one day, and thees not to stop me.'

'Oh, Miss High and Mighty! With that fella too, I'll be bound!'

'He has a name Da, he's called David.'

'Oh, David is it – David Fauntleroy la-la-la Sternby…'

'You'll just have to sell up when you can't work any longer Da, you've made enough money to live reasonable, I don't want any of it. You could move away, buy a little cottage by the sea – you always said you wanted to be somewhere on the coast.'

'My life's work – my life's work: all for nowt! Lass, thees disappointed me…'

This is it, she thought as she blurted out: 'Da, I need to tell you – I'm pregnant!'

IMPORTANT NOTICE

The British Government has issued a new directive with reference to the pending outbreak of Butterfly Bacteria – the latest pandemic to afflict our sceptered isle. Those indulging in picnics need to take stringent precautions. Masks are to be worn at all times, which may prove inhibitive when eating sandwiches. All utensils must be sterilised to 32 degrees centigrade, and used tissues incinerated immediately (note: see article 22/abh-f regarding management and control of forest fires).

Those travelling to exotic climes should take special care, as the insects are larger than their British counterparts and the rate of spread of bacteria is multiplied. Those more vulnerable to attack, such as butterfly catchers, need to take extreme caution and prior to an expedition an anti-bacterial inoculation is mandatory, as is the soaking of nets in cyanide the night before. Extremely windy conditions should be avoided as this may result in butterfly swarming which would exacerbate insect infiltration.

Initially it was considered that caterpillars carried the virus, later research has tended to reject this hypothesis. It seems that the creatures are non-toxic in both the lava and pupa stages; although tests are still continuing concerning infection from the pupa of the Red Admiral and Painted Lady varieties. Essentially keep clear of all open rural spaces where greenery is rife; avoid the following: nettles (they sting), alyssum, aster, aubrietia, bird's-foot-trefoil, knapweed, globe thistle, forget-me-not, wallflower, honesty, geraniums, hyacinth, lavender, purple loostrife, mint, primroses, French marigolds, nasturtiums, and particularly buddleia, also runner beans (this list is not inclusive).

Children are thought to be especially at risk and it is recommended that if at all possible they should wear a jogging suit and balaclava, or preferably be encased in cling-film. When straying into susceptible areas, take all necessary precautions, keep sleeves rolled down and gloves are handy. Covering exposed skin with inflamoxene (available from your local toxicologist) has proved effective; or carry with you a made-up solution of carbolic acid (3 parts) TCP (1 part) and pre-boiled water (6 parts). (Warning: do not exceed stated quantities). Remember you are safer during hours of darkness.

If you suspect contamination ie if you have been 'alighted on' by these creatures, especially in a desultory fashion: Use nearest phone to contact emergency services, or speak to Chris Allis (CEO = Community Entomological Officer) for West Mercia Division (WMD) on 07999012345. If possible make your way directly to your nearest Lepidoptera Clearing Station (see leaflet 592/cabwit/b) and/or cover all exposed parts with the anti-oxidant spray provided (delivered to every household via Royal Mail during the last fortnight along with the Halloween mask and instruction leaflet). Note: if calling by mobile destroy it immediately (extremely important if you or anyone has sneezed on it). Take yourself to the nearest cellar and sit tight until swelling causes death by asphyxia, or help arrives. Relay all symptoms to the medic, the one wearing the red snoopy mask. Don't forget to have your Nat Health nos. to hand or treatment could be refused.

Dept. of Health and other Environmental issues
(Government directive uxb9724/extreme -6 May 2009)

IN DULCI JUBILO

Boxing Day 2019, and the uppermost potshot card glared at me in lurid lime-green demanding to be read: it reminded me that 'just when I was getting used to yesterday, along came today'. Christmas Day was perfectly peaceful until 7.30am, when the phone jangled in my ear.

In recent years I have left frenetic seasonal celebrations to the more agile and adventurous, those who appear to take all-night binging, bopping and buffooning in their stride. I had envisaged my day being one of gentle repose, cuppa then back to bed; to rise seriously at 11 to prepare porridge topped with banana and honey to a backdrop of soothing Christmas music while the mini-tree sparkled away merrily; shower, dress and makeup, to stroll along the street at around 1 o'clock to welcoming friends for Christmas dinner. We would be four in number, an intimate gathering sharing a dry humour and stimulating conversation; perfect for the exchange of gifts, light Christmas quizzes, paper hats and alcohol – shuffled and dealt in the delightful conservatory beneath the large shimmering tree in the bay window overlooking the shrubbery; later to wend a not entirely steady path home as dusk descended. What could be more conducive to indulging the ghost of Christmas Present?

That phone call terminated this vision as my day began to unravel, like a tiny kitten dismembering a knitted scarf. The female element of the congenial couple rang me to croak that she and husband, suffering the sniffles pre-festive season, had finally succumbed to the demon bug currently circulating the neighbourhood; to avoid passing it on she felt it prudent to postpone our little soiree.

Anticipating similar dismal tidings, I was prepared. It was with forewarning not to say a certain foreboding that I visited the local Iceland store on Christmas Eve (Iceland, Iceland, uber alles!). Iceland to the rescue: here I was able to acquire turkey pie (short crust pastry and onion stuffing, with smoked bacon and cranberries); along with a chocolate yule log and some sprouts.

Here's the thing! I like Christmas sprouts; they seem to complement turkey, roast potatoes and parsnips, stuffing and a thick coating of glutinous gravy. The ones at Iceland came in a handy sealed pack of button sprouts retailing at £1: I couldn't go wrong – could I? Answer affirmative! Returning to my kitchen, I realised the suppliers had been a tad generous with their quantity. My ears would be sprouting!

A while back it dawned on me, available space in my mini freezer should be reserved for eatable essentials such as fish fingers, chunky chips, ice cream and ice; no room for seasonal sprouts. I decided the safest option would be to boil the brassica brussels without delay. Again, I had not thought ahead. A friend was due to call for Christmas drinks and my micro-apartment had become permeated with the unsavoury odour of cooked sprouts (did they emanate from the EU?). I greeted Christmas Day with the window wide and the extractor fan on full, noting that out in the world it was a beautifully mild sunny day. I prayed my friend would not call today; how bracing to take a walk beneath a cloudless azure sky?

Christmas Day – brilliant sunlight giving crystal vision – I opted for the hills for a pre-lunch ramble. I had showered and dried off, when I noticed a small black fleck marring my otherwise pristine internal sliding shower door: wouldn't do! With the corner of a J-rag and after several attempts, I was able to remove the offending speck from the sanitary-ware. Jubilantly (in dulci jubilo) I skipped from the shower.

That was the moment I broke a toe. My left foot had made abrupt and violent contact with the the sealing lip of the booth. Emitting howls of pain, wrapped in terminology wholly inappropriate for the time of year, I gingerly manipulated the damaged digit. It seemed to bend in the right places and respond grudgingly to messages from a groggy brain despite emitting painful spasms of shock. Undaunted I felt obliged to carry out my plan, to not waste a glorious day and head for the hills.

Here people are blessed by an extensive variety of venues to exercise the human frame, especially the legs. There are a half dozen places I regularly walk to maintain a degree of well-being. A few are on level terrain; yet on this auspicious occasion I chose Mount Everest. Well, next best thing; from the Malvern Hills there is a true feeling of being on top of the world as one inhales the crisp air and gazes down across the gently undulating picturesque landscape, where tiny grey spires and terracotta roofs are divided by swathes of patchwork fields in varying shades of green. (And Satan tempted Jesus: 'All this could be yours!')

The air was bracing as I slowly climbed the damp narrow path – at times I paused to admire the scene below and catch my breath. People who passed greeted me seasonally, some with backpacks, others taking a post luncheon per-ramble. At one point in my ascent I came across a group of young chatting Chinese buoyed at the opportunity to discover the heights of middle England. This oriental band had paused in their descent after negotiating an extremely muddy stretch of path that extended for about 50 yards. One young man proffered a hand in my direction to assist me over the worst of the oozing mire. I wished them 'merry Christmas' and continued my climb.

On the upper limits, dogs of various shapes and sizes abounded and bounded to add to the colourful exuberance. Crowds were as numerous as those encountered on a Saturday afternoon at Clapham Junction rail station, without the bonhomie and festive adornment. The summits were covered with groups, couples and singles traversing from west to east and east to west in good-natured true festive mood. I made my way to the Worcester Beacon, past the venue of an earlier summer solstice service, turned a bluff and was confronted with a huge guy in a scarlet Santa hat, he and his family, clad accordingly in seasonal bling, were staring towards the Brecon Beacons.

The vivid display assumed a profusion of gleaming flashes of scarlet and white Santa hats or brightly coloured parkas. Faces from time to time paused to turn towards the pastoral panorama below. What shone through, beaming brighter than all the bling, was an air of general jollity and good spirits that prevailed against a backdrop of rolling peaks and winding paths, while above the sun sent warming rays from a patch-less deep blue sky. The moment was Spiritual, my day restored, and I had escaped the commercial chaos and consummate greed that annually assails the 'silly season'; as if the ancient hills were filled with the song that love and good-will might against all the odds prevail.

Despite the warmth of my outing, chill in the shade reminded me of winter, and I returned to a welcome nip of Baileys Cream. This served as a suitable appetiser to my makeshift Christmas dinner which topped with gravy from granules and followed with a healthy chunk of yule log amounted to adequate repast; and all lubricated with a fine red wine.

IN THE BLEAK MID-WINTER

The water was warm and comforting after the hot sand and 75-degree sun. I felt indolently refreshed as I shaded my eyes against the dappled splashes of light that skipped merrily over the surface of the Arabian Sea. My pale pink bikini was starting to suit my colouring, and after the tentative exposure I had afforded it during the latter few days, was beginning to contrast rather pleasingly with my light golden skin. I liked the sun, unfortunately such affection was rather one-sided. Being of pale Caucasian stock I had always envied olive skin-tones. Tariq was a perfect example. He emitted a beautiful mellow glow: a glow that set off his brooding hazel eyes and dark curly hair to perfection. Such an evaluation, I freely admit, may be tainted with a modicum of bias.

Tariq was the reason I was lazily enjoying the temperate waters of the Arabian Gulf off Jumeirah Beach. We had met when he was in London on a Business Studies course just off the Tottenham Court Road. There were a mere half dozen students, and classes took place in a large Georgian house with many doorways. We became acquainted as we attempted to locate the correct room amid the crumbling three storied building. In an embarrassed way I had made some silly quip that Tariq had thought the pinnacle of wit, and we became good friends. Nevertheless an all expenses paid four-day trip to Dubai was certainly beyond my radar.

Time had passed so speedily: Tariq behaved as a perfect gentleman showing me much to savour in future quieter moments. The colourful souks and bazaars were full of absorbing and distracting discoveries, boasting such colourful artefacts as hookahs and ornately painted ceramics. Here I bartered for multi-coloured silk scarves, gleaming jewellery or bagels, (a bargaining process that drew respect from stall-holders along the way). In contrast we visited the Dubai Mall with its glittering arcades of 1200 exclusive shops, where I spotted such prestigious names as Gucchi, Prada, Versace, Seiko and Georg Jensen. Tariq accompanied me on a desert safari, helping me board my camel's saddle, where the sandy dunes glistened away into infinity and I became more than a little saddle-sore. We visited Al Mamzar and the Ras Al Khor Wildlife Sanctuary, the Vaticano and the Global Village. We dined in a prestigious restaurant in the Al Dhiyafah Road and gazed wistfully at the Dubai Fountain with its famous musical intervals: whilst admiring the spectacle we were serenaded by Michael Jackson's 'Thriller'. I marvelled at the Burj Khalifa spire, and the way a multitude of beautiful fountains surrounded the coast and created refreshing oases in the stark terrain. Above all, I was taken by the way the solitude and remoteness of the desert moulded seamlessly with the cosmopolitan frenzy and bustle of the high-rise architecture.

On that final day, following my dip and an early lunch, I joined Tariq who had a surprise in store. We met in the beautiful gardens of the Jebel Ali Hotel with its surrounding palms and enchanting vista across the bay. Then Tariq drove to Dubai Creek where we boarded a dhow. The dhow, an Arabic triangular-sailed vessel common to the Indian Ocean, seemed an extremely romantic craft. As it glided and skimmed the waters of the bay we were afforded the spectacular panorama of the precipitous skyline of Dubai. Ours had been adapted so that fortunate voyagers could enjoy a dinner cruise as they watched the magical city slip by. Tariq explained the Creek had originally been an important port for the pearl trade. The day had been a fitting climax to a delightful interlude.

All too soon my brief sojourn was over. In a rather dazed state I hugged Tariq goodbye and turned my back on the elaborate airport to board my plane in the early hours before dawn. Worse was to follow, the rude awakening that brought me down to earth with a jolt, came after the Boeing finally bounced onto the flight-path. Piled snow lay thick upon the Heath Row runway surrounds as I landed – on that chilly January morning, in the bleak mid-winter...

KISMET

Beth had always been a solitary individual though, thank God, not a hermit like her dear Uncle Will who only went walking when nobody was about, and was particularly fond of dusk and the twilight hours. Living in a rural community close to Abergavenny she felt pangs of isolation. At times her loneliness took over and there were evenings when she could be found sipping gin and tonic, her legs drawn up on the old couch and her faithful kitty Kismet tiny warm and purring beside her; her mind wandering to happier times. Rarely spotting a new face all week, she went for days without entertaining a soul.

In desperation she had put an ad in the *South Wales Echo* but received no response. She had deliberated long and hard before taking the plunge and signing up to a national dating agency. At first she had been contacted by two or three guys, and it was pleasant and mildly decadent to exchange small-talk; then along came Owen.

She found him open and approachable from the start and the feelings appeared mutual. He was charming and thoughtful, and they had much in common. They'd visited similar venues and had both been teachers. Having exchanged photos and confidences for a while, she found herself experiencing withdrawal symptoms if more than three days passed between contact. Not averse to the odd alcoholic beverage she preferred 'olde worlde' pubs, places with character, where on clement days she could enjoy rustic beer gardens. She dreamed that one day he'd take her to the *Angel* at Abergavenny. Often her mind wandered: she pictured them hand-in-hand at Cardiff Docks or

St Fagans; sitting in a tearoom at Caerleon after a trip around the Roman Fortress; or perhaps together on an outing to the Big Pit Mining Museum at Cwmbran. She thought wistfully these are only pipe-dreams; knowing her luck she would end up in the *Crosskeys* at Pontypool, or more likely the *Beleagured Hen* at Blaina. Yet he brought a sense of calm whereby Beth felt able to relax and be herself in a manner that had eluded her for years; flattered with his attention, time passed in a halcyon fog, until the day he insisted they meet.

Beth would much rather continue the relationship from afar. It was a pleasant to know someone was out there, someone with whom she could share her days, her joys and disappointments, secure in the knowledge that distance and sufficient ignorance lay between them. Someone who didn't look too closely at her wrinkles, leave the top off the toothpaste, or prove over-demanding. She felt the current arrangement ideal, one that could continue indefinitely in a comforting cotton-wool cocoon: days would pass in a lethargic limbo without complications. Owen however was adamant they should get together. Yet he lived deep in the valleys and she did not drive. He had alluded briefly to owning a car but it was in a poor state, in need of serious attention; It had remained in this condition for the six months they had been in contact. She had made up her mind, she would meet him and she would travel by bus. And on the day they had chosen to meet, to cap it all, it threatened rain.

Closing her door she entered a greenie-grey breezy world where a mist was rising from the hedgerows and moisture dampened the features. Disconsolately, with stomach churning, she turned up her collar and headed along the lane in the direction of the bus-stop. Entering the high-street she was vaguely aware the grey pavement was covered in a damp glossy sheen. Under the shelter stood a hooded middle-aged woman in a beige raincoat with raindrops dripping from her nose alongside a companion in a red parka; also a dapper young fellow in a suit and tie (off for an interview Beth thought) and another chap in his early seventies, unshaven, sporting a faded navy tracksuit and drawing avidly on a cigarette.

Through steady drizzle and beyond the shelter she spied the hazy reflection of passing headlamps in kerbside puddles. The drabness was alleviated only by half-lit bill-boards and an occasional winking orange-tinted street beacon. Often she was forced to duck towards the interior to avoid spray from passing vehicles. 77s were intermittent, yet she hoped today they would not arrive, she was experiencing deep apprehension – maybe there would be a drivers' strike or fog would descend so thickly that the service would be suspended. She felt the butterflies stir as through the encroaching mist she spied an approaching double-decker and was able to determine a figure 7 before it pulled up alongside; this is it she thought – go girl! A reprieve – a 72.

Her thoughts turned to Kismet. She had acquired him as a tiny helpless ball of fluff six or seven months earlier. She still recalled the night they met, it had been damp and dreary not unlike today on that cold October evening. Returning from a corner-shop where she'd collected a quick microwave macaroni cheese, she became aware of a pitiful miewing from the direction of some recycling bins on the pavement edge. Looking down she made out a miniscule furry countenance peering pathetically in her direction from inside an empty biscuit carton. The pleading eyes she would always remember, eyes effusing raw abandon, beseeching: 'take me home.' Who knows what will happen during ensuing hours she wondered; if she failed to return Katie Jarvis, Beth's neighbour would take him in, she had always held a soft spot for the cuddly feline.

As she waited among the despondent commuters in the murky autumn drizzle and stared with them into the pervading gloom she felt her stomach tremble. How stupid we all are, she thought, standing in a soggy line, zealously defending our assumed territory as we peer optimistically in the same direction through the haze. Each searching expectantly for that illusive number as though eagerly awaiting a lottery draw. Despite wearing trousers she felt cold and the wind was blowing squalls of rain beneath the canopy. The track-suited guy nonchalantly flicked his dog-end towards the gutter, sparks flew as it bounced on the paving before plopping into a puddle with a sharp hiss. Her eyes followed the butt as it drifted along the gutter until its passage was arrested by a crushed Red Bull can.

There had been a substitution in the queue, the beige raincoat and red parka had been replaced by a young couple impossibly entwined and giving each-other mouth to mouth resuscitation, a large percentage of their skin hidden beneath tattoos. She was clad in a tiny silver skirt in polka-dots of large black circles over moth-eaten tights, while the male had on a black cap attributed to Che Guevara. With a disdainful glance at their attempts to swallow tongues, Beth gently moulded her stomach to alleviate her anxiety. At this time of day! she thought, and why so noisy about it – slobbering over one another as if on a life-support machine. A mobile phone broke the spell by issuing a few bars of some Enrique tune and the girl giggled into the mouthpiece for half a minute before returning for another shot of carbon-dioxide from the lips of her beau.

For distraction Beth did sums in her head, such as working out the gas-bill or what age she had been when Bowie became a hit as Ziggy Stardust. She switched her attention to the ridiculous ads. In between the optimistic messages of 'Cut out the fuss, hop on a bus' and a plea to entice travellers to distant parts of the principality the likes of Rhyl, the Royal Mint or the Isle of Anglesey, were a colourful array of enticing products you hadn't realised you couldn't live without. In the past she had thought Olae to be the triumphant cry of a bull-fighter, and Old Spice a seasoning transported along the Silk Roads of China. Then there was that one by Oreall, don't go there she thought, it really wasn't worth it! It was no good the tightness in her chest wouldn't go away. Then, looming towards her out of the murk arrived a 77.

Reluctantly she boarded the bus in front of the two love-birds, who, in danger of saliva-drowning had surfaced momentarily and switched to hugging themselves to suffocation, or clinging to each-other's hands with the tenacity of nervous rope climbers. Fortunately they squeezed upstairs allowing Beth to sit below where she found fresh ads for entertainment: *Become a computer expert…* with mental arithmetic she worked through the sample problems getting each correct in turn. Why hadn't she followed her brother into computers instead of coping with a morass of primary pupils? The brief unsavoury vision of a class of whining, yelling, scrapping snotty-nosed kids was interrupted by arrival at her destination.

She noted the rain had ceased and a burst of sunlight was reflected from a myriad glistening slate rooftops along pleasant terraces with multi-coloured doors. 'Is this Tonypandy?' she asked the driver. Taking a deep breath she alighted on the pavement and made her way to her appointment beneath the clock-tower and into the unknown.

LAST POST

Her heart sank as she stooped to pick up the envelope from the hall-mat. 'Not again' she thought noting the postmark, as with careful deliberation she placed it on the mantelpiece where it was barely visible lurking behind the wide marble clock. It always arrived a couple of days after her birthday, as regular as the ticking seconds behind which it now sulked. She hadn't glimpsed him for over eighteen months, yet still he wouldn't let her go.

She cast her mind back to when she'd opened the first one: it must have been four years ago. In flowing words he enquired about her birthday, then went on to describe how it could have been if they were still together: the places he would have taken her and how he would have spoiled her. All false of course, what he gained in charm he lost in imagination. A stroll in the local park or a sly grope in the back row of the local flea-pit were the most she could hope for. Why couldn't she have seen in advance that it would never have worked out. She had loved him, even dreamt of sharing her life with him in the early days. He was everything she yearned for with his tall stature, careless good looks and quiet smile. He was a child she realised – that was his charm. He made her laugh and was gentle and polite: the sort to often fill a lonely girl's wistful dreams.

Then one dark day the mask had dropped and she discovered his brooding ways. There were times he couldn't hide it when they spent hours in one another's company in oppressive silence. At such moments you could cut the air with a knife and all her efforts to unlock his soul proved fruitless. She knew he was visiting his own private hell and struggling with his demons alone. Later he returned to his usual amicable self. Try as she might she was unable to reconcile these two characters who dominated her life. She had cuddled him, stroked his forehead, made him drinks, cajoled him, ignored him – nothing worked. There was no telling where or when the demons would strike.

She had felt that quiet loving care and tenderness would prevail: perhaps it was a phase and he would mellow. She'd read that men were boys who simply refused to grow up. Well, she would become the life-raft to gently steer him to maturity. Surely one must suffer for love, and if she persevered eventually love would triumph over all? Gradually she came to recognise that this love was destroying her – eating away at her soul. Her health suffered; friends noted her loss of weight as she became a haggard replica of the woman they had known. Of course she also knew if she were honest that love is a debt and when the bill comes you pay in grief.

No, she wouldn't open the letter this year – she would simply keep it for a few days as an emblem that she wasn't forgotten, then she would run it through the shredder. At least it's different, she mused, being stalked by a "mail".

As she pursued her daily tasks she tried to ignore the letter, although perhaps its location wasn't the brightest of ideas. She was surprised how often she needed to know the time, whilst silently wishing the dispatch had vanished – perhaps fallen into the fire. But the off-white edging continued to peer accusingly out at her, defying her to access its contents.

A week later she decided – setting up the shredder she retrieved the letter and took it into the study. It was then she realised it was too thick to go through without jamming the mechanism. Nothing for it, she would have to open the menacing missive to shred it in individual sheets. Tentatively and with pounding heart she slid the thin blade of the brass opener between the folds of the envelope to reveal the contents. With an audible sigh of relief she spied the instantly recognisable bold letter-heading. Lying on her desk was an innocent catalogue for a mail-order company she had completely forgotten requesting. She felt certain she had recognised the handwriting. Maybe this year would be different.

LAST TRAIN

There was a brief click as the door-latch sprang back followed by the slow shuffle along the darkened hallway and furtive footfalls upon the stair. She knew where he went, despite his speech of monosyllables she had gleaned that much information. It was strange, normally men, it was usually men, would prove extremely loquacious. With the result that she would either be bored to tears or sit around chatting into the early morning hours. She pummelled her pillow in vexation, turned over and fell asleep.

It had been almost two years since Veronyka had opened her house to visitors. When she lost Barry she decided she could put the spare room to better use, and being in a coastal location of a not entirely fashionable but respectable resort in Moldova she felt it the thing to do. She enjoyed the casual banter of travellers, and sympathetically joined in their successes and expectations as well as occasionally consoling those minds who had experienced failure and disappointment. Although she had to admit the latter group were growing in number. She also enjoyed the freedom the extra money provided.

Years back she had been a language teacher at primary level, and knew the value of the written word. Here they taught Moldova to half the population, while another quarter were educated in Romanian. Moldova was based on the Romance languages of Spain, France and Italy and contained a musical quality; yet she had to admit it could be a challenge at times introducing young minds to the Cyrillic alphabet, but of course youth was the best time to learn. Rather a recluse as a teenager, her folks were keen to keep her on the right side of the tracks and were strict about her schooling. She had never courted the limelight and fame had slipped past her. She was content to see the sparkle in a child's eye when they had achieved what was to them remarkable.

Famous for its wineries, there was plenty to draw tourists to the Baltic State. Apart from the most famous vineyards of Cricova, Purcari and Ciumai there was much of historical value to visit such as the many monasteries and museums, the Soroca fort or the Secret Lakes. Veronyka had always lived in Moldova. Her parents had survived the earthquake of 1940 when they were forced to shelter in caves in fear for their lives. Her house was in a handy location, close to Nistra Beach in Chisinau and not far from the Milestii Mici winery.

During her more optimistic moods she dreamt of perhaps meeting an amour: not a careless, busy well-off toy-boy with a flashy car and natty feet on the dance floor, and after Barry love didn't enter the equation; no she pictured someone mature and kind – not only for security; someone with a twinkle in his eye to bring her laughter. That's what she missed. At 46 she was still able to turn a male head.

In the running however would not be her current visitor Maxim, whose raison d'etre she had ascertained as trains. He had seemed normal enough when he arrived, although he was rather taciturn and wore a haunted look as if a bird of prey had him in its sights. His clothes were old-fashioned but serviceable, he appeared especially fond of a grimy beige parka (not quite an anorak she had thought) and trousers turned up at the bottoms were certainly not de rigueur. The shabby demeanour was emphasized by the way his eyes always fell to the floor (he'd never look a person in the face), but what was more disconcerting was his habit of clicking his tongue loudly at periodic intervals.

He carried an untidy bundle of 3 notebooks with grubby black covers in which he meticulously logged each and every locomotive he encountered on the tracks. Each morning at sunrise he would trudge disconsolately up the rise towards the bridge that spanned the lines by the small station, unsmilingly clutching the sandwich box and apple she had prepared; to return at dusk, by which time Veronyka had already turned in and their paths seldom crossed. Harmless and pathetic he may appear, but even innocent train-spotters can go off the rails.

He had once murmured that he had been intrigued by numbers since boyhood; A topic of which she was sublimely ignorant and wished to remain, and in her book one which was highly contentious. Everyone was familiar with the hidden menace of 666, and 13 was certainly suspect. As for the inverted 6, well the Devil's work, even the innocent figure five in the wrong hands could appear as a swastika. No, words were more inviting; she thought of the puzzles and crosswords she duly completed every evening before dropping off; yet she couldn't escape the fact that figures had even permeated <u>this</u> sanctum, to indicate the positioning of clues.

The world was changing. Democracy had slipped into the country as stealthily as a night-time thief at the back door; without the loud and heady expectancy of another Tiananmen Square or Egyptian uprising. Moldova was a country that paid lip-service to democracy, yet wasn't that the norm? The populous lived in hope of a brave new future, as she did personally. Luxuries were hard won, such staples as fresh batteries proved elusive. Black market was rife and growing, as was black magic – the country needed something to believe in. Old habits were hard to break and magic involved numbers. Much had changed though not always for the better. Coke machines and American piped music were on every street corner, drugs and McDonalds were available in city centres. It seemed to Veronyka as if the country was selling its soul to the stars and stripes.

Life-styles had been affected; even the humble art of train-spotting had hit the buffers. She'd learnt from Maxim that he no longer had to wait in the sticks until a train hurtled by, that was the reason he did all his 'spotting' from the relative comfort of the station. Apparently nowadays train numbers were given out by helpful train-staff over the tannoy as they warned of a loco's imminent approach.

One night he failed to return and she'd enjoyed a rare night of uninterrupted slumber. Early in the morning she went out to look for him up the incline. A small crowd had gathered around the bridge. She pressed closer and with a gasp made out the silhouette of Maxim's body swaying gently from the ramparts in the morning breeze like a tree weighed down with plums. They had always said the bridge was unsafe and dangerous to walkers. Apparently he had lost his footing and fallen from the parapet where his rucksack had caught the bridge's ironwork to slip noose-like around his neck and this had accounted for his agonising end. The authorities reported 'accidental death', she knew different.

Later she picked up the local paper to read: 'Bridge Claims Another': the power of words, 'a further accident at Bicului bridge...' She was able to read between the lines and knew where the power of numbers could take you...

LOSS

What woke me I cannot tell. Maybe it was the shaft of bright sunlight intruding between the curtains, or the sporadic snuffling beside my pillow. With a start I sat upright and peered apprehensively to my left – a man was sharing my bed, a man I had never before seen. Perhaps we'd met the evening before, but I had no recollection of such a liaison. My mind was blank.

Anxiously I slid from the covers and, covering my bare shoulders with a fluffy gown from behind the door left the room. After a couple of attempts I found the bathroom and dowsed my face with cold water, yet I didn't feel hungover. Then I spied my reflection in the mirror, although it wasn't my face. Where was the 35 year old solicitor? Staring back at me was my mother, a mature face in her late fifties. This couldn't be. I crept around the house tentatively exploring each room in turn, in a frantic search for the familiar – all was strange and new to me.

'What do you fancy for breakfast, dear – cereal or toast? Don't forget your appointment today...'

I decided to confront this man and found him hovering over the toaster: 'I am sorry but I don't know you, and I don't know where I am...'

'Now, sit down and drink your tea darling. I'm Ed, your husband, we've been married for 19 years and have a daughter.'

Things were moving too fast, what appointment? I began to panic; what was happening to me?

At the therapists I requested a private hearing, and my "husband" left us alone. Doctor Montalbano seemed kind and caring. 'Please, tell me, what is going on?'

'Now Sara, I'm a neurologist and you've had a bad accident which has caused memory loss, known as prosopagnosia or face-blindness.' He showed me some photos but none struck a chord.

'But I've lost so many years – how long? And I'm married to a man I don't know!'

'Now, you have the mobile I gave you – you can call me at any time. You also have a diary you keep in your wardrobe which I want you to read – it will help you make some sense of your situation.'

Later in the afternoon after Ed had left the house, I received a call from Doctor Montalbano who instructed me to search at the bottom of the wardrobe for my diary, and to keep it out of sight of Ed as he didn't believe in psychiatrists and their methods. I found it, a mobile phone I didn't recognise and a book lying beneath a threadbare cardigan. I began reading avidly. The book contained dates and entries over the past two years, prior to which I appeared to have been living in some sort of sanatorium.

I had just replaced the diary, after skimming and reading the most recent entries, and was lying on the bed when Ed returned.

'Ed, please can we talk? I feel so lost.'

'I know. But we've been here so many times before!' he sounded irritable. This I knew from my diary. I felt used, soiled in a way, and tomorrow and the day after it would start all over again. Sleep was wiping my memory clean, and each new day was just that – a new day.

Then the door-bell chimed. 'Now, who's that?' Ed strode to the door.

'Hello, does Sara Brinkley live here?' a woman's voice.

'Ye-es, but she's not well at present, she's lying down – who are you?'

'I'm Chelsy Ward, and she's my mother.'

'No, I'm sorry she's-'

'Perfectly well, and pleased to see you –' I cried over Ed's shoulder.

'Darling, we've been so worried about you. We finally got your address from the doctor…'

Ed retreated out the back.

'Now, call me as soon as possible – here's my number', Sara whispered, pushing a slip of paper into my hand. 'You are in trouble, that's not Ed…'

MANIFESTATION

At first she heard the gentle withdrawal of waves sucking the freshly-washed shingle from the fore-shore despite being conscious of the pungent salty aroma. She'd left her car by the ochre dunes and walked along the familiar brief avenue of bright yellow gorse bushes that terminated at the coast. Screeching gulls soared overhead as she rounded the tiny headland and sought out the caves beneath the cliff. In a way it was a sort of homecoming; a homage to her roots.

Raised on this South Devon coast she had not called on her parents, preferring to stay in touch by phone. If she pondered on it, the break-up of her relationship had brought her here. What was she seeking – sympathy, commiseration, comfort? Deswick was a busy market town close to the sea between Painton and Brixham: London work had dictated her habitat, and since meeting the ex partner somehow there was never the time to visit. Deciding to surprise them on a whim she had brought flowers and a half bottle of JD, her father's favourite tipple.

Before arriving at 'Wayward' her parents' restive bungalow, driving along the coastal road, it occurred to her to pause at the tiny cove where as a child she had sought sanctuary. And there it was, the craggy inlet with its kelp and barnacle coated break-water; even on dismal days the scene evoked bitter-sweet memories. As she relived those far-off times a tiny crab scurried around her shoes to the safety of a rocky overhang. This was the soft sand where a barefoot girl had raced beside the ocean and splashed in the incoming foam, bounced beach-balls and played cricket or jokari with her elder brothers, then explored dark caves and teeming rock-pools. Was any part of her left?

Those caves held a deeper significance: it was where she had retreated against the constant feelings of rejection. Here she had run to hide. Here she sulked for hours, curled in a foetal position marking the sand with desperate tears. Here finally she became calm, soothed by the rhythmic flux of a restless tide: she had felt secure in her secret place.

Her marriage had been a travesty where she'd been forced to impose a court injunction to keep the violence at bay. Separated and finally divorced; the recent parting had been less acrimonious, he'd simply admitted to boredom and a dalliance with his PA, however she had been left solvent. Why were men so difficult?

As the sun gradually sank to the horizon she shivered feeling vulnerable. What would her future hold? She strolled to the grassy cliff-top in the enclosing dusk, and from this vantage point watched the small town come to life. Pinpoints of light suddenly appeared as the dim vista was slowly transformed; like a series of radiant fireflies within a forest canopy. Pubs, restaurants, cinema and theatre would be opening to expectant endeavour, and within dwellings people were preparing for the evening's entertainment; all with purpose. A haunted sole, she was unable to ward off a twinge of envy towards the panoramic activity gaining momentum below; the gregarious industry of a community to which she would never belong. She was returning to her father's sullen face and her mother's nervousness where they would sit in awkward silence; or perhaps father would switch off any hope of communion by switching on the television to his designated viewing.

Like a thunderbolt the revelation hit her – no wonder her relationships had failed: there was no love in that restrictive bungalow, there never had been. Her parents were adept at putting on a show for the world; wasn't it Shakespeare who said the world's a stage, well they certainly played their parts well. It was an elaborate ritual, a sham: the respectable couple had taught her many things, except the most important of all – love.

She wondered whether such introspection was worthy of her, or indeed beneficial. Some called it healthy therapy – the exposure of the soul. She wasn't so sure. One thing was certain, she couldn't go to her parents: it would be a backward step. She needed to move forward, organise her life – reinvent herself; attempt to recover what she'd lost. Why was she here playing the prodigal son? She would return to London and confide in a friend: but was such disclosure warranted or desirable? Perhaps she'd simply pick up smoothly where she was: and merely claim her parents were away when she called.

She gazed at the ebb and flow of a mass of loose seaweed gently swaying on the tide reflecting the sinking sun. Watching the hungry waves that lapped briefly at the shore and then withdrew, she felt she too was reaching for her parents merely to recede back into her comfort zone.

With a swift nip of JD, she carefully placed the bouquet inside the cave that had provided comfort to a distressed child, and with measured steps turned towards her car.

MISSING THE POINT

It was Autumn, and the red and gold shades were clearly visible through the rising mist as stray flocks of egrets and whooper swans headed towards Mount Emel and the distant horizon. The rice crop had been good this year, the extra cost for nitrogen had been worthwhile, he would receive a good price at market. There would be rich *niangao* cake to bring Fu at New Year when they wished each-other 'kung hei fat choy' and carried brightly coloured lanterns to appease the dragon as they processed through the village. (Fu = good blessings)

Zhang rested on his hoe and mopped his brow. Perhaps he would buy his wife that washing-machine she coveted. His thoughts were elsewhere as he chopped at the stubborn weeds that grew between and spoilt the symmetry of the neat rows. It took four or five months to grow a crop, and years such as this could produce two. As he cast his eyes over the lush green hills diffused with the swaying crop he became attuned to the beauty of the landscape: a soft breeze rustled the lacy leaves and set them shimmering in the orange glow of a setting sun: for a few moments he allowed his gaze to dwell on the endless shimmering plateaux of stepped rice-fields that continued until they joined the sky.

Mai Li had been looking tired of late, since their daughter's birth, he hoped she was not ailing. Almost done for the day; his colleagues had a further row to work and then they would all head home to the village. Living in the Southern uplands in Zhejiang province south of the Yangste, he had no use for the 'puddling' techniques that beleaguered his northern compatriots. At that moment they would be draining the paddies in preparation for cutting and drying the crop. Zhang lived close to the Water Town of Nanxun on the way to Hangzhou, and <u>had</u> done since his father moved from the north to sample warmer climes.

The next day the cutting process would begin. He allowed his thoughts to dwell on the modern machinery becoming available that took much of the hard labour out of the harvest: some colleagues were still accustomed to the scythe as their forefathers had been before them, others favoured the sickle, but he was more comfortable with a simple knife. A knife that came alive in his experienced calloused hands. He was proud of the prowess with which he wielded the blade: the dexterity he utilized to attack the dense foliage with pinpoint accuracy, in the same smooth movement laying the neat grasses to one side in preparation for gathering. There had been less pests this year, less predators such as beetles or rodents that nibbled at the crop; and viruses and diseases had been kept to a minimum. Following cutting, the gang would transport the rice and lay it to dry beneath the protective open-barns for two to three days.

Zhang was aware that harvesting would take more than six weeks. He reckoned they could spend anything between 40 and 80 hours per hectare gathering in the main crop. With that in mind he decided to retire to bed straight after supper. His thoughts returned to Mai Li and the delicious bean sprouts she would be preparing. How fortunate he had been to meet her, a good wife; she kept the dwelling spotless, cared for their daughter and helped around the farm. She had patiently begun the child's education until she was of an age to catch the bus to school.

Suddenly he was jolted backwards with the shock of a sharp pain to his right index finger. Speedily withdrawing his hand he saw the snake, a pit viper. Natives referred to the reptile as the 'five-step snake': once bitten a person is able to walk a mere five steps before collapsing under the powerful effects of the venom.

Wise Zhang did not panic, although he knew he had to act before the venom had time to substantially enter his bloodstream. Weighing the chances and deciding his only option was amputation, he sprinted to the wagon that contained his tools. His colleagues rushed towards him, aware something was wrong. On his way Zhang broke a short spur from a Yunnan tree. Clamping the twig between his teeth, he selected a small chopper and laid his hand across the flatbed tailgate, his finger folded under the palm with the pointer extended towards the cab. Taking careful aim he brought his weight down onto the infected digit. As blood spurted from the wound he let out an agonising gurgle of muffled pain. The finger rolled along the tailgate to become lost amid the assorted tackle. His companions arrived to be greeted by his collapse at their feet: having completed his grisly task Zhang had fallen unconscious to the ground.

The friends wrapped a handkerchief around his wound, before hurriedly carrying him towards the truck and the fifty mile journey that awaited them. He came round at the hospital in Hangzhou having been heavily sedated. He was given an anti-venom injection and had his wound washed and dressed.

Later he was reprimanded by the medic, Doctor Yang, for not bringing the severed digit with him. He responded that he had other things on his mind! (Presumably it had rolled off the tailboard during their hasty departure.) But the magic persisted, to cut off the finger had been totally unnecessary; the snake involved had not been potent enough to cause mortality. For good measure he added that sucking the venom as, many indulge in or applying a tourniquet, are equally ineffective measures: And amputation had often, in his experience, resulted in gangrene.

Zhang, released from hospital, was reunited with his wife who fussed over him like a doting mother-hen. On the evening of his homecoming she and her sisters prepared a feast of spring rolls, egg-fried rice, sweet and sour pork, chow mein, with spicy tofu and green tea. To accompany this illustrious spread came an acceptable bottle of Riesling with Luzhou Laojiao to follow; while Mai Li wore her treasured golden cheong-sam.

(Note: *niangao cake* is made from rice, egg, sugar, flour and rice-flour)

NEVER A CROSS WORD

Gerald had been her soul mate, her raison d'être, an inspiration with that crazy hair always out of place, cheeky grin and boyish charm. Now she would have to adjust, to adapt, to carve some purpose from the remaining years. She was considered a stoic personality. She had many acquaintances and over the years had secured a few deep friendships: she would pull through, weather the storm. She had never felt the need for religion, yet of late found herself yearning for a little spiritual comfort.

A safari was what Gerald was determined to achieve before he 'shuffled off this mortal coil' and winning the crossword competition for a trip to Africa seemed too good to pass over. Despite the reassurance of the travel operator of luxurious accommodation and the scenic variety of sweeping veldt beneath cloudless skies the holiday had ended in nightmare.

Her earlier premonition had proved tragically true. She held reservations over their visit to Tanzania from the start, but Gerald had been insistent. Drawn to animals from boyhood, especially in the wild, the adolescent had encumbered his patient family with a succession of unlikely pets, including a salamander, a gecko and a bush-baby. His long-suffering mother threatened to leave home when she uncovered a five-foot python in the airing cupboard.

Gerald's wife had sensed that the leopard-skin painted pickup truck they used on safari would be severely restricted for space given the number of tourists as the party were collected outside the hotel, and so it would prove. She wanted to wait for the second vehicle but Gerald was adamant as he pushed to the fore with childish enthusiasm. On board, window seats were at a premium and warnings to stay seated were ignored as passengers competed for prime visual vantage points. The couple had been divided by the central aisle in the scramble. She glanced across at him, he was beaming in expectation as he swung from side to side to avoid missing any treasured sighting, the expensive Leica at the ready.

The perspiring tourists were crammed into the small vehicle and when they picked up the two guards, armed with hunting rifles, the anxious assortment resembled the serenity of a bizarre London tube-train rush hour commute. As they moved along the sandy track, bathed in a fierce heat-haze and civilisation gave way to wide open spaces interspersed with sparse thorny shrubs, the almighty squeeze was beginning to manifest itself. Nerve-ends began to fray and tempers to shrink. A rather plump woman rebuked a tall pimply youth for blocking her line of vision and an opinionated ex-military type was boring everyone to tears with his loud voice and condescending anecdotes. And matters were not helped when the guards instructed passengers that no photos were to be taken without their permission.

She became alerted when Gerald showed signs of agitation – a shortness of breath and rising colour. Gesticulating in crude semaphore she got him to take a pill that he managed to gulp down against the swaying motion of the bus. At the back of her mind was his heart machine and ringing in her ears the consultant's warnings following his last attack.

With a shout of 'Hold tight!' the driver suddenly applied the brakes and slewed the trundling vehicle to a juddering halt, a few moments before a small herd of elephants ambled across their path. 'That was a close one!' the driver commented, reaching for his water flask. The disgruntled tourists were busy disentangling themselves while at the same time jostling for a better view of the giant mammals. It was then that she lost sight of Gerald. Frantically squeezing a path through, she discovered him lying in a contorted heap on the truck floor clutching at his throat, his face now a distorted purple. She had fallen to her knees and cradled him in her arms, but the few urgent gasps were to be his last. As she gently kissed his forehead, he faintly murmured: 'Thank you...'

She had his body shipped home and then he was cremated as was his wish; and resigned herself to what the fates had in store. 'If things had been different?' she pondered, 'If he'd not had this all-consuming obsession...? If he wasn't so headstrong...? if only I had put my foot down? If, if, if...?' The tiny word kept returning to her in varying juxtapositions.

Later, Idling through some of Gerald's effects, she came across his beloved crossword books and paused. He had been an addict, she hadn't attempted one in years. To fill the time, she embarked on one with straightforward clues. Having completed half the puzzle she complemented herself – she was doing rather well. All of a sudden she froze... her whole being became fossilised as she re-read clue 23 down, 6 letters: 'an expedition embarked upon to view wild animals in their natural habitat'.

IN WITH THE NEW

The practice of celebrating the fall of the old year, the beginning of the New and vowing resolutions, has been in existence for millennia. Ancient Persians gave New Year gifts of eggs to symbolise productiveness. Babylonians repaid outstanding debts, while the Romans made promises to Janus (from whence January came). Medieval knights took the 'peacock vow' to reaffirm their commitment to chivalry. Around 600 BC ancient Greeks carried babies in baskets in honour of Dionysus, god of fertility, in order to symbolise annual rebirth: a ceremony continued to this day in parts of Greece. More contemporary is the custom whereby Greek children leave their shoes by the fireside on New Year's Day in the hope that St. Basil, renowned for kindness, will fill them with gifts.

The Meridia or South America is prone to much ritual at this time of year. Argentina, Bolivia and Venezuela hope for travel in the New Year as people carry a suitcase around the house at midnight. Some go further and will take the case around the block to ensure travel at greater distances. Mexico gets down to basics, believing that wearing red underwear on New Year's Eve will bring fresh love in the coming year. Whereas Columbian, Cuban and Puerto Rican families stuff a male life-size doll and then dress it up in old clothes taken from each family member. They call him 'Mr Old Year', and at midnight he is set alight. As the flames destroy him they also destroy the old year's bad memories of sadness and unhappiness and herald happiness for the new one.

Such ritual celebration affects the New World too, with

117

between 40 and 45 percent of American adults making at least one new resolution each year. Such commitment involves an abstention from bad habits and debt to more exercise, weight loss and quitting smoking. Bushels of black-eyed peas are consumed in many parts of the USA, normally accompanied by hog-jowls or ham for good luck. From 1907 a giant ball has been lowered in Times Square as a symbol of the turn of the year.

In Spain, people eat 12 grapes as the clock strikes midnight. This peculiarity began in the 20th century following a bumper grape harvest. Not knowing what to do with the surplus the King and grape growers came up with the New Year ritual. Japan also appeals to the gastronomy of its inhabitants: here on the evening of December 31st they eat a bowl of buckwheat noodles called 'toshikoshisoba' (year-crossing) and listen out for the sound of Buddhist temple bells – these are rung 108 times at midnight. This sound is said to purify listeners of the 108 evil passions that afflict the human psyche. On New Year's Day everyone dresses in new clothes and homes are decorated with pine branches and bamboo, both considered symbols of long life.

China, of course, is famous for its celebrations where crackers are burnt to scare off the evil spirits that roam the earth. Doors and windows are often sealed with paper to keep out evil demons. Many people wear a new pair of slippers bought in the old year: this custom is meant to portray stepping on people who gossip about you.

Various foods are thought to induce happiness, wealth and good luck. The Dutch eat donuts, hog denotes prosperity and the humble cabbage is a good luck vegetable eaten by many on New Year's Day. Cabbage leaves are a sign of prosperity, representing paper currency. In other regions rice is considered lucky.

Closer to home, the Scots celebrate Hogmanay. Here barrels of tar may be set alight and rolled along village streets. Thus the old year is burned up and the new one begins. Robbie Burns 'Auld Lang Syne' written in the 18th century signifies the beginning of the New Year, where participants in the dance link arms and sing along. A Welsh tradition involves giving the gift of the Calennig, an apple with three twig legs stuck with dried fruit, cloves and a spray of evergreens. This is given to friends and family for luck in the New Year and is often placed on window-sills or shelves. The United Kingdom had the custom of 'first-footing'. Here, after midnight, a dark-haired visitor is greeted to the house bearing a lump of coal, a crust of bread, money and some greenery – for good luck, food, cash and long life respectively. Many cultures perceive that anything in a ring shape bears good luck as a symbol of 'coming full circle' or completing an annual cycle.

Religions differ in their recognition of the New Year. Hashanah, the Jewish New Year is a holy time when Jews are reminded of past errors and promise to improve in the future. Special synagogue services are held and children receive gifts of new clothes and New Year loaves are baked to recall the harvest. Christians hold 'watch-night' services to prepare for the coming year by prayer and the making of resolutions.

Widespread and various are the customs and traditions at this special time. One New Year's Eve Marion asked everyone in her local pub to prepare. At the stroke of midnight, she asked every husband to stand alongside the one person who made his life worth living. As the clock struck twelve the bartender was almost crushed to death. Samuel Pepys (1661) admitted making a resolution with the words: 'I have newly taken a solemn oath about abstaining from plays and wine, which I am resolved to keep according to the letter of the oath which I keep by me'.

It wouldn't have done much for his well-being in 1669, when his 29 year-old wife died of typhoid. But my favourite quote is from Oscar Wilde who said: 'Good resolutions are simply cheques that men draw on a bank where they have no account.' Perhaps with the 1.2 million people who profess to being lonely in Britain, a worthy resolution would be to befriend another in the New Year.

ON THE MOVE

Staring disconsolately at the belly-up mosquito on the window ledge she sighed: '...even the mozzies can't stand it here!' It should have been an ideal dwelling situated at a location readily accessible to local amenities, train stations and bus routes, set in its own grounds overlooking the small town with its shops, theatre and swimming-pool, and endowed with ample off-road parking: an estate agent's dream.

That's if she were to repaint the apartment throughout, to hide the encroaching mould on ceiling and walls, and exchange the dreary curtains for fresh ones lacking mildew. Returning the peeling wall-paper to its moorings might add to the ambience and perhaps touching up the dull paint on the chipped radiators might improve the decor of despair. It was a hard water region, where sinks and baths became besmirched with a viscous black deposit, and hapless tenants were serenaded twice daily by a cacophony of unmusical notes emitted by a melange of haphazard plumbing: notes that pervaded the cavernous recesses to echo around the moist walls and forgotten corridors of the dilapidated mansion.

Dating from the 18th century, the property had been annexed in an expeditious ad hoc manner. At an earlier time flowing velvet curtains adorned long sash windows that framed grand views over half a dozen counties, and specific quarters played host to a bevy of Victorian and Edwardian minions who bustled below and addressed calls to service within the house. Fine oak panelling rose four feet from the parquet flooring and a scalloped turned-elm staircase greeted the visitor in the entrance hall beneath art deco lighting. Once it was a school where the rococo architecture and high ceilings rang with eager pupil chatter and session bells. The ravages of time and neglect had ensured a total restoration cost that would leave little change from a million pounds. Eventually the historic edifice would collapse, leaving the owners a highly lucrative investment site.

Little would be done to improve the general air of abandon that pervaded the outside of this grimy white property with its forsaken air of dereliction, where suspended masonry and stucco parted company with the dismal building's facia; and even less regarding the house's shadowy aspect: set into the hillside and encased in rampant woodland, where sunlight was an anathema evoking thoughts of Kafka's *Darkness at Noon*. Years previously she had written a poem about a dark house, it would certainly be applicable here she mused. The exterior would surely have benefited from a comprehensive clearing of brambles and ground elder from the choked flower beds surrounding the house; in contrast to the meticulously cropped lawns that were periodically manicured in deference to an air of respectability.

Inside, the gloomy approach to her apartment was far from impressive. Advisedly ignoring the dozen pairs of mud-encrusted boots and sweaty trainers aligning the stairs, the shabby walls of the bleak corridor (inner dungeon) filled a caller with foreboding. Opposite a couple of rusting bicycles, the entire wall was hung with a series of electric meters and junction boxes worthy of past glories at Battersea power station, and would have done credit to early days at the BBC or Nasser space station. Yet the splendour of this showpiece might be easily missed as, due to a dysfunctional light switch, the hallway was habitually in darkness.

Despite misgivings she knew she had to leave the house on the hill, and there was plenty she would miss on the convenience front. Not included in her regrets was the sight of a pair of grubby long-johns exhibited on the whirly-gig line situated in a derelict backyard outside her kitchen window: this shabby garment and similar belonged to the retired English teacher from number 8 and was the prime reason she kept the blinds permanently closed, adding to the gloom. Nor would she rue not having to run the central heating throughout the year, in a vain attempt to forestall the damp. She could exist comfortably without the noises of the woman above or the draught from the cellar below; and the scampering of mice or thumping of rats across the ceiling over her bed would soon be forgotten. The dark interior with its pervasive cloying atmosphere that resulted in her furniture acquiring a fine coating of green mould, and clothes that attracted a musty odour necessitating regular laundry would soon be distant memories.

She was on her way. But was she turning back the clock, moving to a tiny village with one general store and two pubs? Yet she had her car and would be just five miles out of town, she liked nature and walking and the river was close; and there was an up-market hotel nearby where a weekly night-club was laid on as entertainment...

Within the smart decor she took stock 'What would you like Madam?' asked the brisk young barman, his shiny hair sleeked back above his black and maroon waistcoat. 'N-no, it's ok, I have a drink', she murmured sipping her Campari perched on a gleaming chrome bar stool in the plush surroundings. 'No, it's from the guy in the other bar – he wants to buy you one...' She stared guardedly across the busy space until her blue eyes became locked with a handsome hazel pair. Perhaps...she thought, just maybe: but what happens next?

OVER THE FENCE

According to John, Guy Sullivan was a weird sort of chap. He was forever asking John how he spent his weekend or whether he enjoyed his holidays, or if he could pick him up anything from the shops. Nosey bugger, only wanted to snoop. In John's book people ought to keep themselves to themselves, not pry into others lives. A good neighbour should be seen and not heard: a little privacy wasn't too much to ask.

And of course Sullivan had all the latest gadgets – a loft conversion, like the Treddingtons at 35, with a large dormer window that must have cost a pretty penny: one of those fancy electronic up and over doors to open the garage operated without leaving the car; <u>and</u> an Edwardian conservatory with winter heating, venetian blinds; and a floodlit pool at the back of the house. And, he'd been told, a music system with quadraphonic cinema all-round sound. Colourful Tea roses and Japanese maples ostentatiously adorned the garden, not a michelmas daisy in sight. Of course it was a new car every two years and exotic holidays with that fancy wife (who thought she was better than she was), to all those poncey places like Provence, Marakesh, Acapulco or Lido di Jesolo. Nothing wrong with Hayling Island – he'd gone there every year until he retired and lost Chrissie.

A roaring exhaust accompanied by television interference heralded the return of the blue metallic BMW z4m. You'd imagine a car like that would come fitted with a suppressor John mused, people should spend their money on the important things of life. That's what's wrong with consumerism – too much choice. Now in communist Russia there was less of a problem: one or two makes and one colour. What was the point of all this conspicuous consumption – you couldn't take it with you and the Lord would provide. John certainly worshipped no graven images, plain and simple were his surroundings. When people started living above their station, all social cohesion was lost. And what about the planet with all that extra waste?

Not that Meadowcroft wasn't a pleasant part of town, elegant without being presumptuous; the bungalows stood in neat rows as if on parade and ready for inspection. His house was set back from the road and fronted with a cool avenue of plane trees which gave the street a leafy slumber during the warmer months, and a detached aloofness in bleaker times. Built on green-belt in the nineteen eighties, they remained a tribute to Thatcherite entrepreneurism.

John, a strict Baptist, only last Sunday at St Benedicts had listened while the vicar preached on the conflict between religion and the consumer society: sentiments he wholeheartedly endorsed; nevertheless he may have dozed off when the Reverend drew attention to Exodus 20, 17 ('Thou shalt not covet thy neighbours house…nor anything that is your neighbours').

Through the French-windows and beyond the fence he could see Guy's high-powered lawn-sprinkler in action; revolving pedantically in perfect circles and spasmodically altering direction, like a precise cheer-leader martialling the spray to parts of the lawn John's eyes couldn't reach. There are those you can't get along with in this world, he thought, and they seem designed to make life tiresome.

Over the fence, Guy and Evelyn were occupied with carefully packing their bags in preparation for two weeks at the Algarve timeshare. Evelyn was keen to try out the holiday Portuguese she'd picked up during winter evening classes.

'You know, I'm rather fond of old John next door', Guy observed, wrapping his swimming shorts around the snorkel. Oh, he's a rough diamond who plays his cards close to his chest; yet you know where you stand with a person like that. He's a creature of habit, keeps his garden tidy and his vegetable patch with the neat rows and large crop is a show-piece. Dependable, that's what his is: always up and about at the same time each morning tending his plants, an ideal neighbour in fact.'

'Too surly for me,' was Evelyn's response. 'Would you trust him with anything – I mean *really* trust him? Yes, he keeps himself to himself – but do you know what's on his mind?'

Guy thought for a moment. 'Well, yes, I think I could trust him. He's quiet and level-headed – the sort of stoic chap who keeps the country going; the sort who coupled 'Great' with 'Britain'.

'When was that, dear!?' teased his wife. Then, 'Can we eat out tonight, this packing is exhausting!'

'Why not – perhaps we could try that new Thai restaurant that's opened on the High Street?'

It was on the Sunday evening, the day before Guy and Evelyn's departure, that they received the apologetic phone call from Guy's work colleague Alyson. Someone had left the company in a hurry, and she had to travel to stand in with no notice at a northern branch on the Monday. This meant she would be unable to pop down to feed Guy's prize collection of tropical fish. Panic set in at Meadowcroft, who could fill the breach at the eleventh hour?

"What are we going to do, Guy?" it must have been two hours since Alyson's call and after frantic requests of local acquaintances Evelyn was no closer to getting a fish-minder.

"Well, I know you won't agree with me, but there's nothing for it – we'll just have to ask John if he'd be willing to help us out. He need only drop in a few times while we're away, to feed and check temperatures etc?"

'Are you sure Guy? I have bad vibes about this – '

'Look, what harm can he do, dirty the carpets!? At least he'll be on site and can watch the place for us, and it'll be a good chance to get to know him better.'

'Well – I must say we do have little option,' Evelyn hesitantly agreed.

Calling next-door later that evening Guy put forward his request. John was so taken aback he kept him at the door for a couple of minutes longer than he should have. Inside, Guy was struck with the orderliness of his neighbour's household, the rather modest interior was uncluttered and low maintenance – a place for everything and everything in its place had been his own father's dictum.

'– so you see it would help us out of a jam, if you could pop in just a couple of times a week to see how the little ones are? I'll leave instructions and it'll only take you 10 minutes maximum.' John looked apprehensive.

'There are no man-eaters amongst them, just ornamental really.' added Guy in conciliatory tone. It had been his hobby for 4 or 5 years now, ever since that snorkelling trip to the Caribbean. He had two Sailfin Mollys, one Black Molly, a couple of Guppys, a Swordtail, a few of the smaller Platys, a gold and black Angelfish, and his pride and joy a 6-stripe Frontosa. He'd seen the Frontosa in Tanzania on Lake Tanganyika, and managed to acquire one at a not inconsiderable shipping cost.

'Well, if it's only a couple of times a week, I suppose it'd be ok,' agreed John tentatively.

'Excellent. Here's the key. We'll be back on the Tuesday afternoon, and here's my mobile number if you need me.'

'Alright, see you when you get back – '

'And thanks again,' with that Guy briskly saw himself out before John changed his mind. Pondering his decision John spent a restless night: only partly due to the Sullivan's departure at 5.30 the following morning. Had he been too hasty? He always took time to think through decisions – well, it was too late, next door's key was in his keeping.

Although he was not due to baby-sit the fish until a couple of days' time, curiosity got the better of him and that evening he slipped into the house next door. There, in the lavish living-room, taking pride of place on a huge carved oak plinth swam his charges – ducking and diving around the aquatic plant life and mock shell-castles. John read the note and checked the thermometer – all was as it should be. Then, he thought, it wouldn't hurt to take a little look round since he was there. He had never previously had the opportunity.

As he suspected, the house contained every luxury and labour-saving device known to the 21st century, and some not generally available until the 22nd. He supposed that with no family and two salaries the couple could afford such excesses. After sampling from the spacious cocktail cabinet (no-one would notice) and reminding himself that alcohol did not agree with him, he sauntered upstairs to the dormer, glass in hand. Following a close inspection of the revolving circular bed bedecked in black satin, his view was drawn through the window to the ornate garden and the pool surface that twinkled in the moonlight. It looked so cool and inviting.

He wasn't sure what came over him, but all of a sudden he had a burning desire to skinny-dip beneath the stars. Rushing downstairs he helped himself again from the drinks cabinet this time taking a bottle of spirit with him, opened the French-windows and sneaked across the shadowy lawn. He made a tidy pile of his clothes and lowered himself into the inviting tepid blue water. He became unaware of how long he spent splashing around and taking deeper and deeper swigs from the bottle, which he had to admit was rather enjoyable. So, nothing to this drinking lark, vastly overrated – not bad for a casual teetotaller he chuckled to himself.

Exhausted from his efforts in the pool and the alcohol he staggered back to the luxurious bathroom. Selecting a sumptuous bath-towel, he dried himself down then sat out in the warm night air in a cream bathrobe with a large letter G on the back. Re-entering the house, he decided to try out the superior bed, and with shameless abandon slipped out of the robe and proceeded to romp and wallow on top of the cool satin. After a while, as his brain began to kick in, feeling rather sheepish he dressed himself hurriedly and resolved to replace everything as it had been and return home. He began by tidying the bedding and then went through to the lounge. However the unaccustomed booze was taking affect, and as the room began to spin he collapsed on the plush mink velvet sofa and before he knew it fell into fitful slumber.

He awoke with a start, a bad taste in his mouth and an aching head along with the feeling that something was very wrong. He was filled with a nagging sense of remorse. What <u>was</u> he doing!? Of course, God helped those who helped themselves: but he had definitely overstepped the mark. He had abused his neighbour's trust and acquitted himself none too well. Alright, Guy was a snob and ostentatious to a fault, but even he didn't deserve such treatment. How would John have felt if someone had violated <u>his</u> privacy? After making sure he had re-turned every stone and that the coast was clear he crept back home, "like a thief in the night" he thought.

On the Monday evening before the Sullivans were due to return John heard a sharp rap on the door. "Not those Witnesses again!" he cursed as he switched off the television. At the door stood a tall grey-haired man in a dark blue suit, who identified himself as a detective-sergeant from the local constabulary.

"Mr. Cranshaw?" he enquired. And upon affirmation, "Sorry to trouble you sir, but may I come in for a moment?" No! Someone must have seen him making a fool of himself next-door: how would he deal with the shame at church?

'I'm sorry to be the bearer of bad tidings, sir – but I have to tell you that your neighbours, Mr and Mrs Sullivan, were involved in a tragic fatal accident in Portugal yesterday evening.'

John slumped into a chair: "No, it can't be – there must be some mistake – They're due back tomorrow – "

"I'm afraid the only way they'll be coming back will be in their coffins," the sergeant responded grimly.

It would be about six months later that John received the phone call from the Sullivan's solicitors. It was their duty to inform him that he was to be left a large sum of cash from their estate, running into 4 figures it seemed. He sat rooted to the chair for a long time – how could it be? They had hardly spoken, and all those thoughts he had harboured against them over the years… It was then that he realised his conscience would never let him rest. He would always be a slave to his misgivings.

It was a bright spring morning that penetrated the dim curtains, and allowed the calm blonde nurse to busy around John in Lewisham ward of the General. His injuries were not life-threatening, but he'd had a lucky escape. The Meadowcroft bungalow had been broken into. All the new fixtures, fittings, and furniture John had invested in had been wrecked, and a large sum of cash stolen. In the process of the trashing the intruder had come across John asleep in bed and subjected him to a violent assault that left him with severe concussion and a dislocated shoulder as well as superficial scrapes and bruising.

" – And I never wanted that money anyway!" he regretted to himself. The Jacksons who had moved into Guy's house hadn't heard a thing – no wonder with all the noise they made night and day. Not like the Sullivans – <u>they</u> had standards.

'I tried to defend myself but he just went berserk and wrecked the place, probably on drugs. No, I didn't get a good look at him, wearing a balaclava and wielding a baseball bat. I tried to stop him, but he fixed me up proper – he'd gone when I came round,' he explained to the implacable nurse. Maybe it was divine retribution he cogitated sadly. Since receiving the unexpected windfall, he had been living with the guilt that haunted him by day and kept him awake at night. "No, he just vanished…like a thief in the night," he added as the nurse switched out the light.

PESCE D'APRILE

Delighted with Malcolm and the honeymoon, and having already visited the pasticceria, Laura found herself virtually skipping along the Via Santa Lucia. She felt blessed as she turned her face towards the warming sun of an Italian primavera. She couldn't stop smiling, life was to be explored, sampled and enjoyed in all its multiple complexities.

She had met Malcolm a mere six months earlier and from the start they had clicked. Physiologically chalk and cheese, they nevertheless possessed a rapport beyond imagining. He was tall and skinny whereas she was short and dumpy, she was ebullient and effusive, he was quiet and introspective; he sported a pale Norse pasty pallor while she possessed dark hair and olive skin; she had sultry dark brown eyes, his an incandescent blue; yet, as everyone knows opposites attract. Dissimilar they may have appeared but their spirits found perfect alignment. He was kind and caring and the couple complemented each-other ideally. Both family and friends had warned against premature involvement, but the pair knew what they wanted. The whirlwind romance culminated in the wedding and subsequent honeymoon in southern Italy. They were staying at Sorrento and were taking a final glimpse of Naples prior to their return. Malcolm proved generous to a fault, he had treated her to restaurants and bistros where of an evening she'd been serenaded by guitar, mandolin and even a saxophone –now she wanted to repay his kindness.

He'd taken her to the islands of Procida, Capri, and Ischia: they had visited Positano (the artist's haven), sipped limoncello at Amalfi, strolled the gardens at Ravello where on sultry evenings classical musicians perform Wagner on the cliff high above the waves; they were astonished by Pompei and Herculaneum, and mesmerized by the magical Greco-Roman ruins of Palazzo degli Spiriti as they sat gazing out to sea from the Punta panoramico di Marechiaro. With just a couple of days to go – she would surprise him by cooking them a Neopolitan dish, Sea Bass alla Florentina. With Malcolm's love of seafood she opted for a fish dish. A fish soup for starters, followed by her piece de la resistance. She had seen the recipe (on line from Guida De Laurentiis) and it appeared simple enough, he would be impressed.

She was headed for the famous fish market of Porta Nolana; she passed Via Toledo that led to the Spanish Quarter and then the cobbles of the centro storico. There, she was struck by the local chatter, exuberance and camaraderie of passers-by: here a weeping child consoled by a young woman, there two elderly gents conversing calmly on a park bench. She sailed past Piazza del Plebiscito to her left, and San Giacomo with the old town-hall and university, and when from Via Medina she spied the church towers of Chiesa Santa Maria and Incoronatella she knew she was close to her destination. She navigated the wide Corso Umberto 1 and entered the ancient gateway (she could have followed her nose).

There it was, spread wide before her: rows of stalls beset with bunting, brimming with the most comprehensive range of fruits of the ocean: oysters, shrimps and squids, the colours of black and pink nestled beneath a dousing water-spray. Deep red lobsters rubbed shoulders with octopus that lay alongside bass, sawn-off swordfish and wriggling eels in pans; anchovies and sardines were flanked by an assortment of shellfish and callamari. Cockles and clams, mussels and monkfish accompanied elegant rows of cod, trout, sole, haddock and whiting. The centrepiece was reserved for two giant tuna who reposed within an encircling ring of split lemons and ice. And everywhere, the fresh tang of the sea. To compliment this marine extravaganza were streets of further stalls swaying beneath fresh fruit, vegetables, meats, cheeses, breads and dolce…pastry and poultry…leather goods and smuggled cigarettes, clothes, bags of gnocchi, olives, umbrellas, hanging hams and shoes.

Excitedly she had returned to Sorrento keeping distance between Malcolm and the fish! He had retired to a bar to 'absorb some local flavour' and alone in the self-catering apartment she could hardly wait to begin. Following the recipe from her phone, she rigidly kept to the instructions. The fish she had already rinsed and placed in the oven for a quarter of an hour – although she thought there was something odd about its appearance, it was not dissimilar to the monkfish she had added to the soup. Then to the recipe: 'Wipe pan with paper towel, heat 3 tablespoons olive oil over medium heat. Add garlic, toms, water, parsley, quarter t-spoon salt, half t-spoon pepper, and simmer for 10 mins. Add basil and heat for 2mins, serve immediately. She was in time to slip into a pink frock, apply fresh lipstick, and open a bottle of Pallagrello Bianco before Malcolm returned. She hoped the wine would be compatible with the Peroni or Moretti already beneath his belt.

The meal was rather marred by the couple finding the fish somewhat unpalatable. 'Loved the soup, but this fish…it's a bit chewy! Where did you get the recipe? ' She came clean, admitting to the recipe and the secret acquisition of ingredients…'Sorry darling, no way Sea Bass! Much too tough! But don't worry, nice thought.'

Alighting onto the platform at Naples for the return flight to Gatwick, Laura realised the station was close to the fish market. 'Let's go along, Babe – it's just a couple of streets away, and we have hours before the flight?' With assistance they located the market, where in the shadows behind the counter was the stallholder. Sensing discord, he assumed a weak smile as he called 'Buongiorno' across rows of grey mullet that peered mournfully from beneath vibrant sprays of parsley. To Laura's tale of woe he responded with: 'Alora, mi dispiace …ma what date was it yesterday?' 'Er not sure…' Malcolm answered checking his phone, ' but what's that got to do with it?' he demanded, taking the offensive. (Malcolm protecting his woman displayed a side new to Laura). She asked : 'But what fish was it you sold me?' The man looked towards his shoes and mumbled: 'Squalo.' 'Squalo, squalo…that's oh, um, …<u>shark</u>? You gave me shark, no wonder it was tough! You wretched man…' 'Yesterday was the first of April,' Malcolm affirmed, to which the storeman burst out laughing. ' Si, primo d'aprile! Well it was not bass, but pesce d'aprile!! Mama mia! Yes, very sorry, piacente, piacente… Now I buy us drinks – show I sorry – you – follow with me please…'

After a brief nod to his compatriot on the stall he set off at a fair pace, the couple in his wake. Along backstreets they sped, down narrow alleys, across a piazza and into Via Bisignono and Bar Seventy: a small inn, where Guiseppe the owner/manager greeted them by the door. In the cosy plush interior the bemused pair were treated to cocktails, including some remarkable gin & tonic mixes; later Malcolm approvingly surveyed their colourful surroundings from the rim of a glass of special craft brew. The bar was adorned in a retro style of no particular era and bathed in a soothing purple haze. There were free nibbles on the tables, and the excellent club sandwiches and drinks were on the stallholder - Franco, who seemed to have an accessible grasp of English. He was able to convey via broken dialect and hand gestures that it was customary in Italy to play tricks on people on the first of April, but here this was known as 'pesce d'aprile' (April Fish).

After the second cocktail, Laura felt ready to forgive Franco and after the third the sun was shining once more…'Now I take you to Napoli Centrale…', asserted Franco. The three strolled towards the station in a rather felicitous frame of mind.

PORTOFINO

Lyrics to the popular song *Love in Portofino* hold for many a certain nostalgic resonance; for, as suggested they found love in this 'jewel' of the Italian Riviera. The picturesque fishing port of Portofino can be found in the Italian region of Liguria, which spreads from Tuscany to the southern French border: the coastline boasts stunning scenery though this is often rugged and steep. Brits have enjoyed the enchanting delights of Portofino in substantial numbers since the early 19th century. Although numerous and colourful celebrities 'borrow' this tiny enclave for brief nuptial ceremonies, there is far more to discover along the Riviera di Levante than a romantic hideaway.

According to Pliny the Elder, Portofino was founded by the Romans and was originally named Portus Delphini (the Dolphin Port) –due to the large number of dolphins that inhabited the northern Tyrrhenian Sea region. The name strictly translates as the 'fine port'. In the year 986 the village gained a mention in a *diploma* by Adelaide of Italy. Adelaide was the second wife of the Holy Roman Emperor Otto the Great. As empress, she was probably the most prominent woman of the 10th century – named among the Christian saints of the Middle-Ages. She was associated with the Benedictine Abbey and commune at Cluny in Burgundy, and pressed for fundamental change to monasticism and ecclesiastical reform. She was devoted to the peace and religious culture of Central Europe.

Legend has it that Giustino (Justin) and St Prospero, escaping Spanish persecution, arrived in Liguria with the ashes of three martyrs: Bishop Fruttuoso and the two deacons Eulogio and

Augurio. During the sea passage to Italy, Giustino had a vision where he was visited by a heavenly angel who informed them they would be conducted to an impressive mountain retreat where a dragon lived in a cave. But Giustino was not to be afraid as the martyr's power would drive the beast from its lair. They were told they would find a source of water under a large rock, and there they should build their church. Sailors probably reinforced this legend of a fire breathing, intimidating, dragon in order to keep the water source for themselves.

A further legend concerns the spirits of lost loves: during the night of St John (June 24th) upon the Portofino mountain at the crossing of four paths the spirits of lovers, whose destiny was that they should remain apart, are reunited. It is possible to obtain the magical oak oil (olio di rovere) – a special unguent whose powers come from this special night. The perfumed ointment must be gathered between the first and last strokes of midnight, and is supposed to possess magical qualities.

Nearby, the magnificent Abbey of San Fruttuoso di Capodimonte (a medieval strong-hold) forms part of Portofino's National Park along with the commune of Santa Margherita Ligure, and can only be reached by descending a steep track from the mountain above. It is in this region that the Mediterranean whispers the lyrics of its celebrated bard Eugenio Montale a native of Liguria. His poem 'Cuttlefish Bones' was dedicated to what the Romans called 'our sea' (the Mediterranean). As we approach we may be reminded of his verse:

> *'Here was the dreamed-of homeland rising from the waves*
> *Emerging from confusion, here was clarity*
> *The exile was re-entering his uncorrupted country'*

The best way to see the Abbey (Abbazia di San Fruttuoso) is to approach from the sea (as is the case with St Marks Square in

Venice). Che bella vista ! The abbey fronts the luminous waters of the Mediterranean and was built by Greek monks in the 10th century, rebuilt 100 yrs later, and renovated many times until the 16th cent. The edifice was named after the martyr Bishop Fruttuoso, who was killed in Tarragona in Catalonia in 259 AD during the eighth persecution of the Christians under emperor Valerian. Legend has it, Fruttuoso appeared before five monks telling them where to bury his remains – which today rest inside the church. Two-levels of cloisters and arcades form the impressive layers of the building. For centuries the Abbey was under the rule of the Doria (an influential Genoese family from the twelfth to the sixteenth centuries who were connected with the Crusades; and a Doria commanded 5000 French bowmen at the battle of Crecy).

The Doria tomb lies in the Abbey crypt. The tiny bay is overlooked by a square tower at one wing of the Abbey, built by the Doria in 1550 to withstand Turkish raids. After 1229 Portofino became part of the Republic of Genoa, with its natural harbour and fleet of fishing boats. In 1409 it was sold to the Republic of Florence by Charles VI of France – but when he was ousted the town was returned. It contained a Fief of families in the 15th cent such as the Fieschi, Spinola, Adorno and Doria. In 1815 Portofino became part of the Sardinian kingdom, and from 1861 joined unified Italy. During the late 19th century wealthy European tourists were welcomed as they arrived by horse and cart via Santa Margherita Ligure. By the 1950s expensive holiday homes and tourism began to replace fishing as a form of revenue, and the attractive pastel ex-fisherman's houses along the waterfront assumed the mantle of restaurants, bars and cafes.

Portofino is one of the iconic fashion capitals for high-end designer boutiques, and also arts and crafts. Dining in exclusive restaurants includes traditional cuisine and wine – where dishes of homemade pasta and pesto sauces mingle with veal or seafood. There are also more casual eating venues, all with stunning views. Wine has been produced for centuries from Etruscan and Roman times, some vineyards being only accessed by boat. Popular table wines include the Bardellini variety (despite having once been described as 'a touch rubbery on the nose, with a classic hint of pencil eraser'). Other extremely palatable beverages include the Laura Aschero Vermentino, the Benanti Bianco and the Bisson Abissi Spumante.

Regular tours and ferries run between Portofino, Castello Brown, Santa Margherita Ligure and Camogli during the season of April-September. Overlooking Portofino, from its lofty ridge, perches Castillo Brown: a harbour defence until the 15th century and today a museum. Diving is a popular pastime, and in the small bay that fronts the San Fruttuoso Abbey, between the villages of Camogli and Portofino, a statue of Christ of the Abyss may be encountered at a depth of 17 metres. This was placed there in 1954 to protect fishermen and in memory of Duilio Mercante. Mercante, alongside Ferraro is considered the founding father of underwater diving education. The figure is a sculpture by Guido Galletti of a benedictory Christ looking heavenwards with an opened-armed sign of peace.

The tiny village of Camogli (today not so tiny having spread up the shore slopes above the harbour), lies in the direction of Genoa and is slightly more laid-back than either Portofino or Santa Margherita Ligure. Bordineto, a mountain village 25 km inland with a ruined castle sitting in the centre, is enclosed in spectacular scenery rich with mushrooms, chestnuts, raspberries and local cheeses. Also Bussana Vecchia is worthy of a visit, nestling hills where flowers are grown for export: a former ghost town, today the hamlet is a flourishing artist's colony. 16th century Castello Brown, is renowned for its hotels and shops, and an easy walk along from Portofino Piazzetta (the castle itself casting its shadow from above). In Portofino, the oratory of Santa Maria Assunta is a marvellous example of gothic architecture. Visit the main church of St Martin (12th cent), and also that of St George (housing some of the saints relics). The coast is dotted with picturesque beaches of which Paraggi is the closest – yet nearby are Camogli, Chiavari, Lavagna and Sestri Levante - each possessing their individual charm.

Perhaps lesser known connections to Portofino are the 1950s ballad 'Love in Portofino' a favourite of many crooners from Andrea Boccelli to Paul Anka; Rex Harrison owned a villa there (named after the patron saint of actors – San Genesio); Portofino has spurred enthusiasm for a replica sea-front at Chiba Japan and at Orlando Florida, and is thought to have inspired Sir Clough Williams Ellis with the italianate hamlet of Portmeirion in Wales. The resort featured in *Top Gear* when Richard Hammond in a 1970s Ferrari Daytona raced against James May in a carbon fibre XSR 1000bhp powerboat from Portofino to St Tropez: the outcome was a close finish with May experiencing delaying turbulence and Hammond the traffic police, however the winner by a whisker was James May in the speedboat. Portofino is twinned with Kinsale in Ireland, Palma in Spain, and Nelson Lancashire in the UK.

A trip to Genoa may reap dividends. The sea-port has much to engender interest, including the Acquario di Genoato where there are 50 tanks of marine species. This is Europe's largest aquarium, and second only to Osaka, it is the third most visited museum in Italy and proves especially interesting to children. The Accademia delle Belle Arti (founded in 1751) is the city's most famous art school and hosts paintings from 16-19th cents, with emphasis on Genovese Baroque artists (such as Artemisia

Gentileschi - an admirer of Caravaggio, also Carbone, Benso, Strozzi and Piola). Castelletto, high above Genoa affords some excellent views of the old city. An ivy-covered medieval house and gardens below Porta Soprana was where Christopher Columbus spent his childhood. Visit the Balzi Rossi (Red Rocks) where prehistoric humans left traces and performed magic rites: here the Caves are carved out of sheer rock and visitors are able to view the many objects found in the region.

Further along the coast towards the French border, through Savona and Imperia, one encounters San Remo (the Riviera di Fiori – the Riviera of Flowers) en route to Monaco. An annual televised song contest takes place in San Remo, and this was where Andrea Boccelli became popular in 1995 with the song *Con Te Partiro* (the famous Tuscan tenor recorded a concert at Portofino in 2013).

Though not contemplating marriage, there is much to occupy the imagination among these charming hills overlooking the Gulf of Genoa. It is not obligatory to tie the knot in order to enjoy the hidden treasures of this unspoilt corner that is quintessentially Italian.

PRONTO SOCCORSO

Shafts of sunlight pierced the tiny cabin windows of the 737 as it wheeled in a 90 degree arc and swooped towards Pescara airport. Below, flashes of brilliance lit up the twinkling blue Adriatic. So began an ambitious journey which was to encompass a majority of the colourful and diverse regions of Italy: in these days of acronyms it became known as our IGT (Italian Grand Tour). The first trip to "the Boot" for 2006, it was pleasing to leave the blustery March winds of Essex far behind. It was a vacation come property-hunt.

Within two weeks we were to travel the peninsular in a vast loop; heading first south, then across the instep and up north close to the Tyrrhenian coast, a short detour to Emilia Romagna, across Tuscany to the Marche and back to the Abruzzo our starting point. Although 1000+ kilometres were to be covered in this epic journey, sufficient pit-stops along the route had been built into our itinerary - necessitating about 300 kilometres on the heaviest days between rests. Places of especial interest had been selected along the way with a variety of carefully chosen b&bs selected for respite. Our most relaxing and longest sojourn was to be a 4-night stay in Florence where friends would provide a pleasant interlude, before proceeding east across the mountains to the Marche and returning south to the airport.

The trip had been organised with military precision to the nth degree - every eventuality had been allowed for. To ensure nothing could possibly upset such a finely tuned mission, a campaign map was blue-tacked to the kitchen wall denoting major ports of call with red bullet points: Lists were written and re-written as down to the last detail everything to be included was accounted for. But, of course, life allows us to ride but briefly upon a blissful cloud of delusion before the inevitable bumpy landing.

Peering down, the familiar coastline of Abruzzo came into view adorned with rows of regimented multi-coloured bathing huts that stood as sun-kissed sentinels along the sandy shoreline. Then we were skimming the runway prior to another smooth landing upon the warm tarmac with the congenial small airport awaiting us. "Passengers are reminded to keep their seat-belts fastened until the plane comes to a standstill" came the warning, then: "The captain and crew wish you a pleasant stay in Italy, thank you for flying Ryan Express Airways." Thus the saga began.

The following day our schedule allowed little time to digest breakfast, before we were chaperoned by a contact to visit three or four properties in the region. During one of these forays, we were accompanied by the owner as well as the agent. The senora seemed a nice lady and was constantly chattering away to us and we even got the gist of some of it. Unfortunately she was more entertaining than her property - a vacant shell in need of more care and attention than a large cornetto on a sunny day. Despite a tempting price adjustment, there was no way we were interested in this isolated cowshed -notwithstanding the spectacular views it afforded across open countryside spreading out across the deep lush green valley to the stunning backdrop of the Maiella mountains. Keen to move on to other viewings but with no wish to offend our garrulous host, I faked mild interest with occasional questioning as to the viability of the residence and even decided to take a couple of token camera shots, essentially of the panoramic views.

This casual philanthropic aside proved my literal downfall;

peering through the lens I overlooked a coil of rusty wire at my feet which had become imbedded in the unkempt grass of the property's attendant land and fell heavily to the turf. Failing to free my left foot from the wire my shoulder hit the ground with a resounding thump whilst at the same time twisting my left knee and foot. The heavy thud, that rocked the landscape and reverberated around the adjacent mountain range, ensured the attention of my companions. Feeling a prize loon, I scrambled to a vertical state and casually brushed myself down whilst stoically rejecting suggestions that I should have my throbbing limb inspected by professionals. Dismissing the nagging pain, I hobbled aboard the range-rover eager to re-enter the fray. It was during the night however that despite painkillers it proved unbearable, and Dee cut through the restrictive bonds to reveal my foot a deeper blue than the shirts of Forza Azzuro.

My ankle having doubled in size the next day, I decided to follow advice and pay a visit to the local hospital in Chieti. Anyone who has been unfortunate enough to visit a hospital where no English is spoken (even by the doctors) will instantly sympathise with my plight. Initially, I was given a number and forced to wait in the steamy over-crowded waiting room. Numbers were allocated to patients in the *pronto soccorso* (casualty department) according to the severity of complaint: judging by the list of available options on a nearby wall-chart I was to become very intimate with this room and its environs. After a couple of hours my number was hailed over a loud-speaker and I was ushered through an adjacent pair of swing doors. (Despite noticing many disappearing through this entrance I had spied very few returning).

Shunted and shepherded unsteadily around departments by stone-faced white-coated orderlies, whose pidgin English I answered with pidgin Italian, I was probed, prodded and pinched all around the lower part of my troublesome limb. Eventually they took pity on me (or were anxious to speed up the process and take a siesta) and entrusted me with a wheel-chair. Grunts, groans and guffaws accompanied these procedures (not merely from myself) around a variety of locations on the ground floor of the hospital. After about an hour they became bored and directed me to make an appointment to return the following day for x-rays, after re-strapping the ankle in yards of unforgiving webbing that would have done justice to a Sumo-wrestler's arm-lock.

Not having the slightest clue as to the results of any possible diagnosis, I limped back an hour later to the almost deserted waiting-room. By now it was dark outside and as I would find driving a "bind" (not to mention blind, with no idea in which direction our agiturismo was located) we hit upon the idea of requesting (if it would not inconvenience our hosts) they might call at the hospital and we could then follow them back in the Nissan. Sure enough within a half-hour the brothers Luigi and Salvatore made an impressive entrance, emerging from the swing doors like a pair of Mafia hit-men adorned in dark suits and even darker sun visors and carrying a brief-case large enough to accommodate a Kalashnikov sub-machine gun. They wouldn't allow me to drive and insisted on me going with one whilst the other followed in the hire car. At midnight we were treated to a 4-course dinner, with fine red wine of the Abruzzo fussed over by la mamma.

My stay was more brief on the second appointment at Chieti hospital, this time I hung around for a mere two hours. Shunted perilously along endless corridors, ascending and descending suspect elevators, and crashing through swing doors in my wheel-chair I moved through various departments or waited for long periods in cool clinical corridors. Eventually I ended up on a wheeled-bed in a department specialising in plaster casts and bandaging; where the half dozen staff were kept gainfully employed over a serious hand of poker. Politely interrupting the cards from time to time I was able to practice my meagre Italian. Eventually, realising that my interruptions were costing them too many euros, I found myself grudgingly attended to by a guy who wanted to add to his English vocabulary of' 'How are you?' and 'You German?

He seemed a cheerful sort of guy and with smiles and alacrity began to tightly bandage my aching limb. He had obviously learnt his art to perfection as he held my leg in his vice-like grip and wound and re-wound the restricting material upon my left foot with unforgiving panache. It was then that, suffering from shock, a lack of fluency in the italian language was found wanting. Fearing my numb limb was in danger of being tornique-d straight through, in an attempt to make him release the pressure in deep anguish I cried out 'piu stretto, piu stretto!' Grinning the guy, eager to oblige, nodded furiously and carried on binding inconceivably tighter than ever. It was only later as I hobbled around my room in the agriturismo that my error dawned on me. In my traumatized state, I had inadvertently instructed the obliging hospital orderly to apply the bandage *tighter*, what I should have said was 'troppo stretto' – *too tight!*

Despite conceding valuable time from our itinerary we were able to proceed on our journey omitting one or two places of interest in order to make up time, and we headed south for Puglia.

QUESTIONS

Hilda was tired of life, her life anyhow. It hadn't always been that way, but inevitable advancing years and circumstance had produced a dreary *Weltschmerz* cocktail. She felt trapped in the apartment block, where often the lift was out of action and she had to clamber to the fourth floor weighed down with shopping. She dreamt of living in a small terrace or semi with kindly neighbours. Here nobody spoke from one week to the next, and you were fortunate to be rewarded by a conversation with the neighbourhood cat.

She arrived at the lift at the same time as Madiar from the flat above. 'Madiar – my, but what a young man you are now! – it seems like only yesterday you were at school. How's your mum these days?' she asked feeling guilty for not having visited her. Questions, always questions, 'without questions there'd be no conversation at all. So many questions – but who will answer?' she mused.

'She's ok,' was the terse response. He looked at Hilda as though for the first time, thinking she's really quite sweet. 'Fourth floor isn't it?' he queried, taking charge of the press-buttons.

Hilda left the lift with a brief nod in his direction: 'Say hello to your mother for me', she threw over her shoulder.

'I will – I'm on my way now', the lad said as he pulled the outer door closed, shut the gates and pressed the button.

'Nice boy. Must look up the meaning of his name' she pondered, as she heard the lift continue its grating ascension.

Hilda closed her door behind her and sighed. 'At least the lift was in action today, my bags were heavy' she thought, without remembering what she'd been to the shops for.

**

Madiar paused outside his mother's flat, key in hand. The door was ajar and he heard raised voices inside. Withdrawing his hand, he listened intently; a man was speaking with his mother, questioning her. 'No I don't know where he is, nor when I will see him again – why all these questions?': questions of a disquieting vagueness as from someone in authority. Then it was his mothers turn, 'Why is he wanted? What has he done?' And then with emphasis, 'How do I know who you are? It's easy enough to fake an ID card.' Madiar withdrew silently, taking a couple of backward steps as he heard his mothers raised voice, 'No, you're not going into my sons room. Do you have a warrant?' He'd heard enough as he backed against the handrail. Should he go up or down? Tentatively he peered over and down towards the street where a man stood in the shadows by the mail-boxes. Glancing towards the descending stairs he decided on that option. Adrenalin pumping to full velocity and no longer the kind person who chatted pleasantly with his mother's neighbour in the lift, he hastily retreated and dashed on tiptoe to the lower floor; to the flat directly beneath his mother's and knocked upon the door.

'Who is it?' Hilda called from behind the door

'Miss Hilda – its me, Madiar.'

'Madiar?' she said, letting him in straightaway. 'What's the matter?' She was more surprised than alarmed.

'Nothing, sorry, it's rather a tricky situation'. He was forced to think quickly, 'You see there's this woman I was going out with but now... it's a long story, but I just don't want to see her anymore. Could I ask a favour, can I see if she is outside in the

149

street?' Without waiting for a reply he passed through the rooms to the front window. Hilda marvelled at how he knew the layout, until she remembered his mother lived in an identical apartment. He stopped a yard from the window and slowly peered down, hastily drawing back as he spotted a police uniform alongside a double-parked car by the entrance.

'What have you done?' Hilda dreaded the answer.

His face muscles slackened, his mask slipped and he adopted a defeated expression. 'I'm not going to hurt you, I promise. Just keep your voice down.'

Hilda made a bolt for the door, but he was too quick for her. He placed his hand over her mouth and whispered in her ear: 'Please. I'm not a crook'. Then he took a gun from his trouser pocket.

'Well, what are you then?'

'Sorry I've ended up in your home, but there was nowhere to go.'

'I'm expecting my son this evening,' sobbed Hilda, full of the knowledge she hadn't contacted him for a month.

'Where's your television?' Madiar enquired. Hilda looked in the direction of the kitchen. Pocketing his gun Madiar fiddled with the remote until he found the menu list. Beads of sweat stood out on his forehead. Hilda wrung her skirt in her fingers and wept with frustration in her anguish, she would like to be in control of her destiny just once. She wanted to hurt him, pounce on him – do something. 'Are you going to kill me?'

He gave her the kind of look one gives someone caught blaspheming in church, 'What – are you joking? I'm not a murderer!'

'Oh, you just happen to have a gun…'

Madiars face clouded over: 'It's not my fault there's a war out there.'

Hilda felt herself beginning to doubt his sanity. 'A war?'

'Yes, a war isn't only planes dropping bombs and armies invading lands. War is you too.'

Through clenched teeth she stuttered, 'What do you know about me, about the life I lead?' She calmed a little, 'What will you do when my boy arrives?'

'He won't arrive: because you are going to call him and tell him not to come.' Following an awkward pause, 'He's not coming is he?' She shook her head and fell in a lifeless heap upon the floor, feeling her cheeks blush at being found out in the falsehood.

The TV news mentioned a local murder involving a terrorist group and an uncovered stash of arms. Images flashed by of a person being arrested and bundled into a police vehicle. Madiar's face took on a grimace while an appalled Hilda huddled deeper into her chair.

The news bulletin rambled on: 'wanted for questioning', 'helping with their enquiries'; to be or not to be?

**

Days passed, eventually Madiar allowed Hilda to go shopping – he wasn't sure why he trusted her. Maybe it was because he'd once fallen asleep and she hadn't left the flat.

And she had told him: 'You needn't worry. No-one ever comes here.'

Then there was the time she'd returned from a shopping trip to discover two strangers at her door. Although she felt her legs trembling she took a deep breath and went into action.

'Can I help you?'

'Do you live here?'

'Yes, I live here. What are you doing outside my apartment?'

151

she replied, staggering beneath the weight of her shopping. The eyes of the two men met briefly.

'Police, madam. We'd like to ask you a few questions.'

'Me, why, have I done something?'

'Not at all, we're just gathering information.'

'Ask away,' said Hilda placing her bags on the floor. The speaker looked rather confused, 'Has anything strange happened over the last few days?'

'What do you mean,' she said, eyeing the two men as though they had the plague.

'In this apartment block I mean,' added the man at a loss, 'Have you noticed any strange movements, people you haven't seen before?'

'Well, the cat downstairs has given birth again and the kittens are everywhere. But you are getting me worried now. What are you talking about?'

The other man shook his head as if to say 'we're wasting our time' and responded with 'That'll be fine. Thanks for your time' and the two walked off.

Behind the door Madiar who had been listening in trepidation breathed a heavy sigh. She entered, slammed the door and fell into a chair, exhausted. Madiar comforted her.

'You did smashing, you were absolutely great!' He squeezed her hand. She felt proud and exhilarated. He helped her lie on her bed and retrieved her medicine when she requested it (ten drops in water). Madiar sat by her bed and held her hand as he talked to her. 'Do you know what a risk you've taken. The mess you've got yourself into?'

She answered in a matter of fact tone 'I was terrified they would kill you, you'd probably use that gun of yours and they'd have shot you.'

The following day, Madiar said with conviction 'Now, I must

go. I've stayed here long enough.'

'Please don't go, not just yet. They may still be outside. Stay here, I'll look after you...'

'You know that's not possible,' he told her gently, 'there are people I have to meet up with. Sooner or later they'll come here: but you can help me, you can do me one last favour.' Her face lit up and she freed her hand from his grasp: 'Tell me what I need to do'.

**

Madiar smiled when he saw the new laptop. He fiddled with it and then produced a pen-drive, and became engrossed in the text. Hilda watched him as if he was an alchemist obtaining gold from base metal. 'Now, I'm waiting for a message,' he said.

**

A month later Hilda is standing outside Madiar's mother's flat. Beyond the open door she is listening intently to his mother speaking on the hall phone: 'No, I don't believe it, there must be some mistake, shot down by a police marksman, where, how... not my son?' Then a pause, filled with violent sobbing, 'I told you before I don't know anything...questions, questions – don't you people do anything but ask questions?'

RIVERS

We may reflect upon the inspiring lyrics of Julie London's 'Cry me a river', Paul Robeson's 'Ole man river' or simply 'The River' by Bruce Springsteen; each of these songs evoke the magnetic force of mystical waterways. To indulge in this magic one need not travel far. The most casual of observers, who takes the time to stroll the banks of any of our native water courses, cannot fail to appreciate the engaging appeal drawing him to the riverside.

Despite much of the original canal system falling into disuse, assorted barges may be spotted plying their ponderous routes along our forgotten tributaries, indeed the river boat is proving a compelling pastime for those wishing to escape. Long lazy days may be spent drifting through open countryside at a contented pace, far from the bustle and smell of our congested motorways. Passing vessels may be hailed as they glide by, or a brief interlude may be pirated to moor alongside a fleet of canal-boats riding the tide to revel in the camaraderie of fellow salts. Hour after placid hour are to be treasured, chugging through forgotten hamlets and tranquil backwaters of our rural landscape that provide an idyllic setting for reflection and quiet contemplation. Then to meander with engine silent through old grey-stone bridges or overhanging boughs, with perhaps a welcome lunch break at a riverside pub. Such are the delights awaiting the quasi-mariner.

An enthralling sight to capture the imagination is the obligatory cluster of multi-coloured sails lapping contentedly at anchor, or tacking with the breeze on many of our river estuaries. Energetic types, from bathers to intrepid water-skiers and resolute oarsmen ply the surface, while further along, in the calmer reaches, a patient angler awaits the call to action - his eyes idly following a convoy of soft brown ducks gently riding the rippling surge. Waterways that pass through our towns and cities are often adorned with floating restaurants or nightclubs. From dusk these glow through the dark, their radiant light reflecting a kaleidoscope of colour which ripples in dappled reflections that dance across the surface of the water, perhaps in tune to onboard music.

What is taking place beneath all this human endeavour? A myriad life forms are busy below the raging torrent or gently flowing water-course. Sticklebacks and minnows move in shoals close to the banks, water boatmen and beetles dart and scurry while mosquitoes lazily kiss the moving surface. Further out roach, tench or trout glide between unseen water grasses feeding on life-sustaining plankton, grubs and foliage. Perhaps the busy dipper darts from boulder to boulder beneath the cascading current; or maybe a leaping salmon will break the stillness, to fall back to the water with the resounding smack of re-entry. Perhaps a voracious pike is stalking unwitting prey in the murky depths. A sudden scuffle at the water's edge could reveal the whereabouts of the cunning water rat chasing an eel, or the otter or stealthy beaver will endeavour to shore up its muddy defences. The sudden flash of bright blue among the elders on the far bank may catch the eye as an ever watchful kingfisher streaks across the scene.

Above and below, the river supports a diversity of life forms along its rambling course; as it progresses from the early droplets of a mountain spring through the placid slowly meandering stream to the wide and indomitable force of mighty currents, as it finally disgorges its wrath into the engulfing ocean. Such force has been harnessed by man, and our weirs and water-mills, often still capable of refining corn to flour remain picturesque as well as practical testimony to our heritage. It is not widely known, for instance, that Richard Arkwright's spinning frame patented in the 18th century was powered by water, using the latent power of the relentless river.

Despite such idyllic references, it cannot be overlooked that pollution is a current problem for ghillies and town councils nationwide. From factory effluent and the perpetual detritus associated with modern living, such as Coke-cans, supermarket trollies and non-biodegradable plastics, to vast clusters of choking weed – all are detrimental to the smooth-running of our waterways. Such flotsam and jetsam present a continual challenge to the maintenance of a healthy balance of river life. The Thames is today clearer than it has been for over a century, whereas the Severn estuary constantly makes the headlines as an ecological disaster region. Much-needed money for conservation primarily finds its way to building theme-parks or ever-larger car-parks ahead of the protection and upkeep of our rivers and their environment.

Rivers the writer has known intimately include 'Old Father Thames', the Nene which crosses Northamptonshire and the River Wye on the Welsh border. Sometimes pretentious sometimes serene, but always august, the Thames holds many quiet memories for me within its grey surging fathoms. I recall the proud warships 'President', 'Chrysanthemum' and Nelson's flagship 'Victory' moored alongside the embankment, whose decks became familiar to me as a young rating in the RNVR. Pleasure cruisers ploughing their wake under Tower Bridge and gauche night-club and restaurant crafts clinging tenuously to their moorings come to mind; or the dark sinister barges that glide silently behind diminutive spluttering tugboats moving between their docks and delivery quays; or again, the calm civility of house boats gently nudging sedate moorings further west at Barnes. After Kew, the narrowing river acquires an air of lassitude between its converging banks – with the gay abandon of a woman shedding an over-tight corset as the river begins to assume its rural complexion. Continuing upstream we may meander through Eton, Windsor and Henley, scene of the splendid Royal Regatta held every year since 1839. Henley-on-Thames is close to the river's source in the heart of Oxfordshire (the river runs for over 200 miles and in the process threads its way through 49 locks).

The Thames, referred to as the 'living history of England' is famous for the many interesting bridges which bond north to south along its extensive course: London bridges are particularly notable. Moving against the current, from the central Tower and London bridges (the latter now under American ownership) we arrive at Southwark Bridge the site of Traitors Gate where many lost their heads. Continuing westwards, we pass Blackfriars, Waterloo and Westminster – all city bridges; eventually we reach the suburban fringes of Chelsea, Battersea, Wandsworth and Putney. I fondly recall the spectacle of Boat Race day when annually in a biting March wind, two crews of lusty eights vie for supremacy of the stretch from Putney to Mortlake; where in the company of friends I rowdily, and not strictly soberly, awaited the appearance of the leading 'blue' from around the final bend.

In contrast the Nene is placid and serene as it cuts its irregular course through the flat countryside linking Northampton with Thrapston and Oundle (today the site of a splendid marina) to the north east beside Rockingham Forest. Early memories are of a child, grubby, red-faced and breathless, staring with fascination and awe into the dark void towards the turbulent murky water entrapped between the huge wooden gates, and watching spellbound as the lock-keeper practised his craft. Peering into an empty lock was a daunting experience for a six or seven year-old. Yet on a summer's afternoon, accompanied by a friend or apprehensive relative, I would take tentative steps to the edge of the abyss to peer transfixed towards the turbid water far below. My excitement was heightened when the lock once more filled with the gushing torrent, as thunderous cascades spilled into the vacant chasm and the level gradually rose to meet me. When full the spectacle was much less enthralling, the entrapped tide appearing as a mere extension of the river surface, the innocent ripples concealing any hint of its hidden depths.

The Wye has a chameleon-like quality all its own dependent upon its frequent and varied colour changes. When calm, the water reflects the sky blue canopy – the setting for a thousand jigsaw puzzles, and appears reluctant to reach its destination, as it meanders hither and thither in unhurried softly undulating curves: the surface a smooth sparkling veneer coating its lucid depths. Following torrential rainfall, however, the river is churned and agitated into a sludgy-brown teeming conduit scarred with swirling eddies and dusky backwaters. Swept along on the relentless tide are tree trunks, small trees, mixed debris, even an unfortunate sheep rendered powerless by the swelling advance. At its lowest ebb, such as during the drought of 1989, its force is diminished and it is possible to swim across from Wales to England. That summer we stroked, paddled and floated our way across to where the ghillie's dinghy was moored on the far bank. Thence to return, avoiding submerged boulders and floating shoals of blanket-weed, which clung tenaciously and threatened to punish such audacity by claiming unwary ankles within its slimy fronds, to feel the river's power for at the centre the strong current is in evidence.

This river is a favourite with hikers and canoeists, rambling groups and canoe clubs. Flotillas of canoes may be glimpsed through the trees at the water's edge, often heading towards the welcome of the Boat Inn that nestles the western Welsh bank close to the Forest of Dean. This ancient hostelry marks the climax for participants in an annual pageant, the local raft race held every May, where colourful floats representing Monmouth businesses are scrambled down-stream. The event is always well attended and proceeds go to charity. The rafts usually consist of imaginatively painted oil-drums harnessed together beneath plastic sun-seats. These often consist of appendaged cardboard or light timber framework representing castle turrets or aircraft fuselages. Many themes are manifest, ranging from King Arthur and World War one monoplanes to South Sea islanders or replica Starship Enterprises. No time or effort is spared on these makeshift craft and their crews. Crowds line the route to cheer on the drenched and weary incumbents who are often bedecked in fancy-dress and wearing thick makeup to match their particular theme. The less adventurous stay with the more practical tee-shirt and jeans, although none are waterproof and a ducking is essential.

There is much compelling attraction to the river scene no matter what the season, but perhaps the least expensive yet thoroughly rewarding is an interlude spent beneath a cool willow at the height of summer, as it trails its drooping boughs in the sultry flow: with time enough to ponder the sights and sounds of the teeming aquatic habitat. Incident and drama are never far away, whether it be the fleeting glimpse of a timid otter or wading heron in the marshy reaches; the sudden splash of a thrusting fly-catching fish; the graceful passage of majestic swans or a nervous darting moorhen; a motorboat propelled at speed that causes momentary turmoil among the natural habitat; lovers punting languidly with all the time in the world; or even the aggrieved fisherman helplessly watching his valuable sandwiches float out of reach, adrift on the restless flux.

SHADOWS

The only sound was the periodic clunk of the French-door caught in a cross breeze. Clouds were gathering and the weather was on the turn. As Earth revolved the sun slowly began to cast lengthening shadows across the unkempt lawn to the eastern aspect. The old house wore an uncared-for look as though apologising for its existence, as it peered reticently through a sombre mask of limp acacias and discoloured rhododendrons shielding it from the common. The dull residence made a mockery of the bright sunlight which despite doing its best made no impression on the dismal discoloured stone cottage. The deep wood formed a suitable backdrop with the leaves of blighted beeches and tired oaks reflecting the last golden rays heralding an early autumn.

The dwelling bore a shy and retiring demeanour, as if, having given its all through long years of service wished to retreat into obscurity. The long soft summer was on the wane and evening chills warned of future stagnation. Some windows stood ajar, some firmly closed. The building appeared abandoned to the occasional walker who passed along the derelict footpath that escorted the rotting rear fence and adjoined the remnants of the sultry beech wood. Such was not the case.

Life had never been the same for Marc since returning from a stint with Special Forces close to the Euphrates in Northern Syria. He'd held down a robust job with promise of an adequate pension and adored his loving wife and kids: what went wrong? Along came the demon drink. At first he had one or two with buddies in the mess – then he kept a bottle of Jack Daniels at home and it all began to spiral out of control. Su had enough and disappeared with the children, when he'd been assigned to Syria, on a trip that was to be his last. Well, what more could you expect from this vale of tears. The swaying door interrupted his fitful dozing. Vaguely scratching at his five o'clock shadow and grasping for the bottle he succeeded in knocking his glass to the floor. Cursing he picked up the fallen tumbler and poured a further generous tot of the tawny liquid. So this was it, all he had to show for 20 plus years of service to the army, his wife and kids, and to society.

But, there it was again, by the door! What was it? Peering tentatively around the room, his eyes were drawn towards the darker recesses he knew contained fallow, stagnant, air. As the evening wore on and shadows usurped sunlight in the dim room his stealthy demons returned. He swore at them but they doggedly remained to torment him. They entered in the shades: he laughed hysterically at that, demons in shades! They wouldn't leave him alone, they pursued him as soon as dusk spread its umber cloak. But shadows were everywhere; even Jesus was shadowed by spies who stirred up the crowd against him. There it was again, in the corner this time; a hideous amorphous shape with a blurred outline. 'Hence, horrible shadow! Unreal mockery, hence! ' quoting Macbeth, he shouted towards the darkening void. He'd tried therapy and although diagnosed with PTSD it provided no comfort.

It had begun in Syria, on that assignment. They'd been undercover close to the holy city of Dur-Saalam. The mission into IS territory had gone like clockwork, and a sultry evening found them enjoying some well-earned R&R. They'd fallen back to Dur-Saalam and Marc and a buddy were sight-seeing among some old temple ruins, where protecting the temple doors were a pair of *shedu* or *lammasu*. These were carved stone blocks depicting an Assyrian deity, a man's head on the body of a winged bull; they stood as sturdy silent sentinels on either side of the massive portals in honour of Ishtar: as night fell they were guarding a final outpost to bygone Mesopotamia. Of course in those days he hadn't known a lammasu from a tiramisu. As they scrambled through the irregular rubble Marc felt the sudden urge to relieve himself, assisted no doubt by the warm beer he'd managed to misappropriate back at base. He completed the task feeling secure beneath the unlit arch. At the moment he was zipping towards respectability, a passing lantern-bearer happened by and light from his flaming torch fell across the vacant doorway. In the brief moment he clearly became aware of staring directly into the shimmering sunken red eyes of the winged beast. Too late he recalled the warning a mate had given that the doors to the temple of Ishtar were zealously guarded.

Returning home following discharge on medical grounds he thought no more on the subject. But it was in the empty house that his nightmares began. Through the gloom, through the half-light, he was certain he was being watched. He saw the same hazy figure in room corners, in doorways, or when entering vacuous spaces. A constant feeling of unease accompanied him, until an indistinct form visited him almost every evening, a creeping sombre figure that seemed crowned in a tall head-dress. At first he blamed a trick of the light, or maybe it was his own shadow. He knew people of the East measured time by the length of their shadow. He tried it, measuring his own shadow; try as he may the result was always the same: whatever time of day, even at noon, it inferred midnight! And it <u>wasn't</u> his shadow, at times he'd been seated when the apparition appeared.

In desperation he decided to study Ishtar and the findings filled him with alarm. He learned that in ancient Mesopotamia, the land between two rivers, Ishtar was a major goddess: the sister of Ereshkigal, queen of the underworld; could he expect any less from the daughter of Sin? She had been worshipped at Ninevah and Erbil; where she was known as the 'Star of Lamentation' who caused brothers on good terms to quarrel and friends to forget friendship. The shedu protected the deity. Could the visitation be some high priest of the goddess sent to avenge the outrage of urinating over a sacred shrine?

Slowly but surely Marc was losing his mind. Even in sleep solace escaped him: He was pursued by nightmares of misshapen ghoulish entities that caused him to wake with a start in a cold sweat. The palliative effect of alcohol merely added to his delusion. He'd read somewhere that students of the occult, after certain progress in the black arts, were compelled to run through a subterranean hall with the devil chasing them. If they ran so fast that the devil only caught their shadow they became first-class magicians, but in the process they would lose all or part of their shadow. So "may your shadow never be less" translated as "may you escape the foul fiend". Well, he had not escaped...

It was cold and damp when they came for him. Tormented in mind body and spirit he mirrored the very cause of his distress, having become a shadow of his former self. Mist blanketed the clammy beech-wood and the few remaining bronze leaves hung with moisture and clung desperately to the withering branches. Was Marc mentally disturbed, or did he actually experience the shades? Do the shadow people exist somewhere? Are they figments of imagination, doorways to and from different planes of existence, or simply shadows?

SMOKE AND MIRRORS

*(a metaphor for a deceptive, fraudulent or insubstantial
explanation or description – any sort of presentation
by which the audience is intended to be deceived)*

Hans and Greta lived with their wicked uncle and uncaring mother in a rambling house close to the village. One fine day, the two golden-haired and rosy-cheeked vertically challenged adolescents wandered out through the gate their careless mother had left unlatched, and into the depths of a cold dark forest full of unnatural sounds that echoed through low twisted trees with gnarled branches and tall ferns. The forest floor was set with hidden vines that tripped them and sent them sprawling so Greta's clean gingham became covered in dust and grime. 'Oh dear, what will mummy say?' they pondered as they realised they were completely lost. Greta sat on a tuffet and sobbed her eyes out: 'Come on you silly m–miss, you've only gone and made your dress dirtier, what are you like!' wailed Hans. 'We really ought to find some shelter before nightfall', he added in his protective practical logical male fashion.

All of a sudden a distant light appeared through the gloom and as the two got closer they saw it belonged to a tumbledown cottage beside a sparkling stream. Smoke rose lazily from a crooked chimney. The miserable miscreants rapped hesitantly on the ancient door whilst trying to ignore the rotting wood that fell from its surface. A grizzled hag of indeterminate years shuffled to the entrance and screamed 'Whadoyouwant?' in raucous tones. 'Er, excuse me but we are lost, could you please show us the way to Much Suffrage in the Wold?' And that was how the waifs met the elderly spinster Heidi. Heidi was rather the worse for wear with a permanent squint, a wart on her nose and a penchant for black pointed hats. If anything, the old cottage was in a worst condition than its owner, listing under subsidence and dry rot – that, along with other deficiencies, provided much work for the handy couple over the ensuing weeks and months. Heidi could see the benefits of feeding the little urchins, especially after she determined their expertise at DIY. She was really very kind to the children and let them play in her large garden and care for the many wild animals that frequented the woods. They fed these assorted mammals and birds, giving each a pet name.

One day whilst shopping for groceries in the local supermarket, they followed the crowds drawn by the music and gaiety to a travelling fair that had come to town. They enjoyed the many attractions and had riotous fun, until they discovered the hall of mirrors where nothing was as it seemed. Poor Greta became frightened as the distorted reflections pulled her out of shape giving her two heads, and Hans a big behind. They ran in panic towards where they thought the entrance had been but became horribly disoriented. Tears of tragic frustration flowed across their plump pink cheeks as they hugged each-other and it dawned on them that they were totally lost in that maze of distorting images.

Suddenly they found themselves entrusted to a jolly red-faced policeman who told them: 'Now, don't you worry your little selves. Dry your eyes, all will be well.' Auntie Heidi was located – promptly arrested and reported to the Child Protection Service for abduction, endangerment and neglect. The two children were returned to their wicked uncle and uncaring mother, and nobody lived happily ever after.

(Moral : Beware of reflecting too much on your own image.)

SPECTRE OF THE LOWER FIFTH

It began innocently enough. School had been particularly tiresome: during English Jenkins caught me reading the 'Beano' behind *The Rise and Fall of the Roman Empire* and made me write out one hundred times 'I must not fiddle while Rome burns'; and Tubs Smith hid my store of conkers in the girls' lavatory. After lunch, Hodgson sent me on an errand to call at Jones' minor's house to collect a sick note, as the malingerer had failed to attend for a couple of days.

The bright sunlight contrasted with my mood, as sweating under my cap and tie I distractedly kicked loose stones along the twisting gravel path that led to the old house. Colonies of hungry gnats hovered in the sultry air. An avenue of verdant shrubbery obscured any view of the building and for a spell obliterated the sun, chilling the air about me. As I rounded the final turn through an entanglement of weary rhododendrons the ugly dwelling towered oppressively over me, casting long shadows across the stony approach.

It was clear that some attention had been paid to the freshly-mown lawns and neat rows of bedding plants; such consideration, however, had not extended to the the residence. The ancient edifice appeared threatening, with its sagging gutters and long flakes of dark green paint that hung in dissolute array from the bleached woodwork. Why hadn't his parents delivered the darned sick-note anyhow?

Maybe they had given up on their wayward offspring. Jones remained one of the most obnoxious conniving school mates it could ever be the misfortune of a luckless pupil to encounter. His

166

family, originally of some substance, had fallen on hard times and, as is the wont with the nouveau riche, were desperately attempting to paper over the broadening gaps between themselves and the other Jones'. Ever the optimist, his father decided to invest the remains of their collateral in a misguided attempt to improve his son's education. Despite early aspirations he had failed miserably to make good and was virtually bottom of the class in all except Chemistry, a subject that for some inexplicable vagary he excelled in.

Jones was a loner, without close friends, who put a brash front on life and relied on a gross bullying attitude to persuade others to his will; his rather overweight stature served to enhance this dominant and bragging demeanor. He had taken to me for no other reason than the fact that our fathers had once played in the same foursome for a round of golf. In the parlance of boys' comics, he was Dennis the Menace of Cannock House School.

On tiptoe, I managed to reach the bell-push barely visible beneath a thick ochre stain. After a brief delay in which I was unsure if the bell was indeed connected, for no sound reached from within, I rapped twice with the aid of an ugly black knocker in the shape of a horned beast. Following an interminable wait, the sagging door groaned aside and in its place stood a wizened gent with the censorious scowl and distinct deportment of a butler. The wretched fellow was a shabby caricature of a manservant, and appeared as though he had just emerged from the pages of Punch.

Having informed this outcast the reason for my visit, I was instructed to wait on the step while he made enquiries within. Minutes passed, and finally the resentful retainer returned and handed me a long buff envelope addressed to the headmaster. I was asked whether I wished to exchange pleasantries with Jones, his condition not being contagious. Apparently the miscreant had suffered a twisted ankle; sustained, I was led to believe during a rather frenetic game of tennis. The wretched fellow further advised me that the injury had been tightly bound and Jones, under mild sedation, awaited my attendance in the games-room below.

Obeying the dour character's instructions, I descended to the basement via a dimly lit flight of stone steps and groped my way along an even more dismal corridor. The only illumination came from two widely spaced gas-jets that hissed menacingly and lazily flickered down at me in a miserable attempt to penetrate the gloom. I suppose in earlier days these subterranean repositories had served as storage units to accommodate the large residence; perhaps serving as wine cellars. My footsteps echoed along that passage yet the sound failing to dissipate, and hovered in the cloying air. Unaware of my bearings, I was able to negotiate the correct door by following the Joplinesque strains of an original recording of 'Tea for Two', projecting from what I later discovered was an antique gramophone. As I peered tentatively around the door into the abyss beyond the melody ended and gave way to a curious scraping, a noise I deduced as the gramophone needle catching the outer rim of the recording.

My first wary steps into that unlit room with its indistinct parameters were immediately followed by a resounding crash that reverberated along the corridor behind me to echo through the great house above. I had inadvertently nudged a pair of billiard cues that had been propped behind the door. The sudden clamour did nothing to reduce my rising sense of apprehension. For anxious moments I was incapable of motion, my breath came in short stabbing gasps. It was as though all the air was being sucked from the atmosphere. I was aware of a deep foreboding coupled with a feeling of being stifled. The hairs at the back of my neck began to tingle as my trembling fingers felt along the wall and eventually discovered the light-switch.

Slowly my eyes accustomed themselves to the dusky atmosphere and, in the muted light provided by a single wall-fitting, I was able to survey the dull interior. I appeared to have entered some sort of labyrinthine pavilion, surrounded as I was by an assortment of large wicker hampers that disgorged an untidy collection of sporting accessories. In one corner slouched a moth-eaten canvas golf bag complete with a mismatched plethora of clubs. To one side, grey cricket pads and weathered bats, tennis nets and unstrung rackets lay in casual abandon where they had burst from their confines. Other hampers disgorged a comprehensive miscellany of sporting bric-a-brac, including cricket stumps, faded and scuffed red balls, lacrosse sticks and a selection of croquet hoops.

Then I saw it. Lying full length on a scrolled Edwardian sofa in the furthest corner of that misty cavern was the most loathsome creature any mind could conjure. The very sight of this apparition made my flesh crawl. I wanted to run, to place as much distance between myself and this ghoul as was humanly possible. Yet I remained riveted to that cold floor as surely as if I had been shaped in stone; frozen in abject terror at the sight of the supernatural form that confronted me. This grotesque manifestation, in no way human, possessed tiny pin-pricks of light at the precise position where human eyes should appear; in total, this entity formed a mocking caricature of mortality.

A gruesome head, resembling a large misshapen football, leered at me across the murky haze. Through the gloom it glowed malevolently whilst emitting a greenish sulphurous glow into the stagnant air. This abomination was imperceptibly swaying from side to side in accompaniment to the scratching gramophone needle. Then came the strangest sound, decidedly more intimidating than any I had hitherto encountered. From the faintest rude chuckle it grew in intensity, from a low growl to a chilling crescendo until the walls resounded to the most demonic guffaw imaginable.

It was then that life returned to my quiescent legs; I turned, floundering into a couple of croquet mallets that clattered to the floor as I dashed headlong for the dim hallway. Eventually I burst into blessed daylight, my face felt warm as I clawed at tenacious cobwebs and stumbled down the steps and away from that dreadful place. I didn't slow until I turned into my street, where I fought to recover my breath and a degree of dignity I was in no way feeling. I arrived home breathless and red-faced, with heart pounding and socks around my ankles. Shaking and embarrassed, I hid in my room to collect myself and called to my mother through the closed door to the effect that I had critical homework to attend to and must on no account be disturbed.

In class the following week I was targeted by a cacophony of snorts and jeers as Jonesie revelled in the limelight. With accustomed bluster he relayed his account of my downfall. Draped over a drooping chaise-longue in that cheerless basement had been an antique tailor's dummy. The head was a discarded hollowed-out pumpkin preserved from Hallowe'en, inside which Jones had lit a candle to heighten the macabre effect. An absence of adequate lighting had completed the hideous illusion. Jones, cowering in a spacious hamper, had orchestrated the insane laughter that had sent me careering out of the house in a fit of hysteria. My ears smarted with the derisive guffaws of Jones and company for a long while after that episode. However, I wonder if he was as smug, or indeed confided in the rest of the class, when later returning home one evening he discovered the two upturned inkwells I had slipped into his satchel…

SPIC AND SPAN

He liked his world neat and tidy, believed in order – 'Order out of Chaos' was his favourite dictum. A place for everything and everything in its place. Of course he wasn't obsessed, despite those little nagging doubts that tormented him of late. Ever since that ad on the telly in fact, something like perfume wasn't it... how did it go? Ah, yes: 'somewhere between love and madness lies obsession!' Well he wasn't in love and the alternative was unworthy of serious consideration.

'Breakfast's ready, dear'. He completed the report in front of him, with marked deliberation squared-off the paperwork on the desk top; placed his pencil eraser next to the box of paper-clips and beside the pencil sharpener in the desk drawer labelled 'miscellany'; positioned his black biro to the right of his red biro; returned his pencil to the perpendicular retainer beside the pens then sat back with a sigh of contentment. Slowly he rose and with customary precision placed the chair squarely beneath the desk, ensuring it formed a direct diagonal with the door-frame, flicked off the light and left the room.

'Tea's getting cold, Alf.' This time his wife's voice reached him in the bathroom above the sound of running water as he methodically rinsed his hands. This action reminded him of an article he'd come across in a psychology journal at his work for a City publisher. 'Now that's obsession!' he mused. The feature had portrayed the case study of a woman who couldn't stop washing and rewashing her hands. As soon as she touched something or completed a chore no matter how clinical, she was compelled to return to the kitchen sink. Her condition had become so chronic that she was seen to go through the motion of hand-washing when far from a water supply. The psychiatrist had labelled her a 'compulsive obsessive'. 'Well, I'm definitely not like that!' observed Alfie as he carefully folded the blue hand-towel without any overlap and positioned it in its location to the right of his wife's pink one.

'Morning dear,' he greeted Norma in the dining-room.

'Morning Alf – tea's getting cold.'

'What day is it today, Norma? Well, it's Tuesday, and what do I have on a Tuesday? I have Oatenbrans.'

'I'm sorry dear, I was sure it was Wednesday.' Norma returned the offending grape-fruit to the kitchen.

'It's alright, I'll get it': Alfie followed his wife and opened a cupboard door. Row upon row of regimented cereal cartons blinked back at him in the bright morning sunlight. There were boxes of EveriBran, FruitiBran, Oatenbrans, Crunchi-Bran, Bran-de-lux, Bixie Wheat and cornflakes, Cheeribyes: Pulverised Wheat and Nut Havoc; all standing to attention in preparation for him to inspect their spines. A fleeting vision of his work-place crossed his mind, with the extensive library: 'Just checking the catalogue of that famous publishing house Fibre and Fibre,' he quipped to himself. 'Now, don't forget I've got that committee meeting tonight, Norma. I'll need my dinner early.' he said, tossing a brief thanks over his shoulder as he briskly left the room.

Norma sat for a while at the table, staring towards the high window but failing to notice the streaks of warm sunlight cascading onto the carpet. Slowly she rose and with a deep sigh began to clear the table. Then she heard the door slam as Alfie departed for the 8.22.

The 8.22 arrived at 8.47. Tempers were short and Alfie wasn't able to get a seat until Thornton Halt, the last scheduled stop before London Bridge. He was forced to spend the time standing in the cramped corridor wedged between two smokers: one legitimate the other not. Mr Legit appeared the more accessible, a grey-looking fellow with standard city-clerk uniform and an unfortunate twitch at the corner of one eye. Alfie glanced in his direction meaningfully a couple of times before uttering 'Mussolini!' in forthright tones.

'Er – I beg your pardon?'

'Mussolini, Il Duce,' Alfie reiterated, 'Now he'd have the trains running on time! That's one thing he did for Italy.'

'Uh y-es, I suppose so…' Mr Legit snorted, exuding a cloud of stale smoke in Alfie's direction and forcing him to turn towards Mr Illegit.

'Fascist!' hissed the pockmarked adolescent through stained teeth and looking as though he hadn't washed for weeks. His eyes were already in a semi-glazed state and he wore a filthy military-style jacket, long matted hair and an uncompromising leer to broadcast to all and sundry that he required nothing from anyone. Alfie was forced to turn away, the whiff of the illegal substance was too overpowering – he was beginning to feel its soporific effect. "What on earth do they put in those things?" he pondered to himself, "smells like burnt cabbage! And I should know – I'm married to Norma. Still, I suppose it smothers the smell of BO."

When he eventually found a vacant slot, it was by removing a dishevelled copy of the Guardian which lay open upon the seat. The paper had been turned to a centre page where the lead article caught his eye: 'Are you one of the 10 million who suffer from obsession?' There it was again, the media were certainly obsessed with the big 'O'. Surreptitiously he eyed those around him before scooping up the paper to replace it with his undistinguished rump. Devouring its contents with concentrated deliberation, he began to fold the paper neatly around the small article to leave it surrounded in a tidy rectangle; then realising what he was doing thought better of it as he began to attract the attention of his fellow commuters.

The item was brief and merely stated that approximately1 in 5 people displayed symptoms of the social malaise, quoting an ex-Guards colonel who had scaled-down models of all the major battles of the 19th century on display in glass cases in every room of his Suffolk home. And the woman who had one room crammed from floor to ceiling with shoes of every colour and material imaginable; including a tiny pair from Shanghai fashioned in bamboo, and another from Mexico made from discarded inner-tubes and soled with tyre rubber. One problem she faced was that she could only access those that happened to be on view at any time from the wall of footwear, and finding a 'pair' compared favourably with the proverbial needle in the haystack.

No, he wasn't obsessed, those people were plainly off the wall – one gift token short of a pop-up toaster. 'Perhaps a little over keen on neatness, that's all', he comforted himself, as the steady rhythm of the train sent his mind into a bout of introspection. This 'tendency towards exactness' had accompanied him since his time in the Forces. He had followed his father into military service; nothing grand, he'd been a humble clerk in the Royal Army Service Corps, yet he had to admit he'd fallen on his feet in that job – into every skive imaginable; documenting priceless commodities to depots that didn't exist all over Britain.

Stores originally destined for a Sergeants Mess in Bradford would mysteriously turn up in Kettering; versatile medical supplies such as penicillin, vaccines and hypodermics and even a van-load of male contraceptives had gone astray. He made extra cash by charging over the odds for cigarettes and whisky from a secret cache. Records, papers and ledgers were works of art; all transactions entered in rows of immaculately annotated ruled columns in three shades of ink, and all erroneous. It was a relief when he'd been discharged, that was after a consignment of cooking-oil arrived in place of sherry for an important Brigade Officer's function at Aldershot. Questions began to be asked, and Alfie felt glad he only had a further two months to serve. Yes the Army was responsible he concluded ruefully, and of course his subsequent position as a publishing collator. 'London Bridge!' –, the station tannoy returned him to the present and he joined the scramble for the Underground.

Alfie entered the narrow hallway, placed his umbrella in the rack and solicitously hung his jacket on the right-hand hook.

'I'm home, dear,' he reported dutifully, heading straight for the bathroom. He washed his hands, pausing briefly in front of the mirror to flick a few stray strands of dense silver hair from his brow. 'Handsome sod!' he reflected.

He was greeted by Norma's north country lilt as he entered the living-room, 'Dinner's ready, Alf…Did you have a good day?' she chirped as she sank onto the protesting chair.

'Why on earth doesn't she diet, like other women?' Alfie thought, as he took his seat across the table from his wife's ample form. 'She was so neat and slim when we first met… like that new temp of Ralph's – now she bulges in the <u>right</u> places!' Alfie contemplated. Norma was wearing one of those shiny multicoloured print dresses two sizes too small. 'That's the trouble with women, you think you know them and they change dramatically without a word of warning! They're so unpredictable and disorganised,' he regretted resignedly. 'It's the hormones, that's what it is…' Over dinner Norma, as normal, hardly seemed to interrupt her chatter to ingest any food. Alfie had learnt to relegate this verbal barrage to a dull drone, the way one accepts a whirring fan, an aircraft's hum or a dripping tap.

'– And you'll never guess who was in the supermarket today – ('Bin Laden?' mouthed Alfie silently) that odd Dora Pendleton… you know the one? Well, anyway she was there as usual with her calculator. It must take her hours to get round the store. She compares the price of every item before she puts it in her cart. Then at the checkout she knows exactly how much she's spent, she's caught them out a couple of times with the total. They watch out when she's around. I asked 'er why she bothered, just throw it all in I say.'.

'What's wrong with that? Sounds a good idea to me,' Alfie responded. 'Ugh, liver's a bit tough. How long did it take to cook?' He replaced the salt in the cruet, which he precisely realigned with exactitude on a parallel to the thick place-mat which sat in the centre of the table to protect from the potent ravages of the steaming casserole.

'Well, the time it said in the recipe. It's a new one, I picked it up from the supermarket.'

'Well, it's underdone! What do you want with new recipes, Norma? You've got a perfectly good set of recipe cards out there, and besides we know what we like – '

'I like salads actually! At this time of year anyhow,' she added as an afterthought. 'I'm sorry love, I just felt it would be nice to have a change now and again.'

'Tuesday nights we have meatballs with onions. It takes an hour on Gas Mark 5. What could be simpler? It's what we've always had, we have it because we like it.'

Alfie cleared every morsel from his plate, and peaches and custard followed in hasty pursuit. He left the room to prepare for his meeting. He got out the shoe-cleaning kit from under the kitchen sink, from its home to the right of the uniform rows of cleaning fluids then came to an abrupt halt.

'Norma! The bleach is out of place – you've been moving

things around again. You know it should be next to the multi-purpose cleaner in front of the washing-powder.'

'Oh, I'm sorry Alf. It's just that I was in such a hurry to get to the shops –.'

'Norma, think about it. Lawrence said: 'Man cannot live in chaos!'

Norma re-entered the kitchen her eyes alight. 'Did he say that? That's real poetic is that. I always did like Laurence Harvey, ever since "Room at the Top", you remember?'

'DH Lawrence, dear.'

'Er no, I don't think he was in it…I'm sure I'd have noticed, I'm good with actors. You see I saw it twice, once with you and once – '

'Now Norma, you're slipping. Like the time you used to leave the cleaning fluids out on the dresser so that when I came home I'd think you'd used them. Remember, a tight ship!'

'Alf, really! What does it matter if one or two things are out of place?'

'One or two things can be the thin end of the wedge' Alfie would have been dismayed to learn he'd got his metaphors in a twist.

A frown clouded Norma's normally placid features.' – And like I've said before, you're much too particular at times, right picky you can be!'

'Don't start that again, luv. We're agreed we like to be neat and tidy around the home. If cleanliness is next to godliness, neatness must run a close third.'

'Oh, it's one thing to be neat and tidy, Alf – but you go too far! Thank God we haven't got a garden is all I can say. You'd spend hours getting the hedges all geometric and getting all critical-like with the lawns,' she was into her stride now, '– mowing 'em in chequer-board patterns and finishing 'em off with nail scissors. You'd have a fit if your irises didn't salute you as you inspected their perfect rows. Preening your privets and bevelling your borders – you'd really enjoy that, wouldn't you? At least it would give me a bit of peace.'

Feeling contrite Alfie demurred. 'Now, calm down dear. I'm sorry, but you know what appears in the absence of order – anarchy. The world today's in enough of a mess, at least we can do our bit to restore a little order.'

Following his bath Alfie returned to the bedroom and proceeded to dress meticulously, taking his suit from his side of the walk-in wardrobe and clean underwear and socks from his methodically arranged shelves. Then after attempting to placate his wife with a casual peck on the cheek he glanced at his watch and, with: 'Oh no – is it half past already? Where does the time go?' he tore his raincoat from its hook and raced out of the flat. Norma, in the kitchen, had her thoughts interrupted by his retreating footsteps as he trotted along the street in the direction of the British Legion. She sat pondering. Perhaps he's right she thought to herself – him being so finicky an' all (as they say back 'ome). And in some strange way, his routine did seem to make him secure and content.

**

The chill of early Autumn caused Alfie a momentary shiver as he stood outside the front door delving deep into the folds of his navy overalls for his keys. He had almost reached the hall-stand with his coat over his arm when he realised he was still in his wellies. Briskly he hung up the coat and retreated to the doorstep, where he heaved off the grubby boots. He had to be careful these days, Norma might return early. Alfie slotted his feet into the cord slippers and taking a cup of tea into the living-room collapsed in front of the television. He was just getting into a programme on the social lifestyle of the aborigine, when he heard Norma close the front-door behind her.

'Hello. What are you doing in here like this, you can't possibly have had a bath? You know I like you to have a bath and change before you sit down.'

'Oh Norma, I'm too tired – '

'Now Alf, you know what you said. We do like to keep neat and tidy like, don't we? You just go and spruce up and I'll put the fire on. It'll be nice and cosy.'

'Do I have to?' wailed Alfie.

'How long have you been at the pig-farm, Alf?' she switched off the television to demonstrate resolve.

'Er, I don't know…about three weeks.'

'That's right, and we must have had this conversation at least a couple of times each week. Look luv, we agreed didn't we? We have to have standards.'

Considering the matter closed, she began to hum softly to herself as she ignited the gas. Alfie knew it was pointless to argue any further. Heavily, he dragged himself from the comfort of his chair and left the room. Norma returned from the kitchen and busied herself primping the cushions and setting them individually at precise angles to the chair arms with neatly aligned antimacassars at the centre of each chair-back. After, she positioned each chair at the correct obliquity on each side of the television. Then she turned her attention to the dining-room table upon which sulked a large vase of blue irises. Diligently she snipped the stems until she achieved the desired height for two tiers of flowers to appear symmetrical from every viewpoint. Adjusting the lace doyley beneath the vase she ensured it was in the table centre, equidistant from each corner. She squared off the table chairs until all four were parallel, and with a gentle sigh of pleasure sat for a spell admiring her handiwork. Then she left for the kitchen and a cup of tea.

Poor lamb, he did look tired, but it was all for the best. She'd thought it over good and hard and convinced herself that Alfie had been right all along. It must have been about the time he'd been made redundant from the City book firm that she began to realise it. And now she'd got her own little job, well it was so much easier somehow to have everything spick and span. Thinking back, it must have been very upsetting for him – her being all slovenly an' all. She saw how satisfied it made you feel too: yes, 'a tidy home is a happy home!'

Meanwhile, Alfie had made his weary way to the bedroom, where he shed his clothes in an unruly heap on the floor. He was in such a muddle these days that it took him an eternity to locate his underwear and socks, but eventually he headed for the bathroom. Later, he carelessly climbed into his tracksuit and smelling of bath-soap and shampoo rejoined his wife in the living-room.

'There, that's better isn't it?' she fussed. 'Tidy means neat, and neat means comfortable. Now, what's the time? I mustn't miss Corrie.' She switched on the set.

Alfie looked at the screen but it might as well have been blank. This was all his fault, he could see it now. Around the time of his redundancy he'd been having second thoughts about himself; hadn't he become too fastidious – did it really matter if possessions were too orderly stored – didn't they then possess you? Was it so important after all? His new job at the pig-farm, a couple of miles from the suburban flat, had answered these questions. And he was in danger of making Norma's life a misery into the bargain. He elected to walk to work as it didn't seem worth getting the car out, although it might be different in winter. He found he was far too exhausted to maintain his past regimen of order. It was all he could do to stay awake in the evenings now and he turned in early. 'Only 8 o'clock!' he inwardly groaned as the familiar theme tune signalled the end of the soap.

Yes, at that very time, Norma too seemed to change. 'Well, that was women for you!' he pondered as he gazed with unseeing eyes in the direction of the thriller about the Irish troubles. She had become so infuriatingly neat and tidy and even managed to slim-down, proudly boasting of losing over a stone. Oh, at first it had been a triumph for him – Norma's willingness to join his conspiracy against chaos, an eager ally in his war against disorder. Yet, the curious thing was as she matched his fervour so Alfie gradually lost his appetite for orderliness. There was no longer any quarter to defend, no inconsistency to correct, and dare he think, no more satisfaction – he had become jaded with the enterprise. As he had begun to have doubts she had become more inflexible. How could he protest? It was no good, the rug had been decisively withdrawn from beneath his feet.

As the News jingle roused him from his dark meditation he sneaked a glance in Norma's direction. Yes, they had both suffered a mutual transition and he wasn't at all pleased with the outcome. Since his lapse into disarray he'd not been able to find things and was in serious danger of losing his sense of humour. He'd been more irritable of late and put it down to tiredness. Often, returning from the Farm he would collapse on the sofa before removing his boots, he must be careful though, Norma was hot on that. Yes, the muddy wellie was firmly on the other foot these days! On the other hand, Norma was bright and effusive. He began to long for the good old days.

'You know what day it is, don't you luv?' Norma hinted with a mischievous grin as the News ended and she switched off the television. 'And you know what we do at bedtime on Fridays, don't you?' she teased.

'No, Norma – not tonight, please – '

'Now you just slip into those satin pyjamas I like, and I'll make myself all alluring, just for you. You know I can get into that black neglige now – I've got new perfume too, it's called Obsession, I hope you like it Alf. We've got at least half an hour before our hot chocolate!'

'No, Norma please – I've really got this terrible headache....'

ST. PANCRAS STATION

One of my earliest recollections of vast and extraordinary buildings (late 1940s to early 50s) was as a young child awaiting the arrival of a distant aunt beneath the grand dome of St. Pancras station. This magnificent edifice was designed by William Henry Barlow at the height of steam-power in the 19th century. My Aunt was arriving via the same method of transportation. My father had walked me alongside the Regents Canal and then beneath the daunting glass of the 'cathedral of the railways'; or John Betjeman's 'temple to the age of steam'. St Pancras, a Greek name meaning 'one that holds everything' belonged to a lad of 14 who in ancient Rome converted to Christianity and refused to denounce the faith. He was beheaded in 304 AD and remains to this day the patron saint of children.

By simply closing my eyes I can relive those indulgent childhood days and my first view of that magnificent façade. We were walking briskly along dampened pavements and sucking in the chill autumn air, glad to be above ground again and free of the labyrinthine confines of the metropolitan network. Suddenly, we turned a corner and I was confronted by the magnificent spectacle of tall red turrets contrasting handsomely with the grey background of a November London skyline. Before us stood this palatial monument to engineering enhanced in Gothic splendour. I recall my father's words as I stood, mouth agape staring in awe across the busy street. "…Opened in 1868 it linked London with the East Midlands and Yorkshire…the Grand Union Canal actually runs under it."

As we passed beneath high ostentatious Victorian arches

and soaked up the grandeur, my first impression of that vast arena was of majestic towering domes and sheet glass confined in grandiose wrought-iron filigree. Entering the station sound eclipsed all. From the orderly and businesslike street noises, we were immediately and completely engulfed in an au-dial maelstrom: a continuous roar from which the ears gradually attuned individual strains: humming traffic, snatches of conversation, the roll of trolleys and porter's whistles and news vendors. Within this overwhelming miscellaneous cacophony a public address system emitted a garbled list of indecipherable stations to be encountered along the line towards Derby and Nottingham. (It was many years later that I learnt the celebrated station was then enjoying her swan song as the grand terminus for the now extinct Midland Railway). Amid the relentless hubbub, smartly uniformed porters were sweating beneath trolleys stacked high with teetering suitcases, or stealing a meritorious cigarette behind piles of bulging canvas mail-bags.

My Aunt's arrival not imminent, my Father led me towards a well-lit cafeteria, set as an island in the centre of that seething ocean of people with purpose. We passed steps that disappeared to an underground grotto, with a sign stating 'wash and brush-up' in dark ceramic tiling. Above, bordering the bustling platforms lay a series of cell-like waiting rooms. A few of these dim caverns portrayed the meagre glow of tiny coal fires that twinkled diffidently in an attempt to appear more welcoming. Some chambers bore the pretentious lettering 'Smoking Room' or 'Ladies Only', but the cubby-hole that intrigued me the most was the 'Lost Property Office'.

Here, behind a darkly waxed and splinter-chipped counter, were row upon shelf of black umbrellas enhanced by a wide range of handles from plain bakelite to ornate horn. One I remember was carved in the shape of an elephant's head. There were parcels and packages of every size and contour, and brown paper bags bursting with diverse contents. Smaller objects lay meticulously grouped upon a scrubbed pine table. Such items as pipes, cigarette lighters, purses, wallets, handbags and odd keys were on display; alongside a collection of books and a broken doll with a dejected expression and one arm. Behind the counter and surrounded by this collection of mid-twentieth century and earlier trivia I was able to discern the figure of a wizened railway employee, who despite efforts to remain invisible behind a copy of The Times had nevertheless fallen asleep. He sat hunched beneath bushy grey eyebrows and a walrus moustache, eyes closed and torso rhythmically pulsing: beside him the dark blue cap displaying his badge of office accompanied a half-full mug of tea.

Our's was an insipid grey and barely warm, and if the sandwiches resembled cardboard I did not care – I might have been dining at the Ritz, I was so pleased to be there. Following our refreshment Father purchased two one-penny platform tickets from a seedy booking-clerk, whose greasy strands of dark hair lay sleeked back from his pock-marked features and whose broken pencil stub protruded obtrusively from behind one ear.

We strolled the length of that protracted grey platform, past ornate cast-iron vending machines. Some, for a penny, dispensed an imprint of your name and address on a thin strip of nickel. And others, for the sum of 1d or 2d issued forth a small bar of Nestles chocolate. All along the route were the numerous rows of dull green benches full of sanguine passengers. We finally reached the end of the platform, beyond the roof, and breathed in the damp urban air thick with the heady scent of coal-dust and steel.

Then we heard a dull rumble that gradually grew in intensity to a mighty roar as aunt's train swept imperiously into view around a bend in the track and entered that exalted setting. The noise built to a spitting, deafening crescendo as the mammoth thundered by. The tumult thankfully subsided to a rhythmic snorting, as with whistle hooting and brakes squealing the powerful machine slowed to greet the submissive buffers. All the while, emitting spasmodic gusts of steam from its haughty black smoke-stack; as it belched past I glimpsed a greasy faced driver leaning heavily on the brakes in the bowels of the beast. Dark and indomitable, the monster towed an endless succession of brown and cream coaches in its wake. With a final enormous hiss of escaping air, that caused me to hide in the folds of Father's coat, the hulking monster finally lay at rest as a dark beached whale washed up on the tide.

Doors were slammed and an army of porters rushed to meet the descending wave of humanity like a thin blue line of turtles struggling for the sea. Amid the pressing tumult Father spied Aunt Anna's purple ostrich feather being unceremoniously sucked into the vortex of impatient passengers caught up in the bottleneck of the black wrought-iron ticket-barrier. With certain apprehension we were borne along on the flowing tide, only a single direction was possible. We were extricating ourselves from the maelstrom of dazed commuters who had been drawn through the gate at terrifying speed as we observed my aunt tip a fawning porter, board a waiting taxi and disappear into the anonymity of a London smog.

Of course Father was furious and hardly said a word on the bus home: I sat distractedly playing with a loose sandal strap and reading the colourful adverts above my head. Passing years will never diminish my enjoyment of the day I spent beneath the 'big top.'

THANE OF COULSDON

A North wind wailed in melancholy tones around the long-abandoned and crumbling castle ramparts. The night was bleak. A fluttering white mist blanketed the landscape and concealed a legion of wide-eared bats that jostled together within the fallen masonry on that lonely hillside, in the province of Coulsdon. The opaque pall was whipped to a frenzy and the howling of dogs was muted in the dank air. The proverb was a true one – you can't dodge snowflakes in a blizzard. When it touched the face of a fool caught outside it stung and stuck to the skin like an outbreak of pretty smallpox, causing the owner to clench teeth and lean against the elements. The message in the wind was marshalling one to glory somewhere, somewhere indoors.

From the heart of this melange came the rhythmic beating of giant wings, thrusting onwards through the gloom. Intermittent bursts of flame streaked across the sky and sizzled patches of flakes while briefly lighting the vacant hillside. High over the towers of Downturn Abbey flew the mighty dragon of Thane. Saliva dripping from its greedy jaws instantly froze to lengthy stalactites to adorn the battlements and hang from the town's rooftops as it glided overhead. This scaly beast was also known as the Don of Coulsdon, for work in the black economy and for master-minding an extortion racket throughout the borough whereby protection money was paid for the maintenance of law and order (rather in the manner that future governments were to tax people through their income only less subtle). There were minor DEs, subordinate dragon enforcers, only too willing to do his bidding for a quick buck.

For his work he felt it prudent to transform his appearance. So the hapless dragon was forced to lead a double life. Although the Vatican and the masses were enjoying a post-Lutheran and pre-Calvinistic enlightenment there was still plenty of dragon phobia around, especially during the course of business transactions. For years in human format as Count Drakontos – the Don – had watched blossom, and then stalked, Baron Cameroon's eligible daughter Shalotte: she was the motive for his mission on such a doleful night. First he was making his way to Witch Hazel: she it was who was responsible for his effective transformation to human form. 'Yeah, well, we dragons may have taught humans to speak, but I would fight shy of starting a conversation with Saint George or Beowulf.'

Witch Hazel wasn't really a witch and the Middle Ages weren't what they used to be, nor were they in the middle of anything, except perhaps a turmoil. Somehow at school she had always confused the letter 'w' at the start of a word with the letter 'b', a fault she had yet to rectify: 'Wubble wubble, toil and trouble!' she had spluttered in the Scottish play. She thought the Witches Sabbath was psycho-babble for a few old dears having a Sunday afternoon get-together to slag off their respective partners, later it became known as 'golf'. There had been only one occasion when she'd cast a spell: when her nephew had brought round his scrabble set and she, on a particularly bad day, had hurled it across the room. She didn't practice witchcraft: as she explained in pure innocence: 'Of course I've played snap with tarot cards and dabbled with sorcery and the occult, but who hasn't? The only black mass I've encountered was that hunky sax player I bumped into at the Crown and Anchor; and the closest I ever got to the spirit world was when I experimented with sloe gin.'

She did possess a black cat and a broomstick and kept to herself, all factors which in most peoples' minds qualified her for the position; but, any esoteric knowledge she'd gained from reading. Although, quite by accident, she had magically dispersed her nephew's warts and hiccups, she really had little to say on the subject of the black arts. Hazel altered the dragon's appearance for temporary business reasons, and she had long since warned of the dangerous efficacy of water, one sip and he would immediately revert to type. The process she found quite simple, any man could be made to look like a dragon she felt, although it sometimes proved more difficult to reverse the process. The potion lasted for 28 days (which had caused consternation on at least one leap year he could remember). He was seeking out Hazel for his latest top-up. As Count Drakontos, he had courted Shalotte and all had gone well, finally they married (a ceremony attended with some misgivings by the powerful Baron Cameroon).

Luckily, it was the middle of the night, when following a particularly alcoholic celebration, he had reached for Sharlotte's bedside water without thinking…it was too late when he realised his error. For a dragon he was sweating more than usual. She had turned towards him in an amorous moment and he couldn't escape. He plunged his claws into his ears to block the inevitable screams to follow (from her and him), but they never came. She wasn't screaming but effusing. 'Wow,' she said, 'that was wonderful. Do it again!' He waited for ages but she wouldn't sleep and he was unable to slip into the bathroom for more potion. She pleaded with him to turn on the bedside light, an operation she subsequently completed. 'We must do it this way often' she exclaimed. '– Er, yes', he replied, his back to her. 'And don't worry darling, I won't mention a thing to anyone about your dragon suit!' she added conspiratorially. The Count found his marital duties much in demand from that time onwards, although he was ultra-diligent over dealings with water.

Baron Cameroon from Downturn Abbey and his colleague Jorge Osborne from Grimy Stacks in the Mold (celebrated biscuit barons with regards to their second income) fought hard to be accepted by the residents of Coulsdon domain, however they remained unpopular. This fact caused them much grief – they tried being 'nice', being bad, being indifferent, nothing worked. Finally they attempted a change of appearance – all without success. In a cause celebre, Osborn had notoriously executed a u-turn on Tax hobbits, he bowed to those with accounts in off-shore banks, and even reduced inheritance tax. Yet Ninja turtles still managed to swarm over the walls at dusk in vast numbers to seek asylum in the ivy and gobble up the contents of open tuna cans. Often their tiny heads became entrapped in those metal cases and they took to wandering around in pointless circles in the manner of redundant Daleks.

No one trusted the banks, believing them to be run by Shylocks with Wongo tendencies full of malpractice and corruption, preferring to stash their nest-eggs in the bread oven or on the roof of the four-poster. They lost faith after the PPI scandal, the one that promised to go on longer than (and end with the same result as) the Chilcott enquiry. This Peasant Protection Insurance was the scam of all scams, and at one time had threatened to put the Don himself out of business. Undeterred the bankers awarded themselves an SGB (self-gratification bonus) in honour of past failures.

Barons didn't mix nor mingle, occasionally Cameroon and Osborn visited the swampy mouth of the Thames for meetings to pass fresh laws and edicts, but not very often – for once there they became plagued with the irritating attention of the stinging Boris-fly. To be avoided were Baron Jeremy Corbett, lesser-known brother to the diminuitive Rodnie, both comedians. Jeremy had recently struck lucky by usurping the role of lord of the manor of Barking, this following from his more humble origins as court jester and CND activist or anti-nude photo protester (Campaign for Nudity Discernment). He had even suggested switching the national anthem from the current dirge to one of the themes: Harry Potter or the Archers. Another to watch for at that time was Baron John MacDonald president of the old farmers association (OFA) and subsequent owner of a chain of fast-food outlets from the North Pole to the Zambeze, wherin he gained money for the old rope that often ended up inside the burgers and hot-dogs; aka the gnome of Tooting Beck and a member of the magic circle. Once in the House of Commoners, he produced from his hip-pocket the entire sayings of Confucius while standing at the shadow front bench. Corbett and MacDonald were afforded the welcome normally reserved for the nouveau riche, or survivors of forged tax-returns or overdue parking fines.

Under Cameroon's control the fiefdom was teetering on the brink, less to do with his inane policies than erosion of the white cliffs of Dotage that caused gradual land reclamation. None of the other Barons had any ideas, and simply argued pointlessly among themselves. Brief mention must be made here of the housing crisis as this played a pertinent role. There was no access for first-time buyers to get onto the property ladder, this could have been due to the bar being set too high, the bottom rungs were at an impossible height for tiny hobbits. There was a surfeit of trolls without social housing. Even owners of princely estates lurking behind foreboding castle walls felt the pinch and allowed their properties to fall into shameful neglect. Forget the propaganda about fair maidens with dangling tresses being rescued by dashing young knights in shining armour: the reality of those ugly edifices of social control was somewhat different. Filthy odorous dripping dungeons, where the screams and soft moans of tortured souls, the desperate and forsaken, mingled with the steady grinding of the rack and the rusty rattle of weighty shackles. To the tower Rapunzel!

Anarchy was in the air: discontent lurked beneath many an eye-patch and mop-cap. Stench, malnutrition and corruption were rife. One healthy plague of epidemic proportions would surely bring the country to its knees. The peasants lost faith in the Barons, the banks, the dream of home-ownership, and Shallotte's preference for dragons, and threatened revolt. (Moral: 'Take what you're given.')

THAT SOUND

I knew I would never forget that sound…

It had been a late Spring day of indecisive weather, rain or shine, that we first visited the tiny pub. It was on those far off borders at the edge of the Black mountains, the gateway to a lost goblin land of rough hillsides, quarried stone and forgotten farmsteads; where vengeful chill winds howled through vacant yards and lean-tos. Geoff had taken me on a visit to Hoarwithy chapel with its high Italianate columns and neo-gothic facade.

We stumbled over uneven pasture which pink wild bush roses shared with campion and dark nettle-beds. A forgotten domain where a handful of striped bees were visiting purple thistles, and a meadow lark startled as it took flight when we picked our way through a copse of trembling silver aspens. Approaching the tiny inn the sky darkened and the heavens opened. Geoff grasped my hand and we darted for cover towards the ghosts of bottle-glass windows viewed through lashing rain. The Pitch was surely an abode that held the darkness within.

Crossing the threshold was stepping from a tardis. We were deposited into the 1950s: a red-brick corner fireplace crackled invitingly with burning logs in the dimly lit salon although everywhere appeared coated in a fine patina of dust. Deciding against a glass I opted for a can of Coke. Kramer the landlord was stooped and sullen with eyes, at odds with each other, that followed a person around the room – a taciturn character. Geoff's attempts at conversation with our host elicited low grunts; yet the man pulled a mean pint of rough cider.

The locals were more forthcoming and Joss was even talkative, filling us in with the hostelries history. There was no till, coins fell with a satisfying clink into a grimy chipped glass beer mug that nestled within a wad of notes thrown in an untidy heap on the bar-top. Keeping the books must have been interesting. Chalk on a tiny blackboard informed clientele that Sunday roasts were available. The toilet was a chain-operated affair at the bottom of the garden. Perhaps a mere half dozen souls were in the room yet it was crowded. Apparently Kramer side-lined as an undertaker who laid out bodies on the bar-tables where they were often located overnight, and by the back-door stood a selection of coffins. Geoff felt in his element, smiling as he borrowed a lighter to ignite his cigarillo.

We returned in Autumn, Geoff had a contract in Hereford and he took me along and we called in on the Pitch on our way back. This time the weather was calmer with a waning year chill which brought clear skies and leaves and bracken that were turning colour. Approaching the pub where it lay entrenched in its mossy backdrop, amid rolling thistledown, grey "old-man's beard", and patches of cream hogweed, change was evident.

The brooding old inn lay abandoned, boarded and surrounded with brimming skips. Wandering the desolate landscape we discovered poor Joss, sitting on an empty packing-case. Kramer had been found lying out flat and cold on one of his bar tables. Foul play was ruled out; he had simply become a victim of that unforgiving landscape. As Joss put it: 'He were strange alrit, but a good yun. Never agreed with change…' Change: the clink clink of the coins as they fell into the jar. Turning to leave we noticed, lying on its side on a bright yellow skip, a solitary chipped grime-encrusted glass pint mug, empty of course.

THE END

Although it might be assumed that to begin a narrative on the 'end' is as difficult as to end one on the 'beginning', this is far from the case. Carl Sandberg suggested that there are more ends in the world than anything else. As all things have an end, the subject is extensive, one might say endless – therefore there are many end products to discuss. You may not consider this the be-all and end-all: but if you are at your wit's end, and before you get the wrong end of the stick, the end result is the same.

My first end is appropriate – the thin end of the wedge, from which all others derive. This part of a lost proverb refers to a small beginning that is inevitably followed by a larger or more significant development. Further uses of the end may be found in old sayings: the end of ones tether, meaning that ones patience has become exhausted: the bitter end, which can allude to a meeting with the Grim Reaper or the extremity of a cucumber: the dead end of a road is one that finishes abruptly leading nowhere. We speak of the end of the line, meaning the last station on a railway network or the termination of a relationship. 'You take this end, and I'll take the other,' may allude to a bed-sheet, a length of rope or the limits of a street.

The last page of a book often has a twist to its tale and perhaps an unhappy ending. Rising instrumental crescendos heralded the finale to early Hollywood blockbusters, as the hero and heroine engaged in their ultimate embrace against a sunset backdrop. The spectacle was inevitably closely followed by a fade-out, a blank screen and the words: "le fin", "finito" or "the end".

However we may seek to disguise the fact, all things eventually reach an end, all things that is save death and taxes according to Disraeli; although death is an end in itself and taxes prove the end to many. The process of beginning pre-supposes an end. Time, although relative and continuous, is measured by a series of ends; we speak of 'the end of the day/week or year', but surely time is infinite. However, should mankind reach its ultimate end, time may continue with no-one around to record it.

Approaching our conclusion it might seem that the end is nigh, and this is the time to tidy up any remaining loose-ends. In the Apocrypha, the book of Ecclesiasticus states: 'Whatsoever thou takest in hand, remember the end and thou shalt never do amiss'. Alternatively, Nietzsche wrote: 'Not every end is the goal. The end of a melody is not its goal, and yet if a melody has not reached its end, it has not reached its goal.' Although you may consider there is no end to maxims such as these, we shall end on an optimistic note. At the end of the day, faced with a fait accompli, we are able to weigh the gains and losses of the journey. As you reach the close of this account I trust you agree the end not only justifies the means but also crowns the work, and in the final analysis all's well that ends well.

THE FLYING HADDOCK

Before I met my master I'd been a fish out of water, although I was soon to land on my flippers – all three of them! But I'll come to all that in a moment. I was only a shaggy terrier mismarked in grey and grubby white, "Scruff" Mike called me. I suppose I wasabout toy poodle size and shape and about a foot tall nose to floor, but there the similarity ended: I was definitely from the wrong side of the tracks. I was a mongrel and proud of it, despite some allusion to Old English Sheepdog on my mother's side. Laying aside my dodgy ancestry I was considered quite cute by some; I know I shouldn't say it, but my picture was as good as any of those on the chocolate boxes I came across in dustbins.

We had met in a bleak Welsh January, when the remnants of a heavy snowfall defied the rays of a sickly sun. I hadn't ventured outside, but lay huddled shivering in the red plastic basket they lent me at the home. In any case I had no need to go outside, they slipped my food inside the door before beating a hasty retreat. Somehow, I'd gained a reputation for being the bad boy on the block – I've no idea why.

Notwithstanding, I was in a fairly black mood. I'd just had a dust-up with one of my fellow inmates so they'd put me in an isolation enclosure (cage) to cool off. It smelt and was filthy. It was cold, there wasn't a lot to eat, and my leg was playing up – I wanted to be left alone. I scared the pants off the kennel-maids: I wouldn't really have bitten them, not in earnest, I just flashed my teeth a little. I growled a lot mainly from pain, but they weren't taking any chances.

The Cardiff police had unceremoniously dumped me there two weeks before. I'd been the victim of an RTA in the busy city streets where I had become adept at scavenging for scraps; enough anyway to keep fur and tail together. I'd seen many would-be dog owners thread their way through the corridor in front of those cages; I didn't think much to that – that's how animals in zoos must feel. Still I suppose the Society did their best. Usually the Collies and other working dogs went first, or the macho-status ones the likes of Alsatians, Dobermans and Bull Terriers – I suppose I wasn't much use. I could burrow into rabbit holes if required but I'd rather burrow into a steak pie. It was the greyhounds I really felt sorry for; their racing days behind them they were discarded like a buried bone. Many would have make good companions given the chance, being still quite young and active. Anyhow, when this tall hesitant guy appeared I knew I'd found my meal ticket.

Mike had come with Barb, but he was the one I knew I should cultivate. He didn't say much, which is one reason why I was attracted to him. I think humans can talk a lot of rubbish at times – they just want to rub it in that they're the only animals to speak. Of course, I played hard to get when they made enquiries about me; I'd lain dormant in the basket, merely raising an eyelid at being disturbed: it never does to let them think you're too eager to pander to their whims. No he didn't say much, but he certainly spoke my language, as we drove away he asked me softly if I wanted a biscuit. During that first car journey, he constantly lobbed dog biscuits over his shoulder to me on the back seat. He'd obviously done his homework, I liked that. This guy had style.

As I found my way in my new home, hobbling around in the snow-covered garden of Whitehall Cottage, nestling a lone wooded hillside in the Wye valley, I grew close to this gaunt quiet man. Although they named me Havelock, from a Roath back street where they got lost on their return to the Welsh borders; Mike often referred to me as 'Haddock' – I never found out why. I'd come face to face with many fishy remains during my foraging, but despite a rather washed-out coat that fish and I shared little in common: I was certainly no dogfish. I learnt to trust this person who had rescued me, if he wanted to call me 'bird-brain' I guess I wouldn't have minded. I doted on him and followed his angular frame whenever caninely possible; you humans would say I dogged his heels.

At the time, he was working as an insurance agent in the Forest of Dean and surrounding regions and I normally managed to cadge a lift on the rear car-seat while he made his rounds. Lunch times, although rather irregular, were well worth waiting for. He'd pull over to a layby and we'd share a brief snack, with him tossing peanuts, potato crisps or pie-crusts over the seat in my direction. I must say I became quite good at intercepting these tasty morsels (missiles), even single peanuts or potato crisps I caught in my mouth.

Eventually my leg healed apart from the odd rheumatic twinge, though not until it had been reset expertly by Mike's preferred vet with a three-quarter inch steel screw. I recall Mike anxiously asking whether or not this pin would go rusty if I ventured into the sea. He needn't have worried, you wouldn't catch me going anywhere near water.

Mike and Barb had no children, so I suppose in a way us animals were a substitute – better, I reckon, no nappies nor bawling all night long. I suppose it was bad of me really, but I always let Mike think he was the boss. In fact I could twist him around my tiny paw whenever I felt like it: all it took was a look of total dejection as I turned my moist chestnut eyes towards the carpet. It was really shameful the way I had of getting my own way, especially by putting my head on one side or raising one ear – a trick I picked up when running from the dog patrols in Cardiff.

I guess I was top dog, the other canine resident, also a rescued reject of Heinz 59 heritage, didn't stand a chance against my gutter education. Durham, once referred to as a 'walking hearthrug', was a long low shaggy black Bearded Collie-cross with a white collar, chest and nose, and a distinct absence of leg. As I had adopted Mike, Durham adopted Barb. When they were giving out the lower limbs, this one was away on his stumps somewhere chasing sticks. Once, outside a shop, a passer-by remarked that if he were to stand he would surely be a large dog; to which Mike replied that the wretch was already on his feet! Anyhow I thought it quite fitting that I looked down on him. Yes, I was top dog alright. I was the one to round up the cats and keep them in their place, and got to lick their bowls clean after they fed.

Mike was originally from London, and you can't teach an old human new tricks; he would often return verbally to his Cockney roots. In such a frame of mind, he might use the special term of endearment he reserved for me:"Erbert".This he did as we strolled past a lone barefoot boy on a West Wales beach : "Keep up, 'Erbert," he commanded towards my retreating rump. In response I took a few token steps in his direction before subtly drifting towards where the pebbles met the sand to nose among the interesting debris.

Old habits die hard I thought, as I rummaged keenly among empty plastic containers and jetsam swept in by the tide. I had just discovered a succulent rotting fish carcase when I was aware that the little lad had followed me across the sand. He petted and stroked me. Now, I'm not averse to some of that when I'm in the mood: "humour kids" is my motto – you never know when they may discard their lollipop or candy in your direction. Then, as Mike approached and I'm sure for his benefit, the boy uttered: 'There's a good dog, 'Erbert...Now come along!' The cheek of it – I felt as if I'd been slapped around the muzzle with a wet cod! Now, see here young lad, my name's not... oh, what's the point? Let 'em carry on...

It was during one of these seaside trips that I encountered the second most traumatic experience of my life: I also learnt that humans are, after all, only human. I had followed Mike over some rocks and then we had taken a narrow winding pathway to a cliff-top overlooking the beach. It was always his wont to explore exotic nooks and outcrops, and I thought it best to humour him. It felt quite natural surveying the bustling beach from such an angle. Anyhow I had been busy doing what doggies do when I realised Mike was nowhere in sight. I looked down along the path we had climbed...no sign, though to be honest my eyesight wasn't that good in those days...then I was sure I spied him below on the beach.

Well, I thought to myself, it doesn't look that far down and it would certainly be quicker to ignore the cliff path and jump: anyhow, it quite appealed to my love of adventure: I'd always wanted to abseil ever since I'd seen my first Bat-hound movie, or was it Spider-dog... And of course, Mike was down there, he would catch me – he'd make sure I didn't come to grief. The beach was far from empty, it being a sunny mid-afternoon, and I felt a twinge of pride at the attention of the motionless onlookers below. If my eyesight had been better perhaps I wouldn't have mistaken their shocked expressions for adulation. Taking a deep breath I launched myself off the edge.

Now I know you won't believe this, but Mike joined the other frozen silent spectators; just stood there staring aloft as I plummeted to the rough shingle below to land on my three and a half legs. Of course he made a fuss of me but the damage was done: my faith in him had been dented. I'm afraid he'd gone down in my estimation, as sure as I'd gone down that cliff-face. I suppose I was fortunate no over-hanging branch had intercepted my drop; or I should truly have had a hang-dog expression. I was taken for a check-up by a local vet and passed A1, or is it OK? I managed to restore some wounded pride by limping around for a few days in order to be carried and gain some sympathy. Perhaps Mike had yelled at me to stay put on that tall bluff as I teetered on the verge, but I'd always been a little hard of hearing anyway. It was just my suspicion that he couldn't walk on water after that, although I certainly had no intention of accompanying him if he ever attempted it! You know my feelings about getting wet...

THE GARDEN

Like a skein of blue silk blown against a wall
She walks by the railing of a path
in Kensington Gardens,
And she is dying piece-meal
Of a sort of emotional anaemia.
And round about here is a rabble
Of the filthy, sturdy, unkillable infants of the very poor.
They shall inherit the earth.

In her is the end of breeding.
Her boredom is exquisite and excessive,
She would like someone to speak to her,
And is almost afraid that I
will commit that indiscretion.

Floating iris flags caressed the tall red-brick wall with an assortment of blues from indigo to palest cyan. 'Quite impressive!' Hilary thought to herself as she sauntered along the even stone paving beside the gaily coloured petunias, a slight breeze catching her loose skirt as she headed for the gazebo. The bright sunshine belied her mood – here strolled a woman tormented by demons beyond her control.

Her unsettled contemplation was interrupted by the sound of a vehicle crunching to a halt on the gravel of the front driveway. '– Not that beastly little man again,' she pondered, returning to the house. He'd pestered her off and on for over a week now, 'why couldn't people be reasonable?' She hadn't wanted to go to the Village Barn Dance, but Monica had insisted. Of course she'd longed to dance but rather prayed that no one asked her – a prayer that was duly answered. Oh, why was she so screwed up? Perhaps she should pay a further visit to Dr Renshaw, he had warned her that she might relapse. But this Geoff was an intolerable bore, quite reputable in his old school way but a bore none the less. It's just that, well, if forced to admit it, she was rather wary of men. She liked men; she admired their camaraderie and bravado, unlike catty simpering women; it was simply she felt she couldn't trust them now, not after Peter's charade.

What was she doing here anyway, yet what choice had there been? Following the divorce, Peter had wanted to move speedily to his new pied-a-terre in town and she felt pressured into buying the first amenable property that came along. All that was two years down the road, and two miles down the road was that estate; well they had to be housed somewhere but really – in the Cotswolds? If only Monica was still around, now there was no one left of her set. Still, the garden was nice.

Of course it was the tiresome Geoff.

I suppose I was being rather tiresome, yet she certainly seemed an odd bird. I turned the corner of the house avoiding the hanging baskets where colourful clumps of bacopa and nemesia nestled alongside trailing geraniums. I found her attempting to hide behind the drooping pink and tangerine hollyhocks that stood shackled against the kitchen wall like torture victims in a dungeon. 'Garden's looking good,' I offered, a throw-away comment I could afford. In fact it was rather splendid; my gaze was drawn to the long lawn that had been chequered and manicured to within an inch of its life and stretched into the near distance over the rise and out of sight, accompanied by ordered rows of begonias and anemones. Behind these borderers stood a solid echelon of wall-flowers that stood poised at attention like a column of meer-kats as silent sentinels to political correctness.

Somehow she felt inadequate; there was simply nothing to do. She had tired of the endless attempts to maintain her sylph-like figure in contemporary fashions; books or music no longer amused her, and as for television... Life had become an empty void, a wasted husk of the expectant kernel of yesteryear. Perhaps Peter was right all along – she should have moved into town. The garden was nice; and with more money than she would ever need she of course had a couple of gardeners. Somehow it was all wrong–it wasn't <u>her</u> garden, she only visited it as a tenant, she felt it was on loan to her and never relaxed there. If she happened to move anything, she found it dutifully replaced the next day: a neglected sun-chair, watering-can or trowel found its way to the potting-shed, where tools were neatly stored and replaced on avenues of painted hooks by the zealous grounds-men.

'Yes,' she said, distractedly, '– Although it's the second time today I've had to pick up the litter. Those lads from the estate you know, they cycle up behind the wall and lurk there – God knows what they get up to – sex, drugs and rock and roll I suppose! I always know in the morning after they've been – broken rose-stems, empty beer-cans and other unmentionable refuse on the lawn. Judging by the number of hypodermic needles I've found they obviously suffer from some dreadful ailment or other! I could murder 'em! Never had that sort of riff-raff on the Downs, our neighbours were respectable. Still, they're everywhere these days, they'll take over in the end. The poor will inherit the earth,' she emphasised, misquoting the Bible.

'The Harvey-Beauchamps have all gone now you know – I'm the last of the line. It's all so terribly sad. My brother died in the Tropics. Cyanide-poisoning – caught from the Cassava plant on a visit to the Abuja Botanical Park in Nigeria'.

THE INTERVIEW

I wasn't keen on the assignment when my editor first handed it to me; do a feature on Jorge Davis the famous fashion designer and entrepreneur at his Cotswold factory. Jorge has a fiery reputation and is not known to entertain fools gladly. I am Donna Hilton and I do freelance work for a Worcestershire publishing firm.

On the day in question I motored towards Stroud in plenty of time, having set my SatNav to the correct coordinates and feeling pretty confident with myself. I had dressed in a crisp white blouse, grey business-like skirt and black jacket: no one could quibble with that. I would have to use a Dictaphone but this should be straightforward, the boss and I had given it a brief testing on the day before. I had done my homework and swatted up on the background to this millionaire.

Davis has become successful in the Middle East, launching a range of clothing in Saudi Arabia for the Al-Hokair company. He had an average school experience and, like his father, possessed an abiding allegiance to Liverpool FC; professing among his family friends none other than Bill Shankley. He even attended trials for Liverpool. Although he never achieved such status, he did however play as centre forward for Bangor City, British Universities and England under 18s.

Not settling to higher education despite study at Birmingham University in the 1960s, he took up a post with Littlewoods where he ended up running the Childrens Department. Following Littlewoods, at the age of 28, he started his own business. His background training stood him in good stead as he embarked on a design and buying course in retail clothing. As they say the rest is history. Jorge was responsible for the Next brand and the Per Uno M&S variant as well as input in the clothes range at Asda.

All was going to plan until I was leaving Stow-on-the-Wold, heading for Little Rissington I came across a sign blocking the carriageway and pronouncing the ominous words 'Road Ahead Closed'. To add insult to injury, this was the signal for the clouds to give vent and thunder rumbled overhead. I searched repeatedly for an alternative route but my SatNav resolutely clung to the A429 as my sole means of access. Driving around in desperation I stumbled upon a Garden Centre, where an obliging lady pointed out that I should do well to double back on my journey and seek an alternative. Ought I to call in and explain or would that make me even later? Eventually by negotiating a network of minor roads and re- entering details to the SatNav I was able to retrieve my bearings, but by then I had lost all composure.

With all my methodical preparation this just could not happen. I arrived on site hot and flustered, but with minutes to spare. An astute secretary gauged my situation and offered me a coffee...a glass of water would have been more appropriate. I could have dived in and swam around for a half an hour! I was inside what appeared as a long Nissan hut on an industrial estate, in a unit furthest from the road. 'I don't like being late at all,' I said lamely when the man arrived. He was dressed in what looked like jogging pants with a white shirt flapping over the top. 'But you are not late,' he replied. 'Yes, but...' I tried vainly to explain what had happened in apology for my confused state.

'Do you mind?' I enquired as I slid from my jacket, jettisoned my briefcase and struggled to set up the Dictaphone. 'Not at all,' he answered as he attempted to switch the machine to operational. 'Don't you just hate machines,' I ventured as I threw a few cursory remarks at the tiny black box. Although I had come prepared with about a dozen questions to guide the interview in the right direction, Jorge made it clear from the outset he just wanted to continue in monologue. However I did manage to prompt him on occasions he ran out of steam. I don't know how sensitive the Dictaphone was but it picked up the odd 'Dash it all!' or 'Drink your coffee, it's getting cold' (unlike my glowing cheeks).

I must say Jorge behaved perfectly throughout and did his best to put me at ease. But too late, the damage was done. I did however achieve the intended result, the interview went well and the boss was delighted. Yet I shall always remember my near miss. Returning from the Cotswolds I stopped at the first welcoming hostelry for a much needed double G and T.

THE NOTE

The room felt dark and oppressive despite the streaks of sunlight that filtered through the dull casement to highlight the worn hieroglyphics upon the faded red Persian carpet. I must get out she thought – go to the Hill. She put on a CD of Puccini as she got ready. She had a fondness for music, and in the past especially adored the haunting strains of the violin. The basement flat in Chalk Farm was all Rose could afford: If she stood on tiptoe on a chair she could watch the feet of passers-by as they scurried over the grey pavement above. it was handy and central and often she visited the Zoo or strolled around Regents Park, and sometimes when in the mood took the tube to the West End.

Turning from Gloucester Avenue into Primrose Hill Road she was in a pensive mood: she must have a word with that woman Eleanor who had moved into the apartment above. Rising to the top of Primrose Hill she was again awestruck at the panorama that greeted her. After negotiating the steep bank she paused for breath and surveyed the scene displayed before her: the day was bright and clear and she could make out St Pauls, the Shard, the London Eye and Post Office tower – it was harder to spot the Houses of Parliament and the Gherkin and occasionally she had to consult the information plaque.

Sometimes she had this magnificent view to herself – not today; a curly-haired young man in a red and white check open-necked shirt and faded jeans accompanied by a brindle Staffordshire-Bull terrier, stood gazing across the open space towards the vast urban sprawl. The studs on the dog's collar shone out splendidly as they reflected the vivid sunlight. Hailed as the best view of

London ever, many lyricists had fallen under its spell; tributes had been recorded by a number of artists from the Beatles to the Red Hot Chilli Peppers. The glorious vista never ceased to inspire. She spent a while pondering her thoughts on that grassy knoll before, with raised spirits, skipping back down the hill towards her humble apartment.

The sounds of the violin had been an abiding passion: of course she appreciated Vivaldi's Four Seasons, Mozart and Tchaikovsky, she admired the Mendelssohn and even Shostakovich Concertos but her favourite was Brahms – she could play the CD all day long. She was particularly fond of Hilary Hahn's interpretation; the woman seemed to have such a sympathetic touch as her delicate fingers effortlessly caressed the fret. Rose preferred music of the romantic period and Brahms was her favourite. She had a substantial collection of other concerti, the richest and most seductive was arguably Bruch's, and Mendelssohn's never failed to tweak the heartstrings, but Brahms'…

Alas all had been ruined by her immediate neighbour. Rose's flat was a dismal underworld where bright sunlight was a rare visitor and in that twilight world sleep should have fallen upon her easily, such was not the case. Recently, the peaceful nocturnal hours had been rudely shattered, rent asunder by the piercing shrill cacophony from above. Eleanor practised at the latest or earliest hours unbelievably upon the violin! How she could murder a delicate tuned instrument and cause it to shriek in such defiant anguish she never knew. She was aware the violin was not an easy option, and one of the most challenging of instruments: due, she presumed, to its fretless strings. But she felt the quality of her mercy strained beyond the limits of human endurance.

There was nothing for it, following a particularly restless night she felt it time to raise her objections – perhaps the other woman would prove reasonable and see sense, perhaps <u>she</u>'d find a new friend in that vast and lonely city. With certain trepidation she decided to confront her in the hallway after hearing the Victorian street-door slam shut. She climbed the stairs to the floor above and was in time to catch her neighbour ascending to her rooms. 'Er, excuse me Eleanor, I am very keen on the violin but do you think – ?' she began.

'What a coincidence you should mention the violin!' broke in Eleanor. 'I am having a terrible time trying to get it right, it just refuses to cooperate.'

Suddenly her composure slipped and her normally pleasant face contorted into a grimace: then to her companion's dismay she broke down in tears. 'You see my father was such a good player – once he played at the Albert Hall – he left me his instrument and I vowed to continue in his footsteps. But I am just no good!' she added through her sobs. The beleaguered woman was so distraught that Rose felt this wasn't the time to castigate her. 'I don't know where I'm going wrong, Dad would have put me right in no time flat. Maybe it's my bad hand-shape, but try as I may I just can't find the D sharp on the open string. I just can't find the note…'

THE OLD MILL HOUSE

As dusk descended, it was with a feeling of deep foreboding that I turned into the narrow lane that wound its overgrown and forsaken path towards the old mill house.

*

It was daring enough to visit the place in daylight, yet fears had gradually evaporated in the warmth of a clear summer day. The high lank hedgerows thick with cow parsley and clover throbbing with crickets had provided welcome shade from the unforgiving sun, and the intermittent spears of light that penetrated the rough foliage flecked my path with a kaleidoscope of dappled mosaics: an effect heightened by brilliant silver flashes as the sun's rays caught the silken skeins of spider-webs along the way. The sudden scampering of a lesser mammal and the lazy droning of insects added to a reassuring air of the commonplace.

Of course, the nocturnal visit had been Emma's idea. She was always the first to say where we should go and with whom. We knew it was pointless to argue once she had made up her mind. I had to go to the old mill or Emma would have told the other girls I was afraid, and she would have been very angry. Emma could sulk for England! I had to admire the resolve and velocity with which the others had forwarded their excuses for missing out on our expedition. Julia, Kim and Sarah had each had a cast-iron escape clause: if only I had been quick-witted enough to think of something.

Emma had been waiting impatiently inside the crumbling

ruins of the old barn that flanked the house on the river side. Almost before I had finished tentatively tapping our signal she had appeared from behind the heavy battered door; the gap through which we were just able to squeeze, where it lay at a lazy angle embedded in the soft ground, covered in moss and supported by its remaining rusty hinge. Her freckles and ragged auburn curls contrasted with her plain green dress, which had faded to a washed-out grey. Emma had never liked the curls but every time she had them cut back they bounced. Her socks around her ankles and grubby knees that matched the smudge of dust on her upturned nose, completed the image of reckless abandon.

'You're late, Nancy...', I was greeted. 'Are you ready? Come, let's go inside.' I followed in her wake as she thrashed at the tall grasses that spread from the mill-stream up to the desolate house. We made determined progress through the unkempt brush, pausing briefly to disentangle the more persistent brambles that snatched at our skirts.

The vacant house had appeared almost benign as it basked in the shimmering heat. Even the half-open door with its morbid portent seemed to yawn a drowsy welcome. I remember almost a feeling of relief as I followed Emma into its cool confines, despite the hollow emptiness and pervading musty odour. It had not been as dark as I imagined, shafts of sunlight had managed to penetrate the grime-stained glass to illuminate areas of decaying sallow floor-boards. Bird chatter from the abandoned chimney and the gentle rustle of leaves against a lower casement served to create a mood of airless quiescence.

We had played for hours, running along dusty corridors punctuated only by the neglected peeling woodwork of hollow vacant rooms; sliding down shiny banisters; climbing precariously amongst the ancient rusty pulleys and grinding gear where the sifted flour had once been stored and bagged for dispatch; and hiding in disused and stifling cupboards or beneath dingy forgotten stairways where daylight was permanently banished. As the long afternoon wore on I had become aware of a very dry mouth and nagging thirst; the combination of heat and dust eventually proving unbearable. This urge was inevitably accompanied by the image of the sparkling cool lime-juice my aunt always kept in a venerable misshapen jug for such emergencies.

Exhausted, I had finally flopped in some disarray on the first-floor stairs and absently drew a stray strand of hair from my face. This casual gesture was rewarded with the tackiness of cobwebs and I realised I must look a sight. Retracing my steps to the tiny upstairs room where I had noticed a grimy mirror, I dispassionately examined my appearance. My face glowed an unattractive red beneath dirt-stains traversed by rivulets of sweat. I was covered in grime and webs, my knees were grubby and bruised, my once white socks had turned to a dusty grey and an ugly tear scarred the sleeve of my blouse. What a mess! Hastily I shrugged off the vision of my aunt's agonised features and scolding tone and wondered if Emma could be tempted by the enticing lime-juice…at once I dismissed the idea, it would be a non-starter. I could imagine her response: 'Who wants a drink then? Who's a wilting violet!?'

That was when I lost Emma. We had explored all the upstairs rooms and played the usual games of tag, ladies-in-waiting and I-Spy, and then it had been my turn to hide. After counting to one hundred crouched in a small niche below the stairs, I had set out to find her. I knew she must be on the ground floor, as I had deliberately counted in a whisper to listen for any tell-tale creaking on the stairs above my head. Eliminating a service room and larger chamber, my search had led me towards what must have been the kitchen. The room was large and full of stagnant air where light was prevented from entry by tall overgrown bushes beyond the rotting casements.

Under a high window beside an outside door and barely discernible through the gloom, stood a derelict earthenware sink encrusted in the dirt of ages. The china felt cold to the touch as I stood on tiptoe and peered over the rim. The inside was befouled by a viscous green slime from which a huge spider emerged and scuttled for the safety of its lair behind the blackened taps. But there was no sign of Emma, not in the sink, under the sink, nor in the intimidating recesses of a walk-in cupboard that spanned one whole wall.

Then I felt alone: as dusk closed in I suddenly remembered where I was. Desperately I struggled to suppress my rising anxiety. I wanted to run, to escape the dark menace this house had always held for me. Through the dim window I noticed the sun had almost slipped from view and an involuntary shiver passed over me in the rapidly cooling air.

'Alright Emma, you win…I give up…I can't find you. You can come out now.' Silence. 'Emma…please come out,' I cried I hoped not too pathetically from the kitchen door. More silence. 'I have to be back soon…' I added in apologetic undertones. Then, as the echo of my voice trailed away to be swallowed up by the encroaching shadows along the maze of corridors, I became aware of a faint scratching.

'E-Emma…is that you?' Abandoning any pretence of calm, my apprehension hovered accusingly in the cloying air. With mounting trepidation I became aware of the direction of the scraping. It seemed to be coming from under my feet! Following the indistinct rasping had led me to a shabby wooden table against the far wall of the kitchen, beneath which my groping fingers came away with what felt like rotting wood. The floor-boards under the table appeared to have given way. The scratching stopped, to be replaced by a low whimpering.

'H-Hello…Can you hear me? Is anybody there?' I whispered hoarsely towards the inky void, while kneeling on the hard old boards.

'Nancy, it's me…who did you expect?' returned Emma, sounding far away and affecting a false bravado. 'I was hiding under the table and, well…you took so long to find me – the floor just gave way. I seem to have twisted my ankle – I can't put much weight on it. There's no way back up. I seem to be in some sort of cellar, but without any light I'm not about to investigate – you must go and fetch a torch, a-and the rope-ladder from the old tree-house at the bottom of the orchard. And don't you dare tell anyone, do you hear, Nancy-?' Pause. Then in a more conciliatory tone 'But do be quick! – It's so cold down here…'

I had run all the way to my aunt's, and as I paused to catch my breath was rewarded with fleeting glimpses of the dying sun between the tall branches. Creeping around the corner of the house, I had heard my uncle's snores through the open window of the parlour. I had carried out Emma's instructions. It had been quite a task untangling the rope-ladder and I put my uncle's torch from the woodshed into my cardigan pocket and slipped out, thankful my aunt had gone visiting in the village.

*

I was returning with pounding heart along the shadowy lane, the rolled ladder clutched tightly under one arm and uncle's rubber torch gripped firmly in the other. Purposefully, I intended saving the torch until it would really be needed: it would be sheer folly to go to that place without light. I was able to retrace my steps from memory in the remaining half-light.

Twilight drew its cloak across the brooding landscape, as I advanced pensively along the murky track. This time I stumbled into hidden hollows, and brambles, previously a minor inconvenience, were transformed to malicious barbed thongs that tore at my skin and tripped me, sending me headlong into the dampening grass or unseen nettles. Eventually I arrived at the house. I was aware of its oppressive presence before the towering walls loomed above me veiled in a rising river mist. The encroaching shadows had seemed to reach out for me, to enshroud me in a clammy embrace as I timidly approached. Instinctively I paused before the tall grey stonework, fighting the rising urge for flight: Emma would have made sure the others never forgot. Taking a deep breath, I climbed the steps that led up to the half-open doorway.

*

This time the gloomy hallway offered no reassuring solace, but contained an eerie stillness broken only by the rapid drumming of my heart. I felt a chill that belied the pleasant summer evening. With resolute clenching of teeth I ran into the kitchen. The room looked as it had done earlier. Although it was darker now, the outline of the table was discernible against the distant wall. Leaning into the scarred opening beneath I fought to gain the courage to break the reproachful silence.

'Em-Emma, are you still there…?' No sound. 'Answer me, Emma…please…it's me, Nancy. I did like you said. I brought the ladder, a-and the torch, I-I've got it here, look-' I struggled with the heavy rubber case and applied pressure to the switch. Blackness.

Desperately, I repeated the action with trembling fingers – to no avail. Through waves of mounting fear, I heard my voice croak 'Emma-Emma- speak to me please! …the torch, it won't work!' In rising panic, over and over again I frantically pounded the unyielding boards with the lifeless object: the only response was a series of dull thudding echoes which became swallowed up along those sinister corridors and staircases. Hysterically I kept screaming Emma's name into the black void beneath me as night claimed the old mill house…

THE PURPLE POSTCARD FROM PORTUGAL

With a sharp thwack it smacked onto the smooth parquet, bounced once and skidded along the floor to become partially obscured by the hall runner. Jackie heard it as she descended the stairs: More junk mail she thought. To her surprise she discovered a postcard, it was written in a scrawly hand and extraordinarily it was bright purple! She could appreciate the postman's dilemma, to whom it was intended was unclear; the house-number and postcode were just discernible but the srreet-name was illegible; however the postmark was unmistakeable – Lisbon.

She knew no-one in Lisbon nor anybody visiting the city, her interest grew, to cap it all the card was addressed to a Pam. The closest she had come to Lisbon was that trip she'd made with her sister to Alicante, when Beccy was looking for a holiday rental. And the closest she'd come to a Pam was that frumpy tight-lipped librarian from the council flats.

Oh dear, what to do? With a misdirected letter it was simple, one wrote 'not known' on it and returned the missive to the post-box. What was the procedure with a postcard? There was no room for additional amendment, this would only add to the message's confusion. Perhaps she should consign it to the waste-bin. But, she pondered, what if it was important?

She decided to scan the card for relevant information, no easy task given the poor handwriting, not to mention the deep colour. She expected the usual sentiments that accompany such offerings: "...sun, sea, sand and sex, not necessarily in that order, glad you're not here!" or "...the last time I was in Dubhai I was confronted with a naked snake-charmer...etc. etc." However,

219

it appeared written in a sympathetic tone, what she was able to decipher anyhow. It seemed to be from a person sightseeing the Portuguese capital and contained witty anecdotes. Mention was made of a visit to the San Jorge castle and the Ponte 25 de Abril suspension bridge, the Tagus Estuary, and the experience of Lisboeta (sampling of traditional Portuguese menus at 5 alternative venues). The message ended with an unintelligible signature below the allotted line space, squeezed below this, at the very bottom, was written "in case you've lost the number it is still 0795431288."

Well, not a cry for help, not even a desperate plea for cash; certainly no life or death emergency. Fundamentally she had been privy to a friendly exchange. She should throw the card out after all. Yet, as often happens in these situations, curiosity got the better of her. Perhaps she should inform the sender that she'd received the card. Slightly hesitant, she rang the number provided. She heard the monotonous tone ringing and ringing along the line, but no reply and there was no facility to leave a message.

A week or so passed and she was reminded of the incident when she came across the card beneath some outdated newspapers. She tried the number again. Still no answer; maybe the sender was still in Portugal, maybe they had lost their phone, perhaps the sender had written the details wrongly, her imagination ran riot. She thought again of discarding the card. She decided to make one more attempt at contact, after which she would dispense with the matter.

Third time lucky, or unlucky, she thought a fortnight later as she picked up the receiver. The number rang for a long time and she had almost returned it to its cradle when she heard a voice. Placing it to her ear, she was aware of pleasing male tones. 'Er hello, I'm Jackie and…' 'I'm sorry, but I don't know a Jackie.'

'No, and I don't know you…' 'Excuse me, but why are we having this conversation?' 'Please, let me explain…' It transpired that Dominic had sent the card to his mother, Pam Armitage (he'd always called her Pam), he'd been holidaying in Portugal, and he apologised, the communal phone was at the bottom of the stairs and he didn't always catch it before weary callers hung up.

It happened that he lived in the neighbouring county, and they got along rather well – that first time, they'd chatted on the phone for over an hour. She had explained, had it been legible, she would have forwarded the card to its intended destination. Eventually, following a series of phone conversations wherein Jackie derided him for his poor handwriting and colour blindness, they had met up and dated. Dominic would visit in his renovated red Morris 1100 estate. They shared similar interests and visited castles, ancient monuments and museums. They did the round of local National Trust properties, saw productions on stage and film; and went on long walks during which they discussed the meaning of life and wonders of the universe.

She felt completely at ease in his company, and each time they met they were able to pick up conversation from where they had left off. He was both erudite and witty, and not bad looking in her book. She became aware that they were seeing so much of each-other it was becoming serious.

One bright July morning came a knock on the door. Jackie opened it, prepared to greet Dominic arriving early to take her to the coast. On the step stood a young attractive platinum blonde with piercing baby-blue eyes and bright red lips; and before Jackie could offer 'Can I help you? she was greeted with the words: 'Hello, I'm Pam Walker…'

THE RECKONING

Lyn had worked for over two and a half years on the chicken farm. She enjoyed collecting the warm eggs and feeding the hens – she didn't even mind the mucking out, but she could never get used to the death of any living creature, she never would; since that time, when as a little girl, she had to have her pet cat put down after it had crossed the path of a runaway mink.

The vet had fought valiantly to save the tiny life, but in vain. She had grown up with that cat from its kitten stage and she adored it. Whenever she left the house the cat would follow till she turned the corner, when she knew it would return home. Their close relationship had lasted for 6 years and she retained many happy memories. When the cat died she had been inconsolable, so much so that her uncle had given her a small shot from the bottle of brandy that he kept for 'emergencies' within the dark recesses of his fireside shelves. Of course she had recovered from the immediate trauma and anguish, but her pet's final hours would stay with her forever: the wretched whimpering, her impotence to assist, and all the blood. She struggled to keep the lid firmly closed upon the sorrow that simmered quietly below the surface.

Doubting Tom's old farm cottage lay in a deep valley in a forgotten corner of the Dales. The closest village was half an hour away by foot and there was only a tiny post office and a pub when you got there. Thaxbridge was the nearest town of any significance, and there was one bus a day each way. She felt satisfied with the work and respected the brown hens under her charge; admiring their gentle nature and simplicity. The way they scavenged around the orchard floor in placid contentment, pecking here and there and calmly clucking away to one another of nothing in particular.

There had been times at the farm when injured birds had to be disposed of. Whenever such an incident occurred Lyn always made the excuse of a sudden appointment: a sick relative, or closing time at the post-office, or even locking herself in the toilet as a last resort. On such occasions Tom would take down his old hunting rifle from over the stone fireplace and she knew only too well when the deed was done. One of her jobs in the morning was to clean and dust for old Tom, and this included that gun. She always avoided looking closely at it and loathed even touching that messenger of death. She would flick tentatively at it with the corner of her duster in disgust.

It was about five o'clock on a dull wet Friday evening and she was alone tidying around the living-room, when she heard a hesitant rap on the outside door.

'Yes, w-who is it? she called out, not expecting Tom.

'Sergeant Perkins, ma'am. May I have a quick word?'

Opening the door she was aware of a uniformed police sergeant carrying a wicker-basket, the contents of which she was unable to ascertain.

'Is Tom at home?' the Sergeant's voice was a monotone. Then, 'May I come in, it's a little damp out here?'

'Sorry, of course...'she apologised. 'Er...I'm afraid he's gone to the bank in Thaxbridge. Won't be back till around seven,' she added, wondering what matter had warranted a call from the county constabulary.

Then she saw it, leaking from the basket he was holding were drops of blood and a trail had followed him from the door. Alarmed, she stepped closer to inspect the contents and immediately wished her curiosity hadn't got the better of her. Inside were what appeared to be perhaps half a dozen dead chickens – all mangled in various states of dismemberment, gory and misshapen. Involuntarily her throat tightened and she felt overcome with nausea that sent her weak at the knees as she collapsed into a chair.

The officer noticing how ashen she looked attempted to comfort her. 'Now, now, my dear, don't you go worrying about it, Tom'll be back soon…Uh…I'll just move this, if I may?' With that he took the oozing basket and its grisly contents and left it by the door. 'Tell Tom I'll call back first thing in the morning…'

As an afterthought he returned, 'I'm afraid that young lad of Tom's hasn't got the hang of that tractor…crashed it straight through the first o' them huts out yonder. Birds everywhere! I picked these off the road.' She felt numb all over. 'There's no sign of the boy anywhere, I reckon he must have gone home.' It had finally caught up with her, this was one time she *hadn't* been able to escape.'Well, I'll bid you goodnight ma'am…and don't take on so, Tom'll clear up the mess,' and the retreating man stepped back into the rain.

Despite the downpour, she darted ducked and dived, tripped and rolled over and over on the uneven sodden turf of the broad pasture – screaming, her face warm and streaked with tears as she scrambled she cared not where. She only knew she had to escape the carnage. The ticking of the kitchen clock was the only sound to break the silent scene of death within the dark farmhouse.

THE UNWANTED GIFT

Of the many embarrassing experiences that affect the social sphere, perhaps one of the most egregious to the human condition is the receiving of the unwanted gift. Yuletide is possibly the time when this phenomenon reaches the pinnacle of discomfort. We are all too familiar with the misplaced thong that the darling nephew got Aunt Agatha, and there is just no more space for Uncle Albert to accumulate neither extra socks nor bottles of after-shave. And the doe-eyed puppy is not only for Christmas, one day in the not too distant future, he will morph into an enormous vicious barking brute that will eat you out of house and home.

The enthusiastic donor is equally embarrassed as he elicits the receiver's behaviour, the face often proving the mirror to the soul. People then enjoin a little game and delicately dance around each-other: 'Well, I think it looks good on you.' or 'Is it possible to exchange it, ochre is just not me?' ' It's the thought that counts!' 'Well, perhaps I can take it back', we offer reluctantly, and in our willingness compound the issue with: 'Of course, I still have the receipt, somewhere...' (Then bite the tongue as we realise that the receipt could give away the £3.99 item bargain price). Perhaps we might reach the stage of: 'Don't look a gift horse...' or even 'Beware of Greeks...'

Many, through bitter experience, have become wise and these days decide upon the Gift voucher. An ideal solution, until you realise that none of the participating stores are within a 50 mile radius of the recipient, or the person has to add a considerable sum to the voucher in order to make a reasonable purchase. Large families in particular have thrown in the towel, no space for more; and especially where people live miles apart have become resigned to sending cards only. To give is nobler than to receive, and including postage such esprit de corps can add to a pretty pound.

Even the most clairvoyant can err. How on earth are we supposed to enter another's mind and read their needs? Women are notoriously difficult to please, never second guess size, style or colour; and of course never shop on spec, unless you are one of those demented souls who Christmas shop in October: venturing anywhere in the vicinity of shopping malls at the height of the season is worse than tiptoeing the plank over a pit full of famished crocodiles. We are often heard to say: 'I wouldn't take it as a gift!', and I am ashamed to say some of my offerings have fallen under this heading. Normally this is the result of an exasperated last-minute brain-wave. We also learn of the person who has been endowed with a gift of nature they feel they could live without, such as psychic powers. We may pass on to others more than they bargained for, such as the gift of the common cold. And of course there are recipients of more valuable gifts, the like of the unwanted engagement or wedding ring – that finds its way into the dismal jumble of goods at the local pawn shop.

*

Nowadays it is customary to receive the miscellaneous gadget; we fight hard to suppress the first thought, that this will be yet one more item to clutter the drawers. Nevertheless one puts a brave face on it: 'You really are too kind – just what I needed'. 'Er, what is it exactly?' Inevitably it finds its way to the drawer's further recesses or the garden shed (out of sight, out of mind):

For we are too afraid to discard it at a local charity shop which may be frequented by its original purchaser.

Flowers are often a good stand-by, although they are generally inadvisable for a 15-stone tattooed truck-driver unless of course as a pair you are on amicable terms. It is not always possible to 'Say it with flowers.' It was a certain Charles Dudley Warner who said with a degree of irony in 1873: 'The excellence of a gift lies in its appropriateness rather than in its value.'

A good-natured friend, knowing of my penchant for the occasional wine of the ruby variety, at times regales me with a cabernet-sauvignon, shiraz or merlot; such sweet repast however is somewhat marred, not to say entirely obscured, in that the delectable beverage is invariably imbibed within the confines of her smoke-filled kitchen, wherein her husband continually exhales cigarette smoke. Such is the price of pleasure. And mention of friends reminds me, the storage jars I recently gave as a house-warming token have yet to appear on Ebay.

To avoid the scourge of the unwanted gift, more thought needs to be committed to the choice. Yet this must be weighed against the other valuable commodity that is of the essence – precious time. When in doubt opt for the innocent unbreakable lightweight innocuous versatile redeeming card.

THE WOMAN FROM WREXHAM

Caring and kind neat and tidy, she and her cat were content; that's all life should be about. She visited the gym, walked the hills on a regular basis, played badminton and visited a local swimming baths. She'd been married for 20 years, lost a child during a difficult pregnancy, gone through the traditional rites of passage. She'd didn't want attachment; no way, was over all that – too wearisome. She belonged to several leisure groups from petanque and tai chi to poetry, was a keen photographer, an avid reader, enjoyed pottering in the garden and had made lasting friendships. Yet something was missing, she had felt out of kilter with the world for some years, a state of ennui threatening her: She felt restless, incomplete.

Despite occasional church attendance she found they were neither speaking to, nor for her, and services sounded hollow: despite a wholesome diet her spirit remained under-nourished. She had begun to question the dusty liturgy and paternal presumptions she'd encountered under various denominations. She wasn't alone, she mused, as she'd gazed nostalgically around daunting edifices of cheerless stone to be confronted with row upon row of empty pews and acres of vacant space that had once echoed the praises of Zion.

She had often sat in the expectant contemplation of cool sanctums, her eyes drawn to the votive candles that sputtered in dark corners and enlivened the features of gloomy martyrs as narrow shafts of light furred with dust motes bisected the shadows. The crucifix over the altar appeared blunted by time and apathy, and the pale face of Jesus was blurred and burdened by decades of dust and despair. Who was it that said churches were simply museums wherein the pastor served as curator? Nevertheless they did provide refuge for a scattering of the oppressed, the faithful few. As the 20th century theologian Paul Tillich observed: 'Throughout history the Church has served the function of producing an uneasy conscience in those who have received a new Being but still follow the old ways.'

In soul-searching mode she decided to research less orthodox forms of worship. She studied books by Nietzsche stating that God was dead, then moved on to the honest account of organised religion by John Robinson the ex Bishop of Woolwich; his diagnosis was that the patient (religion) was still breathing yet in intensive care. This had led inevitably via Bonhoeffer and Tillich, to the recently retired American Episcopalian Bishop Spong and the progressive theologian Marcus Borg. To friends, she referred to this quest as 'her spiritual odyssey'. She ordered most books on-line from the popular Zambeze website and with cost in mind opted for 'good-but used' copies. On a crisp morning, as a brazen song-thrush proclaimed her overture on a branch above an array of early primulas, the postman delivered another book: *Taking Leave of God* by the Lancashire born Don Cupitt.

A cursory scan of the publication revealed this was not simply another volume on spiritual themes. She discovered annotations appended at intervals throughout the book in the margins, drawings too; along with a receipt from the Halifax Building Society that had presumably served as a hasty bookmark. These were no random jottings, but a heartfelt and sincere log of human emotion inscribed with raw feeling, presumably the writer expected no one to see them. An open catalogue of soulful sentiments, a profile of a woman etched in pencil.

She had sat perplexed on her bed for a long while after

discovering the defaced pages, the book on her knee. The volume was slim yet it took her over a week to get through the 180 pages, taking care to absorb its contents. The text was profound and thought-provoking, periodically accompanied by an adjunct of these additions; some matter-of-fact, some tragic and heart-rending. On one page marginal notes were accompanied by a sketch of a Greek cross and what appeared to be a sepulchre; and many passages had been poignantly underlined. Reference was made to the author's narrative, involving critique and comments often adjoining a certain line or passage. More than mindless graffiti this was the pathetic wail of a wounded animal. As she read, she found her eyes inescapably drawn toward the carefully pencilled entries accompanying the printed word. In so-doing, she was allowed a rare window into the other woman's soul: this was more than a diary, it was a cry for help.

*

Despair, despair...will it ever end!? I feel so desperate! Of course I feel desperate, of course he left me...there has to be more than this... I discovered that Bunbury dolphins had arrived at Eagle bay. This book? O, something I picked up in the charity shop – about finding peace – try anything. Eat a hearty breakfast Ma always said, what did she know; bacon, toast... No! The kids are coming home today, must tidy round, must get them lunch – fish fingers, Jason's favourite, they seemed happy enough. Order – is order important?... Time and time again I had walked along saying to myself 'it's not a matter of believing if Christ rose from the dead (a meaningless credo) but will I rise out of this abject state of misery ever and begin to believe again that life has meaning? For feeling my own emptiness is death!' (and I don't usually believe I'll rise). Had meal at Over the Moon. This is ridiculous, why's he knocking the metaphysical?... Is that really

so? Like Michal believes in 'guardian angels' or 'white magic'? Hey,
I must stop scribbling on this. Well, it's mine; I can do as I please.
Maybe Nadine might take me and the kids to the beach – they'd
like that. We could go over Blackwater way, to Curracloe, miles of
flat sand...

Thursday, I leave too early, come back, practice today. Nadine
is bringing me unexpectedly into Wrexham, in her car. Ok, ok,
obviously I have revived, and it's not only the tablets, I've come alive
and see life as having meaning (that word again), or I would not
be writing marginal notes here! Hot choc in cafe by Duke Street,
and I get a special salad baguette... Mon Dec 4 2006, I like this,
he's a good writer... I am cast down – Nancy rejects my 'Up Market
Welsh Babe' T shirt. One's whole emotional world perceived is a
myth...two days, three, in a virtual coma – a state of unending
despair (Sat-Mon 16-18 Dec)... oh no, not Christmas! Must get
something for the kids... I've taken £300 out of the Halifax (leaves
me £92.59), should cover my trip and the presents. I have been all
my life using my complex and cunning brain to prove I am sad and
inept. Had kids to lunch, two rolls – they like them, then shops with
Nancy and Jason...Laze – despair again, again, cycle to Scarboro'.
Talk to man from Linlithgo' (Emma with scooter) and to Swansea
(barman from Dundee). 18 Dec, what do I do (I thought in the
toilet) have done always? I hate myself, and I project, attribute the
hatred to other people...

Yes, yes, this is so right; I want that experience 'higher
consciousness' ecstasy, the feeling of being at one with the universe,
because I have time, again, experienced it, and cannot do anything
but seek it frantically. In it, I know the meaning of life! But if life
has no meaning...? Now does he call my yearning extraneous?...
I refuse to crucify myself! Meaninglessness is not rational so I say
(even if I lie) meaning is the core of our and the world's existence!
He's back on 'life after death' again. Since you know nothing – nor

does anyone – about what happens after our body dies – why are you so adamant, so superstitiously positive – that we do not live beyond death? No one on this side knows, not even you...Puffing, walk on beach with my hosts (Glenrothes, Firth of Forth Christmas visit), reading De Bono's crude theology of 1900. On Sat or Fri cycle to, er, Perth...Friday, and return on Sat I think... Where he says: 'You must change your whole life. That is the only way to spiritual integrity and freedom from this false and ugly self that you are, for at present your very selfhood is a pack of lies', I scrawled a big YES of agreement and bracketed off the whole paragraph!

*

Gradually she was able to piece together the puzzle that was 'Cassandra', she had named her after Priam's daughter (who also sought religious truth). At first, she felt like a trespasser who had stumbled unaware upon another's private diary; yet, as she progressed it dawned on her she had found a friend, a being she could totally identify with – a kindred soul. From between these painfully etched lines a pathetic figure emerged; diligent probing and collation of those evocative marred pages rewarded her with a gossamer portrait of the person herself. Little by little the emotive kaleidoscope of Cassandra took shape; until, finally, she was in front of her: a slight slim woman – intelligent, in her fifties with a daughter the age her own would have been; an active woman fond of nature, an attentive mother who kept in touch with friends. All this she had gleaned.

They were similar in many respects she pondered wistfully: both mature women disenchanted with mainstream religion, perhaps they could seek answers together. That quest had cost that person dear, caused her guilt and anxiety, low self esteem and insecurity yet she had resolutely clung to the cause. Her heart reached out to this lost individual; she wanted to comfort her as her flesh and blood, throw her arms around her and console her, the grand-kids too – then she hastily rebuked herself. 'This is silly – stop right there. Where are you going with this!?' O Cassie, if she only had an address, a name…there was nothing she could do…If there was some way to make contact, tell her not to give up hope; to welcome each and every fresh morning; to somehow make her see that she had much to be thankful for, look forward to – she yearned to reach out to this stressed being, to be-friend her for the sake of basic humanity. Yet she felt her own impotence. Had Cassandra enjoyed her Christmas of 2006? 2006 – maybe it was too late…

THREE CAT-ASTROPHES

During those warm dry months of the summer of '84, as in the drought of '76, our walls had proved a benevolent oasis. Whilst providing a cool retreat from sizzling temperatures and simmering fatigue, the thick stone equally insulated against gnawing winter chills. Above, swallows darted, banked and dived in oscillating spirals between the silent chimneys. It was then that our long hours became embroidered by three new arrivals.

The cottage, nestling a precipitous wooded hillside in the Welsh Wye valley, had long been a revival centre for diverse stricken flora and fauna, a rest-home cum soup-kitchen for various waifs and strays – more particularly a haven of content for a succession of furry denizens of the genus felis, simply fugitive felines. To this day I can still recall the expression on the bemused face of a Severn Bridge toll-clerk as I pulled up in a vintage Austin 1100 hatchback (similar to John Cleese's car in *Fawlty Towers*) packed to the gunnels. Straining against the restrictive interior was an assortment of furniture and bric-a-brac, including two year's stock of home-made wine. To top it off, a stuffed stag's head was strapped precariously to the rain-swept roof-rack. A large parrot-cage on the front passenger seat enclosed a dark multi-marked cat of dubious heritage – the other two had opted to travel first class via the removal van.

That was in the past; since that chilly winter eight year's nebulous water had passed beneath that fatigued Bridge's foundations; today an up-to-date version runs alongside. The latest wave of astute appli-cats for our hillside health-farm composed an engaging trio; two thirds of which had shared a similarly bleak and unpromising beginning: the remainder was Sebastian. Of a scruffy litter of six scrawny kittens from the Forest of Dean, first impressions of this aspiring tom were hardly favourable. This litter runt was no more than 5 inches long and had the appearance of a dirty white pygmy rat embossed with nondescript daubs of tabby hue, as though sprayed by a passing muck-spreader. Where his nose should have been, he sported a tiny pink snout that decorated his features with the emphasis of an almond in a plate of trifle. His exterior, lacking any semblance of hair and culminated in a tightly coiled tail, alluding to some forgotten suidian ancestry – surely the tiniest of porkers.

Initial misgivings soon evaporated under the warmth of the little fellow's endearing charm. This miniscule moggie purred at the sound of a friendly voice or chirped in excitement when engaged in such pussy pursuits as the exploration of a cardboard loo-roll interior, a plastic net for oranges or redundant bottle-cap. Diminutive yet thriving, he was capable of devouring all edible (and other) substances that came his way. Such times were his most energetic, when not indulging in his daily hibernation – when he regularly slept for about three weeks, or so it seemed. Cat-napping and still tiny, he was easy to transport around the cottage curled into a tight ball inside a warm pouch or finding a ready hammock in B's tracksuit hood. Like a hairy billiard ball he developed a fondness for deep soft pockets.

A somewhat persistent rust-spot upon the sparkling armour of this little white knight was his unfortunate recurring "brain-damage" (we gave him the benefit of the doubt and referred to these attacks as minor lapses in concentration). Whenever the guileless animal fell, or inadvertently made contact with an occupied wellie, it was invariably his suspect skull that bore the brunt of the impact. He could only manage to consume half a bowl of cat chow at one sitting, being totally unable to fathom that the unreachable area of a saucer contained an equal portion of goodies (maybe it was just his eye-sight; and, to be fair, in those days the saucer was twice his size). Yet this enigmatic phenomenon, named after and bearing no other similarity to Coe the mid-distance runner, was doted on to the perfunctory exclusion of such trivia as his vacant cranium, hair-lip and club-foot; after all, beauty is only fur-deep – his fur did grow eventually.

Equally at home in the plush refuge of his master's favourite chair or snuggled upon a shoulder as the phone began to ring, he would stretch out in deliriums of delight whenever stroked, tickled (or shouted at). Exceptionally quiet, his voice not having broken, and fastidious concerning upholstery, stress-limit of linen union versus four fistfuls of non-retractable grappling hooks unknown! Nor did he break much china, although once or twice he was guilty of sharpening his teeth on the stalwart tape with which we optimistically tethered valuable articles to the shelves. Half-a-dozen dirt-trays proved essential, as the bonehead was incapable of pin-pointing their whereabouts with the slightest degree of accuracy. Should he accidentally stumble upon one of the trays secreted at strategic points around the cottage he was instantly rewarded with an effusion of misplaced compliments. Compliments that died on the lips as the quisling was incapable of perfecting his aim; with the result that often he would sit in the tray and project his bottom over the edge into the living room. In short, this miniature Macenroe proved an im-purrfect example of cat-hood.

On one occasion, accompanying us to a Welsh beach, he entertained us with a beguiling game of hide-and-seek among the rocks; this following a car journey of 100 plus miles throughout which he travelled relaxed and unrestrained verging on the comatose. This maligned miscreant, this puss-icuted head-banger, had found a home.

Sebastian's two sisters by proxy came from the wild untamed terrain of Pembrokeshire. We had stolen a week away from the rigours of paid labour and the herculean task of rebuilding the cottage, and had retreated to spend some time in our retired caravan, or immobile home. This was secreted within a clump of wild gorse amid an abandoned meadow over-looked by a row of bungalows. It was in that summer place where buzzards hovered in the breathless air above pulsing hedgerows that quivered in the sultry heat. Tireless crickets hummed rhythmically and countless flies were busy among patches of bright yellow gorse and purple vetch; brown sorrel and reed grasses reached out in supplication to an unremitting sun. Over arid brooks where barbed brambles bent beneath their ripe shiny burden and desultory multi-coloured butterflies flitted lazily to alight upon majestic thistles that swayed like proud sentinels within the landscape.

Despite having shared a similarly harsh environment, our two orphans were as different as Madonna and Margaret Thatcher. When we first made their aquaintance on a day that heralded the first persistent rainfall for a month, we put their ages between five and six weeks. Both had suffered the traumas of being born wild and the subsequent struggle for survival in a harsh environment. Their initial blind view of life must have been harrowing as they stumbled through the long coarse grasses, ferns and brambles of that derelict pasture. Food was intermittent and the assortment of old doors, tyres and tumbling stacks of tiles discarded by a local builder offered scant shelter amid the uneven turf.

Part of a shabby band of maybe half-dozen feral cats of indistinguishable age and heritage, our two kittens must have used up a high percentage of their nine lives as they acquired sight and foraging techniques. At times the mother would leave the remains of a rabbit, and a few kitchen scraps were infrequently flung over the hedge in the direction of these timid scavengers. Enquiries of the bungalows established that all were strays, and those eluding the local RSPA cat-knapper were about to have their scuba-diving expertise tested in a bucket of water; however, we sentimental English would be more than welcome to any animal we could kit-nap.

Wilderness found us, she staggered out of that Welsh drizzle and into our hearts. A jet-black striped tabby to which the cream inserts of her ears provided the merest relief, she possessed a short spiky coat and a silent miaow. This pathetic creature fixed us with dark soulful eyes that spoke volumes prefaced with despair – thus she came to be named. During our two remaining nights in the caravan, I had awoken to find her nestled in the warm security of my arm-pit. Slowly she thrived and grew to be a handsome queen.

Wilderness had arrived shortly following our participation in a flagrant exhibition of derangement which left the pair of us battered and breathless, and red in the face (not merely from embarrassment). In more relaxed times, I was to refer to this aberration as "moggie-bashing". During a visit to the bungalows B had caught a fleeting glimpse of a fluffy grey kitten, whose long hair and attractive looks placed her apart from her fellow refugees from hell. This tiny waif possessed quite an aristo-catic demeanour, barely visible beneath a mask of wide-eyed wonder at her predicament; truly a mog-Persian.

Excitedly, B had drawn my attention to this "feline friend" (although shortly I was to drop the "r") of whom I was treated to a transitory image as she darted for cover. Frightened saucer-large blue eyes circled in amber were set perfectly into a soft grey furry head framed ignominiously by the grimy rim of a

6-inch soil-pipe. While B busied herself navigating a path between the numerous obstacles of building detritus that littered the landscape, Fluffy and I continued our eye-ball to eye-ball confrontation. My keen gaze was disdainfully returned with an irreverence born of freedom. B's appearance at the further end of the pipe provided the catalyst to unlock our visual intercourse. Then B was in position, and that was that, just a simple manoeuvre to drop the tiny beauty into the vacant basket – or so we thought.

Flapping net from rural bungalow windows betrayed the location of curious Welsh voyeurs. No doubt at that very moment they were reaching for their Rennies in desperation, in a vain attempt to dispel the dyspeptic disturbances brought on by the extra lunch-course we were providing. To our consternation there was no sign of Fluffy, and we found ourselves gazing at one another along the grubby ceramic tube like a pair of gibbering chimpanzees. Two adults, on the surface of reasonably sound minds, kneeling gingerly in thigh-length soggy grass and peering vacantly at each-other along a length of discarded glazed piping was obviously more compelling entertainment than that on offer from the television; the 'Antiques Road Show' or the life-cycle of the indigenous Alaskan ice-mole simply could not compete.

The fun then began in earnest. Ignoring snagging briars that played noughts and crosses over our smart green wellies, we crashed and cavorted around that meadow like Druids at a Solstice. Oaths were mercifully drowned in the rampant foliage, as we flung ourselves unflinchingly into succulent nettle-beds of Triffid proportions; or fell head-long over trip-wires of entwined brambles and coils of thick wire, to emerge in a sodden melange of sweat and rain topped off with a liberal coating of furry burrs. There followed a brief lull in the spectacular, as the weary forces regrouped; at this moment I was prepared to throw in the towel (although had a towel been to hand I should have dried myself off first!) Judging by the still curtains, our audience had taken this as the intermission; I imagined the power-surge as fifty kettles instantly went into over-drive. There must have been a frantic dash to warm tea-pots and prepare Welsh cakes in morbid anticipation of further indignities to follow.

Predator B again sighted her prey and, following primitive sign-language that would have done credit to a mental institution for Amazonian bush-men, I also managed to locate the hapless hairy Houdini; cringing in trepidation, she had assumed the form of a dark patch between a breeze-block wall and a dilapidated peeling door. B tiptoed, as only one can in wellies, towards our quaking quarry; while I approached from the direction of the stalls exercising all the stealth I could muster. Unfortunately the desired surprise of our pincer movement was thwarted by my cry of anguish as I inadvertently disclosed my whereabouts by tripping over a concealed hillock. I ended up buttocks over apex, albeit in the correct place – namely blocking off any viable escape in my direction.

This was it, we had reached the moment of truth, no turning back. I made offensive noises from my direction, while B courageously stuck her hands in the general direction of the timid shadow lurking close to her end of the rotten timber. The tranquillity of that Sunday afternoon was irretrievably shattered by B's howl of pain as she withdrew her hands; one clutched a bleeding thumb and the other a violently protesting fluffy grenade. As the hissing spitting varmint was temporarily floored, I approached panting; and using my superior guile, and one hundred and thirty pound weight advantage, pinned the unfortunate grey bundle to the damp turf whilst yelling for B to fetch the basket.

I had no intention of letting this mesmerised mouser

escape due to any ineptitude on my part, especially after the imbroglio we had already endured. Besides, the audience deserved a positive outcome. B duly arrived and the furry fiend was unceremoniously deposited within the wicker enclosure, the catch was drawn and we gasped with relief. By this time, the spectators were probably rolling about on their Wiltons, reduced to paroxysms of uncontrollable mirth. Triumphant though battle-scarred, like mud-spattered commandos, we slunk towards the cover of the caravan; B sucking her injured digit, I had to admire her fortitude. This had been the antithesis of our meeting with Wilderness, who had calmly walked into our lives.

First suggestions for a name for this grey grimalkin were understandably censored. Early realistic options such as various battle grounds held a certain fascination; names such as Pearl Harbour, Paschendale, or Culloden were echoed sympathetically. Eventually we arrived at Islandwhana, site of a telling British defeat at the hand of Zulu warriors. The latter appealed to B, who preferred the abbreviated Isa; so she became Isadora, the one who had led us a merry dance.

Of these redeemed pussies, Wilderness was the one who related to us from the start – she had the need. Isadora, although shy and retiring, slowly began to mellow and with daily doses of TLC learnt to overcome her anxieties. An environment of calm and plenty of patience we found can work miracles. As for Sebastian, he never succeeded in getting a mention in the Guiness Cat-alogue of Records for the longest cat-nap in history! All three immigrants meeting at a similar age grew up together. They were each individuals and successfully imprinted their unique personalities on our lives. A healthy inquisitive spirit allied with a naïve trust and natural exuberance formed the ingredients for an intoxicating cocktail that served as a constant delight to their benefactors.

These aspiring "wild"-cats all grew to maturity in a cosseted environment and readily succumbed to domesticity. The trio settled in with other deserving vagrants equally rescued from impending disaster and graciously accepted succour, shelter and security. Further feline asylum-seekers rested awhile at the old black and white stone cottage on the banks of the river Wye, in the company of various canines they roamed our woods, marked our hours and decorated our days.

TILL WE MEET AGAIN-

It had been a while since I returned to Balby, and not a lot had changed – I could almost pick it all up where I left off, figuratively speaking that is.

I knew where to find Granville of course, his bicycle was lying outside No 34 Lister Avenue, skiving as usual on the pretext of delivering to Nurse Emanuel. I found him busy cleaning her best chintz upholstery with the seat of his filthy overalls.

She was reclining on her chaise-longue, as voluptuous and inviting as ever. I sidled across to her side: 'Gladys, Gladys, I kneel at your feet. You once asked me what my meringues were like, well, now I'll show you!

Come on, come on, don't crit there sitizing lad. Thik shop'll be full o' customers be now, and you'm missin' all them sales.' Granville sprang to his feet with a shiver, as though directed by some malignant force that set the hairs of his neck twitching, 'You know, Gladys, sometimes I've the feeling uncle is still here, he never went away. I feel his beady eyes watching to see I don't pocket the small change! Now he's calling me back to the shop.'

'Aye, that'll be Arkwright. If there's one thing worse than a furtive grocer, it's the ghost of one.'

*

'A tin of luncheon meat Mavis, that'll be two shillings and nine-pence.'

Well done Missus, and you certainly have been. Granville, don't forget to charge for the p-p-pepper, I know she's not buying it but she's sprinkled some all over t'floor. Granville, fetch your cloth! Don't dally lad, and t-take her money before she changes her mind. Face like a fit that one!

Now, I want a w-w-word wi' you our lad. That Big Edna, have you been knock-knock-knocking coppers off her order? That's alrit, if you put 'em all back on 't somewhere else!

Where was I, oh yes, that silver coin collection...now, the old Oxo tin? Of course under the kitchen sink. Couple of these are pre 1922 and solid silver... It's bright in here – the lad's using too much 'lectricity...must arrange for a power cut...

Now, one last thing – check the cash is still rolling in. On the counter, somewhere along here, behind the sherbet dips and liquorice torpedoes, ah yes. Yaah! It's got a mind of its own – Till, we meet again! Heh, heh, I wonder how many times they've stitched Granville's fingers back on?'

Granville jumped as the till sprung open: 'Yaah! Mind of its own that machine, must get a new one – the old skinflint wouldn't, said it deterred burglars.'

'Yes, it were a g-great burden Granville, being 'olier than everyone else. But I enjoyed it! Aye lad, remember I told you one day all this would be y-yours, lock-lock-lock-lock-lock, stock and barrel? Well, now it is, and a right pig's breakfast thees making of it. You'll be late for your own funeral youth, you were certainly late for mine!'

TIPPING POINT

Jake Crochett was a hard man on a short fuse. He lived in a cottage close to a tiny hamlet at the bottom of Spillbrook lane, about four miles from Norwich, with his only daughter Sal; having lost his wife in childbirth three years previously, her with baby and another baby before that. A country boy, his father was a carter, he grew up around horses.

When he was ten years old the family moved to London, which he hated. But his father had a job working for The Pantechnicon Ltd in Belgrave Square, a furniture shop and picture gallery, where he drove a horse-drawn van. Magnificent beasts were those vans – tall black and sleek with the firm's name in gold on the side; 12-18 feet long by 7 feet wide and pulled by a pair of shires. Seated on high, the driver was afforded a panoramic viewpoint, master of all he surveyed, and loading these mammoths was made easier by cranking down the back axle then dropping a rear bay.

After losing his father to over-work and his mother to TB Jake had returned to the rural life. He acquired an un-sprung oxcart (or 'jinker') and a roan Clydesdale named Trooper. Roans were less popular, the white hairs intermingled with the brown, so Jake was able to do a good deal on him. With white splashes on his face he was often taken for a skewbald Irish Cob or Tinker Horse, the favourite of the Romanies, despite lacking the tell-tale feathered heels. Jake refused to move to the city like most folk, clinging to the notion he could use his skills transporting customers' goods, and handling occasional removals.

A shady chancer: he was always on the lookout for a quick deal and forged most of his dubious contacts in the dingy chasms of ale-houses. Here he frequently came off second-best in drunken brawls, although that failed to silence him: many's the time he would return to Sal the worse for wear to receive nursing and a piece of her tongue. To some, Jake was 'street-wise, savvy, a rough diamond', others kept their counsel. It was a hard life putting bread in his and his daughter's mouth, although Jake felt equal to the task: she was surly like him – a chip from the same rotten woodpile.

One day he was sought out to dispose of some refuse from the new metal bins that had been introduced to cope with the ash-pit privies' in the late 1800s. He had emptied the rubbish into a handy ditch and was walking away when he spied a glinting in the long grass. He uncovered an embossed silver butter-knife with an ivory handle. It dawned on him: maybe he should collect rubbish more often – people unwittingly discarded what they didn't intend: treasure for the taking to eagle-eyed Jake.

Beside removals, he built up steady work collecting others' rubbish and often found worthy objects to pass on: Items such as silver spoons, fairground jewellery, chipped china, sometimes coins or fancy buttons; jewelled hat-pins, a pocket watch and once a broken set of bellows; and even a pair of valuable antique silver sugar-tongs. His main problem was the disposal of waste. For this purpose he sought out quiet woodland regions, although at times he would use hedgerows or deep ditches to abandon the refuse. All shades of detritus including hot ashes had to be sifted through, some more pleasant than others. He didn't care, it was definitely worth it: 'Where there's muck there's brass!' He considered himself a fully paid-up member of the AFT (the Affiliation of Fly Tippers).

Then, fortune smiled on him: filtering a particular load he uncovered what appeared to be a small cheap brooch. On closer inspection he discovered it was in the form of a cross, about an inch and a half in length but with fluted edges. Thomas Mathias, the fence he'd known from the years they'd played truant together, said it wasn't worth a bean. Jake wasn't so sure. He weighed it – it was twice as heavy as brass; he rubbed it between grubby fingers and smelt it, no smell – brass would have one; he rolled it on his tongue, no taste – brass had a definite tang. He gently scratched the back, it didn't react as any brass he'd stumbled upon: he was becoming quietly excited. Cleaning it, he found the cross was studded with stones, a large one in the centre with smaller ones on the arms.

Feeling buoyed up he decided to take it to a Norwich pawnbroker, and chuckled as the man dropped his eye-glass in enthusiasm: 'What do you want for it?' 'What'll you gi' me?' 'Well, it's a fine looking piece, I'd say it'd fetch about a thousand punds on the market.' Jake couldn't conceal his delight: 'N-no, I'll keep hold o' it for the time being. It were a special o' the wife's,' he lied with a grin. Roaming the streets, he felt in a fever: a thousand? That meant it was worth double. Leaving the Black Swan he found himself treading the cobbles of Elm Hill where he straightened his neckerchief, ran his fingers through his greying locks, and entered an elegant-fronted jeweller's shop.

The salesman looked him up and down with certain disdain, but when he saw the object his eyes grew brighter than the centre gem. 'Well, well, what do we have here,' he said reaching for his eye-glass. His slow deliberate examination of the piece was accompanied by a gentle clicking of the tongue. Finally he spoke: 'Sir, we have here a 17th century Byzantine Greek Orthodox Cross, previously used as a pendant, in 18 karat yellow gold centrally embedded with a quality diamond and surrounded by emeralds. Are you looking to sell it? I would put on it a price of £2500. Maybe more if you went to auction…' he added. Jake swallowed hard: 'No, just wanted to value it,' he croaked and hurtled out of the shop and back to the Black Swan. On his rather wayward journey home he began to whistle, something he wasn't noted for, as he fingered the cross to assure himself it was real.

Arriving home he ignored the house and made straight for the stables. Sal had fed Trooper, who stood in the corner of his stall contentedly munching hay. In a dark cubbyhole where the spare shoes, tools and harnesses were stored was a grubby old jacket and Jake slipped the cross into one of the deep pockets. He wasn't going to mention his find to Sal just yet, not until he had decided on a plan of action. He was free, he would live a life of ease, he could have a fine house, perhaps a servant…Best keep it quiet for now, don't want Sal gossiping in the village or wasting it on fripperies. In the next few weeks he'd decide, after all he was the man of the house.

It was a fresh Spring morning and Sal had beaten the carpets, washed out the sheets and checked the hens for eggs. She then fed and watered Trooper and was about to leave the stable when she decided to tidy up. She took the Besom broom and swept the floor, then grabbing an old pair of Dad's long-johns from the bench she scooped them together with an old jacket she noticed in the corner, telling herself she had enough rags about the place. Rounding the cottage she dropped the items in the bin and proceeded to the kitchen where she placed a couple of logs in the black stove and settled the kettle on top.

The following week Jake searched high and low for the old garment, eventually confronting Sal who said she may have tidied the barn. Unable to make a fuss, he covered his distress in alcohol which did nothing for his temperament. From then on, he spent all available daylight hours fretfully visiting the tipping sites he could remember, and others besides, to no avail.

He ate little, failed to sleep, and became trapped in a spiral of decline: he took to walking in circles and muttering to himself in indecipherable monotones. What really rankled was that he and Trooper had brought about their destruction by including their bin in the waste disposal dodge. Ultimately, the stress proved too great and tipped him over the edge. His final journey was in a van similar to the one his father had driven with pride; however this one was painted white and manned by two burley assistants with coats to match.

TWENTY THINGS TO DO BEFORE BREAKFAST

Tom was a staunch sceptic, always had been. As an Apostle he would have been Doubting Thomas; he had to be assured before in the morning placing a foot on the bedside rug. He had never believed the moon landings, although certain that the planet was not made of cheese (now confirmed by the Chinese) and he was not a member of the Flat Earth Society; however he was the sort who had to experience something to believe in its existence. His long-suffering partner Patti was constantly telling him to be a more trusting soul, but old habits die hard. He attributed this blemish to his mother who, until she had a rude awakening with Tom, thought babies were dropped by a stork: however, the only large bill Tom encountered was the one that dropped through his letter-box courtesy of his Energy supplier.

Currently Tom was beset with the farcical fiasco daily enacted at Westminster concerning exit from the European Union; as a staunch Re-moaner in the debacle he spent hours agonising over the multiple twists and turns of the debate: he was convinced the UK should not leave the protective canopy of the EU, having himself visited the Continent on several occasions and made various contacts abroad. He simply could not understand why people would wish to leave the Union. We couldn't go it alone, the British empire had long since ceased to exist, and in his mind many were now championing a contrary myth. The confusion, while providing him with anguish, gave him and his nearest and dearest some humorous entertainment.

For instance the shenanigans of Dominic Grief, and John Burk's contempt for parliamentary protocol in the office of

Mr Squeaker provided much merriment. Burk's antics in the imbroglio, encapsulated in his amateur enactment of a music-hall impresario when addressing ''orrible' and right ''orrible' members of the House, contrasted with the eloquent sonorous timbre of the Attorney General's baritone. The participant names on each side of the divide caused him certain schadenfreude: the likes of Jacob Sea-Smog, David Devious, Dominic Rhubarb, Anna Sodbry and Kia Stammer came to mind, or Father of the Horse Kenneth Nark. Others worthy of reference included the leading exponent to massacre party unity, Boris Johnstown, and the belligerent parliamentary leader of the SNP (Separate Nation Party) Ian Blackhead. Talk prevailed of a No-Confidence vote, surely the <u>country</u> should have one, with no confidence in any of them.

He spent fruitless hours at the shrine of the little screen, watching endless parliamentary debates and news bulletins. He was particularly fond of the fiery catch-phrases that erupted from discussion, the likes of 'avoiding the backstop' (the backstop – a fielding position in cricket), 'Nation First' (echoes of an American president); and he had always looked on an 'Irish border' as either next-door's tenant or a particular breed of dog. He was becoming more and more confused; should he 'build a wall' to keep out the neighbour's cat, or would he be more profitably employed by 'taking back control' of the finances? Everybody seemed to have their 'red lines'; more so than a Mao Tse-Tung march-past. And what was in the National Interest anyway? He was totally bemused. Was he becoming a reluctant victim of 'Project Fear'?

He leapt from his chair to cavort around the room when the government lost another parliamentary vote, keeping tally on his private 'chuff-chart'. To Tom it was a paltry pantomime, Mother Theresa had a fair majority which she proceeded to squander on a General Election. As for Jeremy Corbet calling her a 'stupid woman', well Tom had to admit to addressing Patti at times in far more decorous terms. On the Andrew Besmirch program the PM had insisted hers was the only option; was she simply, like the Hickory Dickory mouse, 'running down the clock'. Gripped by the skirmish, he wondered would the PM receive the backing of the DUP (Duff Up Parliament party), or would she succumb to the Grieve-ous back-stabbing of the former Attorney General? Despite the feeling common sense would prevail, nagging doubt assailed his mind that perhaps the country might be drawn into a No Deal black-hole. So he avidly kept pace with News throughout the day, which caused some wearisome conjugal friction as well as a degree of mutual mirth.

*

True to the run of things, on the day of the Meaningless Vote, persistent drizzle fell out of deep grey clouds (obviously the heavens were none too pleased with the circus below); by evening a violent gale broke with malicious vengeance. To the accompaniment of sudden thunder claps and ugly bright yellow lightening flashes Tom added a reasonable representation of Victor Mildew's 'I don't believe it!.' At this signal, the television decided it was overdue to throw a wobbly, and began to produce an agonising series of intermittent picture snatches and an unintelligible smattering of sound. A tsumnami of erratic multi-coloured streaks and crackling protestations crazily crossed the screen, resulting in 32 inches of havoc. Tom was incensed to the point of deciding between three hazardous options; ejecting the set through the picture window; evacuating to France to join the Yellow Vests; or cutting his losses with a litre of Theakstons Old Peculiar. 'Think of your blood pressure, dear,' Patti soothed. Following a full minute's urgent deliberation he settled for the third option. In the meantime, the TV picture returned for a spell before capitulating in a miasma of static and turning black: Sound had ceased entirely, a perfect storm.

Exercising suitable feminine guile Patti gently adjusted the set to achieve the faltering earlier picture, lamentably without sound. Expectantly, Tom attempted to watch what was possible as MPs returned through the Lobbies and the crucial vote was returned to the Speaker; he had the briefest of windows to discern the House in uproar, albeit in eerie silence. He was certain he had glimpsed jubilant Tories on Front Benches before the intransigent technology gave way to the forces of Nature, and with a despairing cough called it a day. Tom, totally demoralised, retired to the study with afore-mentioned alcohol not to be seen by Patti until the next day. Essentially, he locked himself away in the study until the alcohol dried up; and he then slipped out to disturb the silent street by 'kicking the can down the road' for a good hundred yards.

The following morning dawned bright, breezy and dry, in contrast to Tom's demeanour. Awaking with the head from hell and an early morning appointment in the offing, he weighed up the option to leave the appointment and remain in bed; but he was made aware that 'the clock was ticking' by Patti's call from below stairs. Noting his lack-lustre appearance, Patti offered to do breakfast; and promised to cook him his favourite Moussaka for dinner if he would pick up some fresh aubergines on his way. He thought about that, though not for long, he was experiencing feelings of both nausea and inadequacy; he would be forced to leave without breakfast to get the best aubergines. it was going to be her deal or no breakfast at all as he would have to leave imminently.

Suddenly recalling yesterday's turmoil he dashed for the living room and managed to achieve the 9.00am news bulletin where he learnt the truth (supported by Patti's confirmation); the government's grip on power was tenuous and Conservatives were coming to terms with losing the Motion by over 100 votes. A delighted Tom took Patti in his arms and as they danced a quasi-quickstep across the living room carpet Patti declared: 'Oo-oh, you do get in a tiz darling!' After their mini-polka, regaining her breath she said: 'Why get so heated over something we can do nothing about, something that won't affect us anyhow? Now, just sit yourself down and I'll fetch us a nice cup of tea. Forget your appointment for today, we'll go shopping later. I never forgot what my dear old gramps used to say: "Believe nothing of what you hear, and only half of what you see".'

UNLIKELY LIAISON

One day in Heaven there were ructions at the collision of two great minds:

NAPOLEON: Aha! And oo do vee 'ave 'ere? Turn yer pritti face to ze light, madame.

THATCHER: No, no, no – this lady's not for turning!

N: Come on darleene, until you spread your wings, you'll have no idea how far you can fly. It states 'ere on yure record you were ze daughter of a grocer, iz zis true? As I thought, a nation of shopkeepers! Per'aps I should sample your peaches, no?

T: Get off me, you horrible little Frenchman! Your crass cross-channel chat-up-lines have no effect on me. Josephine told me, you're all trousers!

N: But I like... a strong woman. What did zey call you – ze iron lady?

T: Yes, and I thrived on it. In my book if you want something said, ask a man; if you want something done, ask a woman.

N: But if you want a thing done well, do it yourself, come si, come sa? Oh, you're so sexy...I like ...ow you say, a feisty woman. You said yourself: you 'ave to fight a battle more than once to win it, n'est pas? (Maybe I should revisit Waterloo?) In England they said you could walk on water.

T: Yes, well, if my critics saw me walking over the Thames

they would say it was because I couldn't swim. You do not achieve anything without trouble, ever. You Europeans are all the same! What do you know about the facts of life? You sir are nothing but a trumped up French socialist. The facts of life are conservative. It may be the cock that crows, but it's the hen that lays the eggs!

N: Oh la la!

T: Most women defend themselves. It is the female of the species, it is the tigress and lioness in you – which tends to defend when attacked.

N: Oh you English, always so independent – wanting to go your own way. With me I am a proud Frenchman, and you know where you stand: I wear my 'art on my sleeve.

T: Not good: wear it inside, where it functions best.

N: I was great! Revered throughout ze world! Why, at my instigation zey signed ze treaty of Austerlitz…

T: Treatys, treatys! Europe is larger than the Treaty of Rome, the EU is merely the practical means of cooperation between independent sovereign states. A man may climb Everest for himself, but at the summit he plants his country's flag. Constitutions have to be written on hearts not just paper. As I said at Bruges, we did not roll back the frontiers of the state in Britain, to have them reimposed by the EU.

N: Fighting talk indeed – and so saucy! I'm glad you stayed at Bruges and didn't visit Versailles. We could not afford to replace all zose glass ceilings!

T: I've always believed in action, not words. During my lifetime most of the problems the world has faced have come, in one fashion or other, from mainland Europe, and the solutions from outside it. Europe was created by history, America by philosophy.

N: Phooey! I was ze one that created zat history, I redrew ze map of Europe!

T: You're nothing but a despot, a dictator.

N: I 'ave been accused of 'aving a 'eavy 'and...

T: Heavy hand!? History will judge you as 'ruthless'.

N: Some might call me that – but could be guillotined for less. Anyhow history is a set of lies agreed upon. Were you never ruthless; the all-powerful woman of the state, the fearless Amazon, the 20 century Boadicea?

T: Being powerful is like being a lady, if you have to tell people you are, you aren't. I was in politics because of the conflict between good and evil, and I believe that in the end good will triumph.

N: How sanctimonious of you, carrying enlightenment behind the shield of Brittania to the darkest corners of the globe. What about ze rape of your Commonwealth?

T: No-one would remember the Good Samaritan if he'd only gone with good intentions; he had money too.

N: But, had 'e not met ze victim in ze gutter, he would not be remembered either. Ability is nothing without opportunity.

T: I usually make up my mind about a man in 10 secs, and I very rarely change it. In your case it took half the time.

N: Oh, ze drawing room etiquette of ze Brontes!

T: I pursued a course with purpose. Defeat!? I do not recognise the meaning of the word.

N: Yes, and 'impossible' is a word to be found only in the dictionary of fools! Were you popular with ze people?

T: Well, I did select the weapon of choice for the Northern Ireland police force, the American Ruger.

N: All I did was fire on a rowdy Paris mob with nothing but a whiff of grapeshot.

T: When all's said and done, we <u>will</u> be remembered (perhaps for all the wrong reasons). Nevertheless, we have two things in common.

N: And what are zey, my sweet? I was never one to interrupt an enemy when zey were making a mistake.

T: Although I seem to smell the stench of appeasement, I concur. We were marmite, and had a thirst for power.

N: Oui, boring weren't we!?

WAITING IN THE WINGS

The old man groped gingerly along the dusty wall with grubby fingers protruding from tattered woollen gloves: finding the switch he blinked as the stage before him was suddenly splashed in brilliant light. What memories that scene conjured for him. In earlier days Len had been considered a not unsuccessful entertainer 'on the boards' and on one occasion was almost a stand-in for the great Benezzi. However since those happy days too much grimy water had passed under the old canal bridge, close to the rundown tenement where he rented the single room he called home.

His story began in the heyday of the music-hall when it vied with the circus for entertainment. It was in the 1930s that his greatest moments were realised: the glory days when the halls still enjoyed a full box-office, before the television dream became a nightmare. He had accompanied such acts as the trapeze artists the Delamere brothers; comedians the like of young Jimmy Withers with his cheeky red face; Mr Black the conjuror whose speciality was sawing ladies in half; and the singing and tap-dancing of the beautiful Belle Summers. Many were the nights he would watch the incredible feats or listen spellbound to one of Belles songs from the wings.

As a lad Len had been a clown before he added to his repertoire. His father and his father's father had been born into the circus, it seemed only right that he too should have his own act. He'd accompanied his father to such diverse places, places he'd only seen on picture posters in railway stations: towns with obscure sounding names like York, Liverpool, Leeds, Pontefract,

Caerphilly and Glasgow. He loved the thrill of the road and the camaraderie of the troupe – as the youngest he was their favourite. Yet, as he grew older he grew unsure of his own performance, it could never compare with his father's juggling: the man had 'proper coordination' as everyone said – a master of his craft as his own father had been before him. Len knew the crowd were laughing at him and not with him – often jeering and once a banana skin had been lobbed in his direction as he sweated beneath thick layers of cheap makeup.

Then he'd met Toby and his career took a turn for the better. Toby was a brown and white terrier, with a smudge to one side of his nose that Len called his beauty spot. He had taught Toby tricks from the age of three months and the dog was good. Toby could jump fire-covered hoops, bark from one to five and even walk blind-folded on his hind-legs with a bottle of beer tied to his neck. He always accompanied his master, as Len repeated the same old tired gags and lampooned his way around the sawdust ring dressed in baggy pantaloons and sporting a large comic red nose: the nose complemented Toby's ruched white collar adorned with scarlet trimming.

Life had become harder for him since he lost Mabel. He missed her squeaky laugh, her cuddles and her cakes – she always sent him off with a large chunk of her latest baking. She had supported his hair-brain suggestions, although not always. Once he had in mind to spend money on an old beaten up ambulance to take his travelling act around the country. She'd put her foot down then, told him he was being childish. She was right of course: the old vehicle wouldn't have reached halfway to London before breaking down. Without Mabel he had just drifted, but he had his memories.

After leaving the circus there seemed no point in continuing, returning each night to false acclaim. The truth was he never trusted the crowds who jested and jibed him from the ringside seats. They were not real; they came to watch the spectacular elephants, performing tigers, the gravity defying feats on the high-wire or the horsemanship of exotic Zara. They weren't interested in the 'fill-in' entertainment – but he was an entertainer, it was in his blood – what else was there?

It had been around this time that he and Toby had tried the music hall. He'd begun with some casual jobs around the theatre, carrying and shifting props – not work for the soul. Of course Benezzi topped the bill. Impresarios such as he were special; radiating a brilliance that outshone lesser constellations. Benezzi always gave a polished performance and proclaimed confidence and poise while the audience sat spellbound. With his handsome Neapolitan features and dashing smile, flashing dark eyes and shiny black hair he turned many a young girl's head. A mellow tenor with a silken voice conceived of simmering olive groves and sultry southern vineyards: he achieved the impossible with the silver cane that was his trademark; transforming it one moment into a ladies parasol the next a flashing duelling sword as he danced and swaggered across the stage. As he swung his famous cape, studded with diamante until it flashed and glittered in the footlights, appreciative onlookers glimpsed an elegant blazer and bow-tie above neatly pressed flannels. Then he would discard the flowing mantle and crown his dark curls with a straw boater to compliment the cane. Pure elegance.

Gradually Len had attained assisting roles with various performers, this awarded him the chance to watch Benezzi at close quarters. He had zealously trained, practised and rehearsed in the hope that one day he would be called on to stand-in for his idol: and had waited his chance filled with awe and admiration a few steps away. Recalling these times, he lamented that he never saw his name in lights.

There was the time he left his favourite post in the wings to take some air during the interval. That was the night he first set eyes on tiny Annie. Abandoned by her parents when times were hard, at the age of ten she had found her way to the Manchester Hardwicke Road Orphanage. She explained she was seeking any scraps available around the theatre, as the hostel food was alright but there just wasn't enough to go round. Len had given her his lunch including a thick wedge of fruitcake, although not a patch on Mabel's, and a mug of warming tea. They had talked and talked about nothing in particular: the child was a good listener and very bright. Her tired face lit up when she was introduced to Toby. She gave him a big hug and the little dog responded by giving her a lick on the nose. She said she had always wanted a dog of her own.

Befriending the little urchin Len noted the sadness she carried in her young eyes. Yet no-one was more surprised than he, for he always felt awkward around children. Annie told him she had often watched the performers arriving and leaving the theatre, playing a guessing game of each ones role on the stage. She longed to one day watch them from inside, but she knew that was only a dream. After he had escorted Annie to the orphanage where she was reunited with some thirty other waifs and strays, an idea began to form in his mind. If he were honest, nobody would miss his stop-gap appearances, but if he should find an audience of his own – one that would truly appreciate him…

The performance went better than he'd hoped – the children had cheered and laughed with gusto, cheeks glistening with joyful tears. 'Uncle' Len was an overnight success but Toby stole the Christmas show. The warden had asked him to return, to again enthral his eager young audience. Len had agreed and visited once a month over two years, receiving a warm meal at the orphanage on each occasion. Mabel would have been so proud.

The small children loved the delightful duo, and were always peering anxiously from the tall murky windows to watch them arrive. Len seemed to possess some special way with them to which they responded wholeheartedly. They would fetch him mugs of steaming tea or cocoa in the intermission and always made a great fuss of Toby. But Annie was his favourite, in a way she had found *him*: he was forever slipping her small tokens of sweets; and on one occasion an inexpensive bangle he'd bought on a market stall. They always found some topic of conversation. He knew Mabel would have loved Annie and treated her as the little girl she never had.

Then there was the night he found the performance ticket beneath the door on the foyer floor. He knew he ought to have returned it to the box-office and was on his way to do so, when he suddenly thought of little Annie and her dream. Could it be done he pondered? The unused ticket was for the Saturday evening and luck was on his side in that he was friendly with the usher for that night. He would meet Annie and bring her to the steward who would escort her to the vacant seat. Annie looked so smart, she had scrubbed her skin until it shone and she wore her favourite chequered frock with two bright matching bows in her hair.

The spectacular was a success. The theatre hummed that night and little Annie felt so honoured to be sharing the exalted atmosphere. A packed house gave the various and colourful performers a generous reception. A mini-drama was being simultaneously enacted from Annie's seat as she experienced a spectrum of emotions: in turn she clapped, laughed and briefly cried. She joined the applause for the juggling; laughed out loud at the comedian, although she couldn't understand it all; and shed a tear at one of Belle's sadder renderings. After the show Len treated her to a fine meal at a small bistro round the corner from the theatre before dropping her back to the orphanage. How happy she had been.

The theatre often holds cruel plays of fortune, and so it was that fickle Mistress Fate was to intervene centre-stage once more. The friendly warden was promoted and transferred to a London home. Annie was fostered and moved to Newcastle, leaving Len praying that she was loved and happy. A fresh warden took over at the orphanage – a svenghali figure who felt children should be seen and not heard; if children came to the orphanage they had obviously done something wrong, deserving whatever hardship the institution meted out. Len returned to doing odd jobs about the theatre and at times assisting the entertaining artists.

They never asked him to take the place of Benezzi. As he turned down the stage lighting and in the gloom stumbled through ancient hampers brimming with theatrical costumery and assorted props, a solitary tear rolled across his cheek. A tear not for unrealised ambition, but for little orphan Annie and the night he brought the house down…

WAITING ROOM BLUES

Continuous rain gusting relentlessly against the glass panes heightened the early Monday morning gloom of the waiting room interior, whilst simultaneously deflating the spirits of the room's occupants. Peeling jaded cream paintwork merely served to increase the drabness expected of such institutions. In order to lift my flagging humour I opted for a little mind game. I concentrated upon my fellow occupants seated on the painted wooden bench opposite. As my imagination took control these ordinary folk became alive to me: I began to muse over their position in life, their social status, their ambitions, their fortunes and their failures.

A rather dapper young woman in knee-high boots was gradually yet inevitably losing the battle to control a pair of miniature demons of either gender; she was making a vain attempt to keep her temper, and, after remonstrating with the hapless pair, she surreptitiously glanced around the room to see if anyone was concerned by their antics. I saw her returning to a tidy semi, situated at the corner of a smart suburban estate surrounded by neatly trimmed lawns. Her kitchen contained the latest gadgets, here she prepared dinner for her tight-lipped executive husband, the successful executive returning on the train from some distant office. Sliding into slippers, he casually flicked through the TV chanels: 'Nothing on again!' This woman's wardrobe was stocked with the latest fashions and she attended keep-fit classes in order that she would fit into them.

Beside this self-possessed trio, or to be perfectly correct, beside the young woman – the two miniature monsters were unable to stay in one place for any length of time, sat a trim elderly lady, knees pressed tightly together and encased in stout navy tights. Her long silver-grey locks were spun into a high bun behind her ears, her plump hands rested protectively upon the black leather bag on her lap. She must have been in her sixties, and possessed an air of Dickensian authority in the way she sat straight-backed and prim. Her clothes were tidy, although inexpensive. I wondered whose maiden aunt she might be, perhaps a teacher?

She had begun by making overtures to the two little goblins, displaying a frustrated maternal instinct, however this led to minimal response followed by molestation to the point of embarrassment, so she had resorted to a pose of cold indifference. Apparently the male infant had become obsessed with the elastic of her pink knickerbockers barely visible beneath her tweed skirt, and had acquired the not inconsiderable knack of twanging the elastic above her knee. Behaviour to which the mother appeared to remain in blissful ignorance.

My final companion in that dreary setting was a short stocky man perhaps in his early fifties who sported a careless mop of mousy brown hair that insisted on raising itself skywards, despite the restriction of a greasy check cap. From the open-neck shirt, red glowing cheeks and calloused hands I saw him as a man of the soil. Further proof if required could be attained from faded corduroy trousers that flapped abandonedly above scuffed heavy boots. Little appeared to bother this weathered man, whose craggy features and casual bearing suggested someone at home in any situation. Curiously the pair of tiny wretches seemed to sense this and, after having been unceremoniously bounced upon his knee they were careful to avoid his end of the bench.

What intriguing personalities we conceal within our various frames. I was left to ponder on the thoughts my five companions had entertained concerning the stooped pallid-featured inquisitive middle-aged woman seated facing them, dallying in deference to Sudoku.

WHAT'S IN A NAME?

I have long been a great believer that man is master of his own destiny. Bronowski said the world can be grasped by action, not by contemplation. With this in mind I have seized upon every opportunity to further my endeavours with a passion. It's not every day that one is invited to both the Lobby of the House of Commons and a top show-biz award ceremony: carpe diem.

I had spent the day at Lords, watching England attempting to stall a particularly venomous Indian spin onslaught. It was an overcast day with low cloud-cover and rain-spots in deference to which the umpires had called an early tea interval. Upon entering the ground, I met up with Carl Simmons an old journalist buddy and during the break he invited me to accompany him into the Long Room.

For years I suffered that perennial complaint known as dramatis frustratus. Despite strutting and stumbling various amateur stages, making up the numbers of a parade of 'extra' roles, I had never lost the chance to spot my name in lights. Carl, as all my other acquaintances, knew of my aspiration and happened to mention he had been invited to cover an auspicious annual award ceremony that very evening and could get me a spare press ticket. Delighted as I was to accept this gracious offer, I was less enthusiastic to learn we would be making a detour to Westminster beforehand, as Carl had to pick up some leads on the current debate in the House. Politics had never inspired me and the rather claustrophobic prospect of being surrounded by a multitude of querulous and suspect octogenarians in a fusty atmosphere of smoke and confusion held no appeal; then, of course there was the House of Lords.

As journalists do, Carl was acquainted with a plethora of the inaccessible and famous. He once introduced me to the great Nicholas Lloyd, Sir as he now is; who in his day worked for a spell with the Mail before moving on to the Sunday Times. As I recall, at the time we had a lengthy chat on World War One; Sir Nicholas being a member of the Centre for First World War Studies. The ubiquitous Carl was of value to me.

Entering the Long Room, the great hall was quite packed on that damp August day and most tables were full due to the inclement conditions and England's poor performance at the crease. Carl guided me to a corner table where there were a couple of vacant seats and we discussed the match. Sharing our table were a collection of citizens of retirement age, and I discovered their identities as we debated the merits of the googlie. One fellow, as I rightly guessed from his bearing to be of military persuasion turned out to be the former Adjutant-General, General Sir Geoffrey Musson; he still lamented the saddest day of his life – 13th July 1968, when the Light Infantry Brigade was disbanded. He then attempted to beguile me with fond memories of bygone campaigns.

*

It transpired that our table was occupied by such notables as the studious Professor Geraint Gruffydd, an amateur theologian and retired Vice Principal of the University of Wales at Aberystwyth, not to mention his presidency of the Congress of Celtic Studies. Next to him sat Sir Peter Heatly the former chairman of the Commonwealth Games Federation, who had been a diver and sportsman earning a CBE in 1971 as well as a founder member of the Scottish Sports Hall of Fame in 2002. Across the divide, sat

Sir Roger Hurn, former deputy chairman of GlaxoSmithKline, who in his day had been chairman of Prudential and Marconi. Apparently he had put Smiths Aerospace and Smiths industries on the map despite moving on in 1996.

Conspiratorial conversation came from the further reaches of the table where a mature couple bent towards each-other in impassioned dialogue. The gent was Mr Peter Sanders, former Chief Executive for the Commission for Racial Equality; and the sole female turned out to be none other than Mrs June O'Dell, the chair of Probus Women's Housing Society and deputy CEO for the Equal Opportunities Commission. Although I should have delighted in furthering our deliberations we were interrupted by the bell for the resumption of play. 'Delighted to make your acquaintance, old boy,' huffed Sir Geoffrey as we returned to the stands. 'Shame about the cricket!'

England as usual were rescued by the weather as the contest drizzled to a dismal draw. It speaks volumes for the capricious English character that they should invent an important national sport wholly unsuitable to the climactic conditions. 'Jammy buggers!' was Carl's only comment on the match as we sped into the city in the direction of the seat of power. As we drew close to the Towers I tried to display an optimism I in no way felt. We passed through security and, at the end of a long corridor littered with portraits of a milieu of past leaders, entered the dim cloudy bar, where my initial expectations were realised.

So much for the smoking ban I thought as our eyes pierced the heavy gloom, and we ended up squeezed at one end of the long bar by a horde of snorting, loquacious, overweight red-nosed parliamentarians – all with too much to say in too loud a voice. Surveying that scene of cackling corpulent humanity, I had sympathy for a comment attributed to Hitler, that no politician should ever let himself be photographed in a bathing suit. Amid the haze opinions were being voiced in boring monotones on every issue from terrorism to fox-hunting.

*

In fact the Hunting Bill was the topic Carl was addressing, and with this purpose in mind had obtained an unofficial interview with Lt. Col. Michael Mates MP. Mates, Con. for East Hampshire was on record as being moderately against the hunting ban. By all accounts he was also moderately against student top-up fees, anti-terrorism laws, the smoking ban and ID cards (virtually all the Government's manifesto). Off the record, it has to be said, he held somewhat different views. As Carl conducted his impromptu interview in a no-smoking room through a doorway off the bar, I was able to mingle in the misty melange. I soon found myself in the company of such parliamentary stalwarts as Douglas Henderson MP a member of the SNP, and Peter Kilfoyle MP who had been very vociferous during the Iraq debate in 2003 (as well as during the EU debate of 2005). It was during the latter that he notoriously referred to the Commision as a Geronimo scalping the taxpayer for propaganda purposes. Alongside the aforementioned was Professsor Eric Hobsbawn, the renowned historian famous for his Marxist leanings: To this day he admits to being an 'unrepentant communist'.

At the bar, attempting to replenish my glass before re-entering the fray, I found myself waiting alongside no less a personage than Robert Mcnamara, US Secretary of Defense during JFK's administration. I was about to quiz him over the Bay of Pigs when along came a waitress. Incidentally, you will be interested to know that whilst at the bar across the room I'm sure I caught sight of Charles Saatchi. No doubt he was stating his price for doing a similar makeover of the current incumbent of No.10 as he had for Margaret Thatcher. Actually, Saatchi is the Hebrew word for watchmaker and he certainly appeared to have plenty of time on his hands. And if time hadn't been so pressing I should have liked to chat to him about his famous art gallery. However as we were leaving the Lobby I can't be certain but I'm fairly sure I spotted Sir Roy Meadows, the discredited paediatrician, who at the height of his career had been struck off by the GMC for his radical views on cot-death babies.

Later that evening Carl called round to take us on to the Awards. Show-biz glitz and glamour oozed from the Leicester Square venue and onto the pavement beyond, where it mingled with a legion of paparazzi. Stars and groupies were arriving in a blaze of bling. Avoiding the red carpet we were ushered through the expectant crowds into a side entrance and along a brightly-lit corridor of purple and gold. We were directed towards an open door through which sparkled a dazzling array of lighting, emitted from huge spinning silver spheres that focused soft beams upon the tables below. To one of these we were shown towards the rear of the proceedings, whilst in front of us the stage shone forth brightly-lit for television.

*

The alacrity with which I grasped a proffered dry sherry from a passing waiter was matched only by my embarrassment when I collided with a pretty young starlet on a similar mission. She turned out to be none other than the screen-star Natalie Portman. I have long been a fan of this vivacious 25 yr-old after watching *Cold Mountain* in 2003. Natalie was also prominent in *Star Wars 3* in 2005 and *Goya's Ghosts* in 2006. I'm not entirely sure whether it was my winning way with women, or maybe she was merely attracted to my prominent press-badge and sensed some impending publicity; but I do know that I was invited to join her at her table towards the front where I was introduced to her current beau, someone high in finance I understand.

I couldn't believe my luck to have alighted upon such illustrious companions. Although I had recognised him, Natalie introduced me first of all to Tony Britton the Birmingham born comic actor; among other productions Tony had starred in the sit-coms *Father, Dear Father* in 1968-73 and *Don't Tell Father* in 1992, as well as many other diverse roles. Then there was the guitarist Les Paul who, in 1924, had become popular for his rendition of *Tiptoe Through the Tulips*. And the stand-up comedian Jackie Mason, born in Wisconsin of Jewish parents, whose male relatives were all rabbis; his sit-com 'Chicken Soup' was a great success and he was later honoured by Nelson Mandela.

Michael J. Fox was there too, who had starred in such note-worthy productions as *Back to the Future 3* 1990, *The American President* in 1999, and *Atlantis* in 2001. A sufferer himself, he had been responsible for the Parkinson Research Foundation. Then there was the mystery thriller writer, Patricia Cornwell from Miami; and also present the incomparable Johnny Depp, movie star of high acclaim for his interpretation of *Sweeny Todd* and a host of other screen performances. In 2004, his most prolific year, he appeared in such blockbusters as *The Libertine*, *Finding Neverland*, *And They Lived Happily Ever After*, *King of the Hill*, and *Secret Window*. More recently he starred as a swash-buckling buccaneer in the multi-million dollar production *Pirates of the Caribbean*.

Unfortunately I lost Carl in the milling crowds at that ceremony, and indeed have heard nothing of him since. My new-found friends however enjoyed the proceedings and applauded each nomination with gusto. I forget who achieved the coveted accolades that year, suffice it to say that the whole arena was awash with esteemed celebrities too numerous to record. I did however notice Fiona Bruce and James Nesbitt at some point. Needless to say, despite dropping the odd subtle hint to all and sundry, my personal quest for acclaim has yet to be realised. That elusive big break remains stoically unattainable. However it is a comfort to relax in the knowledge that I have made such eminent and numerous contacts. I always say it's <u>who</u> you know that really counts.